DEADLY
DRIFTS

The Macduff Brooks Fly Fishing Mysteries

BY M.W. GORDON

THE WESTERN MOUNTAINS TRILOGY
DEADLY DRIFTS
CROSSES TO BEAR
"YOU'RE NEXT!"

THE FLORIDA TRILOGY
GILL NET GAMES
BARRACUDA PENS
TBA

DEADLY DRIFTS

A MACDUFF BROOKS FLY FISHING MYSTERY

by

award winning author

M.W.GORDON

SWIFT CREEKS PRESS EDITION, FEBRUARY 2012

Mill Creek, Paradise Valley, Pellicer Creek, and the areas around Bozeman, Emigrant, Jackson Hole, St. Augustine, and Grand Teton and Yellowstone national parks are real places, hopefully described accurately but used fictionally in this novel. The same is true of certain businesses used by Macduff Brooks and his friends and adversaries. This is a work of fiction, and the characters are either the product of the author's imagination or are used fictionally. Any resemblance to actual persons, living or dead, or to actual events or locales is unintentional and coincidental.

Library of Congress Cataloging-in-Publication Data
Gordon, M.W.
Deadly Drifts/ M.W.Gordon

ISBN-13 978-0-9848723-0-5

Printed in the United States of America

This book is for Buff, who encouraged me first to build a wooden drift boat and second to become a fly fishing guide. But not to move to Montana or Wyoming, forsaking our *spartina* and mangrove laden salt-water coastal marshes of Northeast Florida.

ACKNOWLEDGMENTS

This book would not have been attempted or completed without the encouragement of family and friends. In addition to our wonderful daughter and son, and my wife Buff, I would not have started or, having done so, would have stopped at many points – and likely gone fly fishing. Others who have helped include Jeffrey Harrison, Roy Hunt, Johnnie Irby, Marilyn Henderson, and Shelley Fraser Mickle.

Readers will undoubtedly join me in thanking Iris Rose Hart, who edited the manuscript, and made me wish she had been my high school grammar teacher.

AUTHOR'S NOTE

After years of writing on various aspects of foreign and international law, I turned to this novel, gloriously escaping the confines of citations and footnotes. Law books lack one of the most intriguing characteristics of a novel — dialogue. That is not because lawyers are silent folk.

When writing about the law, the principal sources are cases and statutes. Writing this novel took me searching for information about such things as the al-Qaeda and the Taliban; private jets; wine, food and restaurants; fashion; oboe literature; trout species; and weapons. Undue time was spent on distinguishing between Beemers (motorcycles) and Bimmers (automobiles), when referring in only one brief sentence to the BMW product. Believing readers would be unfamiliar with that distinction and the correct use of Bimmers in referring to the automobile, I chose the easy way out and opted to use "BMWs."

This book was written partly at a desk in a cottage overlooking acres of salt water marshes south of St. Augustine, Florida, and partly in a cabin in the woods by the side of Mill Creek in Paradise Valley, Montana — often very late at night. Always with me were my wife Buff and our sheltie, Macduff.

I am an avid trout fly-fisherman, strictly applying a catch and release and barbless hook practice. From catching my first brook trout at nine, *every* trout I have caught over the years has been carefully returned to its home.

PROLOGUE

Mr. Macduff Brooks
Mill Creek Road
Pray, Montana 59065

Dad

Mac and I are home on Captiva after five interminable days on the road from Montana. Thank you for all the books, especially the ones you wrote decades ago when you were law professor Maxwell Hunt. When I opened one of the books, out fell a tenth wedding anniversary card and a letter to Maxwell from El. It was such an endearing love letter that I was embarrassed to have invaded your privacy. It ended with a postscript saying how much she was looking forward both to floating again the following week on the Deadman's Bar to Moose section of the Snake River in Jackson Hole, Wyoming, and especially to having their soon-to-be-born first child!

You took me on that very same float so many times. Do you remember those trips? The first was when our sweet sheltie, Wuff, was getting on in years. We had to lift her into and out of the boat. That beautiful wooden boat we called Osprey *that you built.*

As I think back to my wonderful times on Mill Creek, I realize there are some parts of your life I have never known about. If my curiosity in the least bit brings back memories best left undisturbed, I will understand that you wish to preserve the secrecy of those years.

Your loving daughter
Elsbeth

It was time she learned the full story of my life. With the effort of age, I wrote back:

Ms. Elsbeth Hunt Brooks
14 Seahorse Way
Captiva Island, Florida 33924

Dearest Daughter
Please forgive your aging father for faltering penmanship and lapses in memory. You two were wonderful to drive here and surprise me on my 90th birthday.
I have never told you the full story of my life. It's time you knew. I lived a private life that was on occasion filled with tragedy. You were never told of the danger because it might have placed you at risk. When you are back for Christmas, you will have had time to read part of the story, and I will try to answer your questions.
I've enclosed a manuscript that will tell you many things you should know. I intended to leave it to you — it has been in the safe with my will. I do not want to read it again; the horror of trying to escape Juan Pablo Herzog's vengeance is not something I wish to relive.
When you were in college, I received a residency at the Rockefeller Foundation's Institute at Bellagio, Italy, to write a novel. I was not writing a novel but rather my memoirs. The novel form was to protect my identity, if such protection remained necessary. You were in graduate school in London and came to visit on your spring break. I remember how much you enjoyed sitting on the porch of the villa with evening cappuccino, looking out as the sun set over Lake Como.
I never intended to have the manuscript published. Once it was written, I thought the full story was too personal to share with anyone. Read as much of the manuscript as you desire and do with it what you wish.
You are the brightest star in my galaxy. I cherish every moment you have been part of my life.
Your loving father
Macduff

In a small weather-challenged home on the Pine Island Sound side of Captiva Island, surrounded by sea grape, hibiscus, and bougainvillea, under stately palms that leaned in consort with the prevailing winds, Elsbeth ground some Guatemalan coffee beans she had brought from a vacation in Antigua, and made a cup of coffee. She took the coffee to the screened porch, settled deeply into a sea-grape leaf-print covered chair, looked out over the sound, opened the manuscript, and began to read. Her sheltie, Mac, lay curled at her feet, looking at her through his dark, understanding eyes.

Deadly Drifts

THE MANUSCRIPT

1

EVEN WHISPERING THE NAME JUAN PABLO HERZOG provokes fear throughout his ancestral village that hangs precipitously on a mountainside in Sacatepéquez Province in Guatemala. Mists often descend and obscure the village, lending the terrified pueblo a bizarre illusion of safety. The villagers have been agitated by the nearby volcano, Fuego, for the past dozen years. They have been agitated by Juan Pablo Herzog for much longer.

His village overlooks a fertile valley that three generations ago provided a new beginning to an industrious immigrant family from Germany. Fleeing Prussian oppression and conscription, Juan Pablo's great grandfather, Werner, and his bride, Katja, found a new life cultivating coffee. That life offered them a sense of permanence, and they gave their children names with the Spanish lilt of Alejandro and María Luisa. María

Luisa married into another coffee growing immigrant family from Europe. He married a fertile daughter of immigrants from Majorca who presented him with five boys and one girl. In time, the family relinquished many of their European characteristics that had defined them as German, but they always protected and honored the Herzog name.

The coffee plantations grew and generations passed. The Herzog name became part of the coffee legends of the country. But somewhere among the seeds that had been planted, not in the coffee fields but within the family tree, the Herzogs produced a boy who, among family members but always behind closed doors, would one day be called the Antichrist of Guatemala. He was christened Juan Pablo.

Juan Pablo was provided all the benefits of Guatemala's primitive form of aristocracy. He was educated in a Catholic monastery school that catered to members of the wealthy Guatemalan elites, families that controlled the production of the richly flavored coffee bean, as well as sugar, cotton, and other agricultural products that flourished in the yielding soils of this jewel-like country.

Juan Pablo was exceptionally handsome. Taller, more athletic, and more intelligent than any of his siblings, cousins, or fellow students, he lacked only one thing that might have allowed him to surpass the fame of his great-grandfather as a "Man of Guatemala" — one of the first recipients of the rarely bestowed Great Collar degree of the Order of the Quetzal. Juan Pablo lacked even the smallest trace of a conscience.

By sixteen, Juan Pablo had impregnated a half-dozen fellow students and also two young postulants who had taught him the ways of Christ in preparing him for his Confirmation. He learned that the deep passages of the convent of the novices connected him to the quarters of the young women, newly into vows they were not always certain they could fulfill. One of the young women, her long, flowing habit covering a growing life within, confronted Juan Pablo and did something no one had ever done. She *threatened* him. Not to see that he was excommunicated — that would not trouble his soul but only heighten his implacable spirit of self — but to blackmail him unless he married her.

The next day her body was discovered in one of the chambers of the subterranean passageways. She had been crucified on a soaring, 17th-century, wooden cross. Her womb had been carefully excised from her body to leave no sign of her expectancy. No trace of the unborn child was ever found.

There was a quiet, private burial after a closed casket service at which Juan Pablo was a smiling altar boy. The grieving mother, with whom her departed daughter had shared knowledge of her condition, saw the smile and, in the darkening afternoon in her small house behind the church, took her own life.

Juan Pablo soon thereafter was sent to the United States, to an all-male military academy isolated in the mountains of Tennessee. He knew he had walked on a precipice from which he might well have fallen, and devoted much of the next two years to his studies and sports. But with an unhindered urge that came to him at times, he frequented unfavorable sections of Knoxville, where the value of a woman was negotiable. From these encounters he learned that many people were as weak as the young women of his youth. He began to buy drugs for sale in his dormitory to numerous classmates who were attending the academy, not because of their desire to pursue military careers, but because their parents were too busy to spend time raising them and, with pretended pride and considerable relief, had sent them off to the academy's hands.

Juan Pablo was thrilled by the risks he assumed and amused by the naivety of the academy's administration in not detecting his breach of rules. The head of the academy was a failed Army major who had been given the assignment after acts of incompetence beyond the call of duty, which were buried in a series of military messages that remained top secret. After graduating near the top of his class, Juan Pablo enrolled in a dual business and agriculture program at the University of Florida in Gainesville, well-known throughout the Americas for its studies in tropical agriculture.

At times there seemed to be hope that this handsome, brilliant young man might find a life at home in the Herzog family businesses, which were growing at a pace that might justify the family excusing his earlier transgressions in trade for his needed intelligence and knowledge. While in Gainesville, Juan Pablo especially embraced the benefits offered by the university's Center for Latin American Studies. He found his friends among other foreign students at the university, particularly Abdul Khaliq Isfahani, an Iranian-born young man who had completed two years of undergraduate study at the University of Khartoum in the Sudan. Abdul Khaliq was strikingly distinguished in appearance — a rail-thin, olive-skin, meticulously dressed, soft-spoken, serious student, who wore elaborate Muslim high-collar robes and prayer caps, edged with gold thread. He was a good influence in keeping Juan Pablo focused on his studies.

One of their courses was a seminar on contemporary issues in Latin America, jointly taught by professors from various departments, including two whom they particularly admired — Maxwell Hunt and Roy Palladio — both from the law college. Hunt had lost his wife in an accident and had no family to go home to after long days at the law college. He often spent evenings with students, mentoring them on a wide expanse of life's challenges. He invited foreign students to his home for Thanksgiving dinners, Juan Pablo and Abdul Khaliq among them. Juan Pablo especially admired Professor Hunt's collection of pre-Columbian ceramics. Such experiences encouraged Juan Pablo to learn more about his own nation and, on vacations home, he spent hours in the Guatemalan museums. As the semesters passed, these two — professor and student — became friends, but in the way that was limited by the age-old academic partition of status.

Soon after Juan Pablo finished his studies he returned to his country and settled in a penthouse condominium in Guatemala City. But his life soon turned dark. He was in an automobile accident, struck his head, and received a severe concussion. As he slowly recovered he began to suffer from nightmares, often waking abruptly to the agonizing screams of the young postulant. He discontinued the careful dressing and grooming habits for which he had been known. He consumed numerous medications prescribed by terrified doctors. He began to frequent parts of the city at night not traveled by anyone who valued his life. His friends believed that his substantial intellect was increasingly consumed by an animal intensity. He did not carry out plans. And he began to use profanity as though it were part of his natural manner of speaking, which it had never been. Friends who had been worried for him began to be worried about him.

Juan Pablo learned who controlled prostitution and the sale of infants to foreigners. But most importantly, he learned that Luís Boca was the Guatemalan godfather of organized crime who dominated the drug trade. Boca was a former army private who had advanced by stages to general, failed at an attempt for the country's presidency, and withdrew into his various illegal businesses.

5

Guatemala was long known as a country where modest amounts of money could be exchanged for the disappearance of a disliked business associate, an estranged male or female companion, or even a family member. The price varied on a sliding scale according to the relationship and stature of the victim, and his ability to remain hidden from public sight.

Juan Pablo's favorite movie, *Scarface*, was the only DVD he owned. He watched it often and imagined himself as Al Pacino portraying the Cuban immigrant Tony Montana, who rose to control the drug world of Miami. Juan Pablo applauded the tools of Montana's trade.

One afternoon, Juan Pablo cornered Luís Boca playing tennis at a small private club. Juan Pablo walked undauntedly onto the court after he and two friends had dispatched Boca's three guards. Juan Pablo yanked the starting cord on a chainsaw as he walked straight to Boca, and with no more emotion than a gardener would show trimming a hedge, left Boca in eight bloody parts strewn about the tennis court.

While Boca's blood was absorbed by the recently resurfaced red clay, his tennis opponent, horrified while he watched the death of Boca, graciously conceded the match. Not to what remained of his friend Boca, but to Juan Pablo. Smiling, Juan Pablo picked up the tennis balls, returned them to their can, presented the can to Boca's shocked opponent, and sent him on his way. Later that day the opponent's body was found in his car by his house. The can of tennis balls was on the front seat, each ball showing crimson stains on the soft yellow felt. No one was ever charged with Boca's murder and the authorities did not even investigate the murder of his tennis opponent.

Within a week, Juan Pablo had gone from a swaggering, small-time thug, to the immaculately dressed, soft-spoken, self-crowned *jefe* of Guatemalan organized crime. Paid homage to by Boca's leaderless followers — who had never imagined that the raw violence of ambition could be exhibited so brutally — Juan Pablo began to extend his activities to the control of legitimate businesses, including the one that funded his ambition — coffee. Sugar, cotton, poultry, and the other traditionally oligarchy-controlled businesses increasingly came under his protection and often ownership. Seeking further wealth, Juan Pablo began to expand to the development of cattle in the rich tropical forests of the Petén, on land he cleared of trees and cleansed of local inhabitants. He also made contacts with the Mexican drug cartels, careful not to yield his own local power, desiring only to learn from them the harsh tactics that would assist him in extending his control of drugs south of Guatemala, all the way to Panama.

No man as ruthless as Juan Pablo can cause the *universe* to cower. There are *always* Tony Montanas breeding in the sewers of society. Sometimes there are men determined to challenge such evil. There was a priest of such determination in Guatemala. He was a very good man, known simply as Padre Bueno — in English translated as one chose: "the father of good" or "the good father." His full name within the church was Padre Augustino Herzog. He was Juan Pablo's first-cousin.

Padre Bueno knew many secrets about Juan Pablo. Together they had attended school, until Juan Pablo was sent to America. As a priest Padre Bueno had learned the true details of the death of the young postulant. He could not allow Juan Pablo to continue destroying the name of the Herzog family and the country Padre Bueno loved. He talked frequently to Juan Pablo, who went beyond denying his actions; he ridiculed his saintly cousin and the institution of the church from which Padre Bueno received his strength.

After deep thought and prayer, Padre Bueno took the matter public, denouncing Juan Pablo in the Catholic newspaper, in letters to the Attorney General's office, and, most dangerous of all, from his pulpit. It was the latter that enraged Juan Pablo.

As Padre Bueno led his parishioners on Easter morning through Antigua's narrow streets, treading gently on the religious scenes which the devout had crafted for days in colored sawdust, and before hundreds of onlookers, Padre Bueno was hacked to death by four machete-wielding, drug-crazed disciples — not of Christ but of Juan Pablo.

From the oldest living members of the Herzog families to the youngest, even to third and fourth cousins, came condemnation for the murder of their Padre Bueno. They spoke out, but they had acted too late.

On the day that Padre Bueno was to be buried in a gleaming, polished, white Carrera marble mausoleum, among the tree-lined pathways of Antigua's San Lázaro Cemetery, Juan Pablo struck his family with the fury of his deranged mind.

Antigua, designated by the Spanish conquistadores as "La Muy Noble y Muy Leal Ciudad de Santiago de los Caballeros de Guatemala," served as the country's capital until successive earthquakes severely tested the will of God by burying His great edifices in rubble and ash. These buildings had been constructed largely by impoverished, non-believing indios, who rarely understood the fairness of trading their labor for conversion to Christianity. Overlooking Antigua, the volcano Agua, as well as both the more distant Acatenango and the eternally smoking Fuego, seemed prepared to once again spill molten fury on the heathens below.

The mass for Padre Bueno was held at the 1543 Cathedral Metropolitana, a towering colonial fusion of stone, terracotta, and sweat that had been severely damaged by earthquakes and eruptions, but had lingered on in varying stages of decay over two centuries from the consequences of the nation's poverty. Those unable to pay their respects by entering the overflowing cathedral waited patiently across from the main entrance, among the spring flowers in the Plaza Mayor. Flowers that were given life by water in the Plaza's central fountain that burst in streams from the breasts of a quartet of angels.

While life was being regenerated in the Central Plaza's fountain, the cadaver of Padre Bueno lay in a closed casket in front of the cathedral's altar where he had celebrated hundreds of masses. The casket received from many the veneration his life had earned.

Juan Pablo stood in the rear during the funeral mass and departed quietly after the service. The funeral cortege that assembled was the longest people could remember. They walked in silence the few blocks toward San Lázaro, heads bowed in respect and personal grief, the cobblestone streets dotted with many flowing tears. It was their last walk for Padre Bueno, and for many the last walk of their own lives.

As the cortege, led by many family members, came within view of Padre Bueno's final resting place, two dozen men wearing wooden ceremonial masks depicting the hated conquistador Don Pedro Alvarado, attacked the funeral procession. They first threw grenades among the hundreds of mourners walking behind the casket, then selectively machine-gunned every member of the Herzog family they could find, and some three dozen others who were unfortunate to have been friends of the grieving family. This episode would take more lives than the last eruption of Agua, which had killed scores of the city's sleeping inhabitants.

As the slaughter of the mourners subsided, the aroma of coffee drifted over the area from one of the Herzog's plantations behind the cemetery. That very product had brought great wealth to a family which in minutes was reduced to the aged and the infirm few who had been unable to attend the service.

When the smoke of the explosives lifted, the survivors of the procession looked to the front, where the casket of Padre Bueno had been torn apart by a grenade. Hanging from a hole in the casket's side was his embalmed, bloodless but broken hand, clutching a rosary from which a silver cross dangled and turned, reflecting the rays of the sun streaming through the trees.

High above the city Agua began to smoke for the first time in decades. On the streets of Antigua, starting with those who had barely survived the slaughter and extending for blocks, there commenced a wail from the women that increased to a deafening crescendo and continued for half an hour. Thereafter, on the anniversary of this brutal massacre, there would be awakenings by citizens of Antigua who would swear that the wailing of these women of Antigua had stirred them.

The world was outraged; newspapers on every continent showed grisly photos of the deaths. The Vatican held special masses for Padre Bueno, while at the same time publishing embellished statements adorned with Vatican seals and tassels, cautioning that the perpetrators had souls that must be prayed for and saved.

Juan Pablo was unseen for weeks. During his absence the public was so terrified that throughout Guatemala his name was spoken only in whispers.

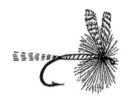

2

I WAS UNEXPECTEDLY THRUST into the macabre world of Juan Pablo Herzog as Professor Maxwell Hunt at the University of Florida law college in Gainesville.

While snowbirds fleeing the oncoming summer humidity were racing home northwards, uncluttering the roads of thousands of geriatric drivers, I was in my third floor office where I'd been teaching for twenty years. The Cuban Buena Vista Social Club's *Chan Chan* was playing in the background. Compay Segundo was singing:

> *El cariño que te tengo (The love I have for you)*
> *Yo no lo puedo negar (I cannot deny)*
> *Se me sale la babita (My mouth is watering)*
> *Yo no lo puedo evitar (I just can't help myself)*

Except for *Chan Chan* the day was evolving miserably.

After my eight a.m. class a student followed me upstairs to my office.

"Professor Hunt, you *have* to change my fall grade in International Law from a *D* to a *B*."

"Let's review *why* you received a *D*," I suggested.

"You don't understand. I'm too busy with campus politics to go over my exam. I *need* the higher grade. A *D* looks lousy on my record when I interview for a job. I'm not challenging the merits of my exam. I just *have* to have a better grade."

"If I review your exam, I'm as likely to lower the grade as raise it."

He left.

At the ten a.m. faculty meeting a female professor moved that: "The faculty of law shall cease hiring *any* male faculty until women represent a minimum of one-half the faculty, in accordance with Title IX."

"Ms. Wade," I responded, "it appears you're unaware that Title IX applies to sports programs, not law faculty. I suggest you differentiate between *women in sports* and *sporting women.*"

Assistant Dean Rodney Jones dropped by as I was about to leave for lunch and pleaded, "Maxwell, you have to repaint your office. This dreadful red is not an authorized office color."

"Rodney, the only *authorized* color is *pallid gray*. It's the same gray that's on every wall of this law school, and makes the place look like my old destroyer." One weekend a decade ago when no one was around, my wife El and I had painted the walls an energetic Chinese red. Then we'd hung a dozen late 18th-century Japanese woodblock prints by Kitagawa Utamaro.

"Your office must be *uniform*, Maxwell. *Uniform!* Additionally, it would be *more* so if you removed those ugly foreign cartoons and replaced them with your diplomas and awards."

I didn't go to lunch. My hunger had already departed.

Other than that, it was a clear, eighty degrees, early spring day. Florida's seasonal humidity was late arriving, and nobody was complaining.

I closed my door. That was enough visitors for one day. . . . Five minutes later I had a call from Frank Cisco at the CIA mission at the U.S. embassy in Guatemala. Reviewing the sparse file on Juan Pablo Herzog in the embassy files, Cisco had found only one brief reference to Juan Pablo's friends at the University of Florida. One name stood out. *Mine.*

"Professor," Cisco began, "there's been some new trouble here in Guatemala City that likely involves Juan Pablo Herzog. Thought you'd be interested."

"Frank, I read some time ago about the murder of Padre Bueno, and the butchery in Antigua at the funeral. Hard to believe it was Juan Pablo. I was fond of him when he was a UF student. Brilliant. Polite. Elegant dresser. What I've read makes me wonder if he's the same person."

"He's the same. We have information only about Juan Pablo's activities in Guatemala. We need to fill in his time line in the U.S. You can do that. We need you here to help."

"I'm tied up the next two weeks, ending with a lecture in D.C. I suppose I could fly to Guatemala City from Washington as soon as that lecture is over." I told him my D.C. schedule.

"We'll make the travel arrangements. Thanks, Professor."

The next day, a fortyish man in a dark blue suit, wearing sunglasses even in the law building's dimly lighted halls, hand delivered airline tickets to my office. The mission has plans for me. In less than twenty-four hours it had arranged the "purpose" of my visit — to give lectures at both the Francisco Marroquín University and the Guatemalan Chamber of Commerce.

Ten days later on a soggy Friday I flew to D.C. for the annual meeting of the American Society of International Law. The cordial, attractive receptionist at the Army and Navy Club gave me my favored room, decorated with Chinese antique furniture and art donated by the widow of Chiang Kai-Shek. After attending the opening reception at the State Department, and presenting my lecture Saturday morning, I checked out of the club — less than twenty-four hours after arriving. A car was waiting. The driver said only "good afternoon, Mr. Johnson,"

13

and handed me an envelope, which I opened with curiosity to avoid watching him drive eighty mph to Dulles. The envelope contained a diplomatic passport and new first-class tickets, both in the name of Richard Johnson. Why was this necessary if I were only going to spend a few hours at the U.S. embassy talking about Juan Pablo's years studying at Florida, and give two public lectures? Cisco obviously hadn't told me everything.

On the way out of the La Aurora International Airport on the outskirts of Guatemala City, I bought flowers for a lady professor friend at Marroquín from a woman sitting on the sidewalk, wearing the dress of the highland village of Sololá. I gave her four quetzales, worth a week's food for a family of ten. She smiled as much as her poverty allowed.

A man from the U.S. embassy was waiting. He stood by a large Suburban. Both man and car were dressed in black. The driver never told me his name. I sat in the back holding the flowers. Before we left the airport the driver turned his head and said, "Sir, please place your hands in your lap."

I put the flowers down and placed my hands in my lap — unquestioning but uncertain. I heard several solid clicks.

"Those were door locks," he said. "You're secure. The vehicle is heavily armored. No one can get in."

"Or out," I murmured.

"Open the compartment on the back of the front seat." This time he didn't say "please."

I pushed the button on the panel. It opened forming a tray.

"There are two, identical Uzi SMGs in the compartment. They're unloaded. Take one out."

I felt the cold, blackened steel of a weapon I hadn't handled for years, not since the Sudan.

Take an empty clip from the compartment . . . insert it into the weapon." He worked me through the process all the way to

14

pulling the trigger. I cradled the lethal weapon more carefully than the flowers, which were now strewn on the seat. The driver concluded my lesson: "If we should have any trouble, you may need the weapon. Now, take the empty clip out and insert one of the loaded thirty-two cartridge clips. Put the gun back. Close the compartment . . . sit back, relax, and enjoy the ride."

I sat back. I didn't relax. And I didn't much enjoy the ride.

The desk clerk at the Camino Real was a pretty, dark-eyed twenty-something. As attractive as the receptionist at the Army and Navy Club, but with slightly ochered skin that evolution had adjusted to the tropics.

"Professor Hunt, welcome to Guatemala. You'll have the ninth floor."

"The whole floor? One room is fine," I said, perhaps unfairly responding to what I thought her reasonably proficient English had intended to say — "You'll *be on* the ninth floor."

"*Room* 904," she said quietly, leaning over the counter. "But you do *have* the ninth floor. The *whole* floor. No one else will be using that floor during your stay." She smiled in a way to let me know she had said what she intended to say.

I could smell her perfume. Chanel No.5, blending nicely with copal burning in a small incensario on the counter.

Sunday morning, after a breakfast kaleidoscope of fresh fruits grown close-by — mango, papaya, watermelon, and banana — I went to the nearby U.S. embassy in the same SUV. A different driver. I wondered if the Uzi was still loaded. I didn't ask, and I didn't touch the button on the compartment.

The day passed quickly talking about Juan Pablo with a half-dozen mission agents. Their names included Smith, Jones, Johnson, and Rogers. The ambassador was elsewhere working on matters essential to U.S. foreign policy. At noon he was scheduled to cut a ribbon to open a new McDonald's franchise. In the afternoon he'd escort two visiting, lame-duck D.C. congressmen on a tour of Antigua, followed by a private dinner at the historic Popenoe House, hosted by several members of the coffee oligarchy. The coffee growers likely know more about Juan Pablo than the mission agents. The ambassador has probably never heard of him.

Dropped off at the hotel, I was told I'd be picked up at nine the following morning for my lecture at Marroquín. After a leisurely hour in the hotel dining room, entertained by a four-piece marimba group from Totonicapán, I went to my room and began revising my lecture notes. I sat near the window overlooking the pool and Avenida Roosevelt beyond; my view of the surrounding hills at night obscured the poverty. The lights all twinkled. I felt like Peter Pan.

While scribbling a note about something I wanted to remember to say at the morning lecture, I heard noise behind me. It was after midnight. Someone was trying to unlock my door. I thought my room was secure. *I thought the whole ninth floor was secure.* It must be either hotel security or people from the embassy. Even that disturbs me. I like people to knock.

The door opened as I rose and three men entered. Juan Pablo Herzog was first. Impressively dressed, as I remembered. A little aging that I wouldn't have noticed had I seen him every day. In the half-dozen years since his UF graduation, his face had become more severe: tightness at the corners of his mouth, a firmer jaw, and a scar below his left ear I wouldn't ask about.

Behind Juan Pablo was Abdul Khaliq Isfahani, elegant and immaculate in a tailored silk suit. He looked as though he had come from a photo shoot at *Gentlemen's Quarterly*. His unblinking raven eyes were different. I remembered them as kind eyes, but now they carried a hint of suspicion and mistrust.

The third person was neither familiar nor introduced. He spoke only to Juan Pablo, in a Spanish with the lyrical rhythm of the western highlands. He stood a little behind Juan Pablo, a telling bulge under the left arm of his suit jacket.

Juan Pablo did most of the talking. It began cordially.

"*Professor* Hunt, it has been too many years since Abdul Khaliq and I were the fortunate recipients of your kind hospitality in Gainesville. It is very good to see you again. You appear to be in excellent health."

The sentence was spoken carefully in impeccable English, occasionally infused with the soft Latin musicality characteristic of the successive generations of Herzogs. Juan Pablo drew his words out as though there were twice the number in a sentence, making each word appear to carry special meaning. I remembered it was such a pleasure to hear him speak; I had to listen carefully to what his sentences were intended to convey, or I became lost in the elegance of their construction and delivery.

"Juan Pablo, you've burst into my room . . . in the middle of the night! How did you get in?" I erred in focusing on *how* they found me here, rather than *why* they were here.

"That is not important, Professor." The lines where his eyes blended into his temples wrinkled.

I wanted to defuse my poor beginning. "I'm sorry about the death of so many members of your family, Juan Pablo. I hope what's been in the international papers about your alleged involvement was not true." That may have been more like *lighting* the fuse. But he smiled. Had I perhaps reminded him of a *happy* time?

"None of it is true, Professor. I assure you. Merely the ranting of a few adversaries jealous of my business successes."

17

I turned to Abdul Khaliq, who'd remained motionless beside Juan Pablo. "What brings you to Guatemala, Abdul?"

"My friend Juan Pablo, of course. I came on the anniversary of the tragic death of his cousin, Padre Bueno, and have stayed on to console him and reminisce about better times. And *you*, Professor Hunt, what has brought *you* here? And why would you come to Guatemala without first contacting Juan Pablo?"

"I've come a few times over the past years . . . nearly always to lecture at the Marroquín law faculty. Just for a day or two; unfortunately no time for seeing friends. I love this country — the Maya ruins, the Colonial history, Antigua and. . . ."

Juan Pablo's tone changed abruptly as he interrupted with a more forceful voice. "You first visited here *nineteen* years ago, Professor."

Juan Pablo picked up the desk chair, set it in the middle of the room, motioned me to sit down, and stood close enough that I could smell a mix of garlic and after-shave.

"On that visit you spoke at a bar association meeting, met with U.S. embassy staff . . . *including CIA agents* . . . and traveled outside Guatemala City by private vehicle."

His information was chillingly accurate.

"Juan Pablo, I'm surprised you have any interest in the travel schedule of a law professor whose reputation hardly extends beyond Gainesville, and whose lectures concern such esoteric subjects as rights of colonization in space or the settlement of disputes over international boundaries. Your information is correct, except for contacts with the CIA. I doubt the CIA has any interest in Guatemala. My contacts within the embassy have always been with the cultural affairs staff."

"You returned nine years ago and again lectured, that time at both the Chamber of Commerce and the Francisco Marroquín law faculty?" Each inquiry came from his lips as a statement, but was twisted into a question at the end.

"True. I was invited by the law faculty to give two lectures, one to the faculty at a luncheon, the other as a lecture to . . ."

"You also appeared on a local radio talk program."

"I did. When Marroquín invited me I called the Guatemalan desk at our State Department. Years ago they asked me to let them know when I was invited here funded by a Guatemalan institution. The State Department's cultural affairs people scheduled me for the lecture at the Chamber of Commerce and the radio interview."

Beads of perspiration were migrating from my forehead to my chin and dripping onto my lap. Juan Pablo showed no emotion. He was enjoying the conversation.

Abdul Khaliq remained silent. He puzzled me. Was he really in Guatemala to commiserate with Juan Pablo? Or was he possibly associated with an al-Qaeda training center in Guatemala? I was beginning to understand why the CIA mission had wanted to talk and why part of the morning's discussion had been about a terrorist training center in the highlands.

Juan Pablo interrupted my thoughts. "You spoke disparagingly about our government, and especially our justice system. And, more recently, you've written expert opinion letters for cases in the United States that allege a breakdown in our legal system, plus widespread corruption throughout the executive branch. Do you think you, as a *foreigner* with little time in Guatemala, know enough to make such statements?"

"Juan Pablo, it's common knowledge the Guatemalan justice system is broken. Your country's been studied closely by the United Nations, the World Bank, Amnesty International — even the Vatican. Not one report has presented an attractive picture about Guatemala's adherence to the rule of law."

"You omitted reference to the CIA Country Reports. Are you familiar with them, Professor?"

"I am. The CIA prepares its own country evaluations. The reports on Guatemala haven't been flattering."

"Did you contribute to the most recent CIA report?"

"No." I didn't know whether I had made contributions by general conversations with mission staff over the past years.

"Did you speak with CIA agents *today* at the embassy?" His face suddenly reddened. Juan Pablo was struggling to control his anger with my responses. He reached into his pocket and withdrew several pills, which he quickly swallowed. He was aware one dropped to the floor, but ignored it. He seemed momentarily confused. Mixed with anger that signaled trouble.

I thought about his questions carefully, and answered, "No, I was with cultural affairs and economic staff people today." That *was* true; the mission agents *officially* have more benign embassy assignments. My answer wasn't what Juan Pablo wanted to hear. I saw his blow coming and twisted to the right as it landed, reducing the harm to cuts around my mouth. Fortunately, his high living and low exercise softened the blow.

The third visitor grabbed me from behind as I struggled to get up. I couldn't escape from several more blows. Apparently the conversational part of our meeting was over. I hoped Juan Pablo had never heard of water-boarding. But even that was better than crucifixion. Or chain saws.

Abdul Khaliq's expression remained stoic. He never moved while Juan Pablo spoke and repeatedly struck me. Juan Pablo's voice became louder, emitting staccato phrases that were less questions than preludes to further blows. "We know *exactly* where you've been in Guatemala on your visits over the past few years. Who you talked to. Receptions you attended. Parcels you dropped off. Messages you sent from your hotel. You were *spying* on the El Molino Alemania coffee plantation in the highlands a decade ago. *You were spying for the CIA.* You disappeared into the woodlands with a guide and didn't return for two hours. Where did you go?"

"If you know my every move, you must know where I went." Clearly the wrong answer. This time I didn't see the worst blow coming, from his left fist that held a roll of Guatemalan twenty-five centavo coins. It caught me on the right temple, momentarily scrambled my vision, and sent me skidding off the chair into the dresser, knocking the mirror off the wall. I could see my distorted, bloodied face as the mirror shattered. I had thrust my hands in front to break the fall, but landed amidst the coins and jagged shards of the mirror. Blood was flowing from one wrist.

The breaking glass attracted attention. A knock on the door. But it wasn't the noisy questioning that had brought the knock. It was a colleague of my visitors.

"Hurry, Señor Herzog, a black SUV has pulled up at the front entrance. It may be from the embassy."

Juan Pablo gave me several parting stomps I was certain damaged ribs, and maybe a kidney. Exiting, he turned in the door frame and said, with a soft grace and smile, "Dear Professor, we didn't come intending to kill you — at least not tonight. Abdul Khaliq and I owe you that. *Leave Guatemala immediately. . . .* If we conclude you're working with the CIA, we *will* come to Gainesville and kill you. Goodbye — *my very dear friend.*"

I never want to be his enemy. As soon as they left, I struggled with bloody hands to dial a number Frank Cisco had given me, but after the first digit lapsed into a void of pain and illusion. Filled with blurred visions of being moved. Of bright lights and close-up faces staring at me. Of bitter taste and conversations I couldn't comprehend.

Two men had carried me down the rear service stairs, out through the laundry to the SUV, and in minutes I was in the embassy. A pathetic, bleeding heap on an examining table. Most of me hurt. The other parts I couldn't feel. But I was safe. Guarded by one of "the few, the proud, the brave." *Semper Fi.* I liked his uniform better than the dark blue suits. Then someone fuzzy looking in a white coat stuck a long needle into one arm.

A dozen hours passed before I regained any semblance of consciousness. I was wrapped with enough bandages to be stored for eternity in a sarcophagus displayed in the CIA museum. Two men carried me to a vehicle that sped to the private aviation side of La Aurora airport. They lifted me into a private jet. Shortly before dusk, four hours later, the plane landed at what appeared to be a military base. I could hear a band playing a military march, followed by a single, mournful bugle playing taps. I hoped it wasn't playing for me.

Borderline conscious and cognizant, I was carried into a grim room in a building so old it could have housed the wounded during the Civil War. I collapsed on a Spartan, metal-framed bed, surrendered to another white coat with another long needle, and missed Tuesday altogether.

Wednesday morning I tried to bathe the few parts that weren't bandaged, and clumsily put my clothes back on. They were torn and darkened by dried blood. I couldn't do my socks or shoes. I didn't dare look in the mirror. While I was sitting on the edge of the bed, trying to remember how to stand, something was slid under my door. It was a downloaded copy of an obituary from my hometown paper, the *Gainesville Gazette*. I like to read obituaries. But not this time. *It was mine:*

Professor Maxwell W. Hunt, of this city, died of a massive stroke Monday in Washington, D.C. He was known to be in good health and his death was unexpected. Hunt received degrees from U.S., Mexican, and

French universities and taught at the law college for twenty years. He was recently elected to the Académie Internationale de Droit Comparé in Paris.

Professor Hunt was preceded in death by his wife El, who was killed in a tragic accident while they were fly fishing on the Snake River in Wyoming a decade ago. They left no children.

No services are planned. The decedent's lawyer recommended that friends might donate to the Grand Teton Coalition, which advocates for better protection of wildlife in Grand Teton National Park, where the Hunts vacationed annually. His ashes will be scattered on Wyoming's Snake River, near the location where his wife died a decade earlier.

Reading my own obituary was a bizarre way to begin a day. I was dumbfounded. Not that *I* planned to write my obituary, but *who* wrote it? I was beaten Sunday night and brought here Monday. The Wednesday paper says I died Monday. How can the CIA be making these decisions without me? Do they *want* me dead? If that's true, they would have let Juan Pablo finish the job and shipped my body home.

I've never thought about cremation. Maybe I'd want an open casket funeral. Not appropriate *this* time. No corpse — yet. Cremation isn't a bad idea. But I have a lot of questions about *why* I had to die.

No one ever knew that a CIA agent carried a small, plastic sandwich bag containing the "ashes" of Maxwell Hunt to the bank of the Snake River in Wyoming. Dressed in the dark blue suit, white shirt, and blue tie masquerade that served his agency well for espionage or funerals, what the agent actually scattered on the river were the ashes of the Sunday edition of *The New York Times* he had read on the plane to Jackson Hole.

3

THE FOLLOWING DAY WAS BETTER, except when I looked in the mirror. It took me only half the usual time to shave — half my face was bandaged. Over the years, I've reached a mutual understanding with the accumulated nicks, sun blotches, age spots, and diminishing color and abundance of hair. But in a mere fifteen minutes Juan Pablo had added more than his fair share of new impediments.

Clean clothes beckoned across a chair. Dressing usually isn't a painful act, but it took me a half-hour. As I pulled the lace tight on my second shoe, I suddenly grasped I was not performing a final dressing task in preparation for heading to the law college. I wouldn't arrive early, make the first morning coffee in the faculty lounge, and teach my class at eight. I wouldn't teach my ten a.m. class either, nor tomorrow's, nor tomorrow's tomorrow.

About now students would be arriving. A quarter normally arrived prepared, another quarter less so — hung over from the night before. The remaining half sat mute, with earplugs connected to their laptops, watching me mouth an hour's unheard words, while they listened to music and sent text messages to friends.

My first class this week was likely greeted by Dean Roscoe Stein, playing the role of saddened leader, and saying a few nice things about my law career. He's a smug, middle-aged, big city swashbuckler, who'd come last year to save the South. I suspect he'll last a year, maybe two. We clashed the first week he arrived, and he's probably thinking about to whom among his few cronies he'll give my endowed professorship. Instead of retiring in a couple of decades as professor *emeritus*, I've gone directly to being "the *late* professor."

Around nine I was escorted to breakfast by a mirror-image of Judi Dench playing M in a James Bond film.

"Relax for the day," she said with a frown. "You have the run of the place."

She meant *only* within "the place." I needed a key to get *out*.

"Where's the swimming pool, the tennis courts, the bar . . . the coed dorms?" I asked.

Her frown became a glare. "The medication you were given that made you nauseous will take another day to wear off. Impertinence will get you a second injection with another week's worth."

"Are we in D.C.?" I asked.

"More or less."

"Can you narrow that a little? My watch says eight a.m. — Guatemalan time. Yours says nine a.m. East coast?"

"More or less. Be happy you're safe and alive." I had doubts about both, but that was all she'd tell me. Then she smiled, tilted her head at me, and made a little chuckling sound. Compared to my Guatemalan episode, being alive was enough.

As we approached the cafeteria I asked M, "How's the food? What do you recommend? A couple of Bloody Marys? Eggs Benedict or Huevos Rancheros?"

"You're not at the Four Seasons. Are you familiar with airline food?" she asked.

"That bad?"

"Worse." She made the chuckling sound again. "I think we buy airline leftovers. I've *never* eaten here. Try *three* Bloody Marys first." Another little chuckle and she left me at the cafeteria door.

I stuck my head in and sniffed. A mix of Pine Sol, Clorox, and vinegar. Plus a touch of garlic. I wasn't sure whether they'd been cleaning or it was the food. My stomach was growling. Not because I was hungry. This time it was growling *at* the food. I chose reconstituted orange juice that came in a sealed carton, plus three small boxes of corn flakes. I may lose twenty extra pounds I've been carrying around, without paying Jenny Craig a dime.

Escorting me to my room after breakfast, M pointed to a lounge she said was mine to enjoy. She gave me a file labeled IIPA, along with a couple of DVDs.

IIPA, I soon discovered, means the Intelligence Identities Protection Act, mainly directed to stopping the disclosure of information that would identify a covert agent, but extended to something like the federal witness security and protection schemes that hide witnesses who give evidence in trials, usually involving organized crime. The idea is to help the good guys. Why me? I want to go home to Gainesville as Maxwell Hunt and report to everyone what Mark Twain said when his death was announced: "Rumors of my death have been greatly exaggerated."

Watching the DVDs, I learned that there's humor after all within the agency. One of the DVDs was a comedy about the witness protection program. In the morning I'll ask M whether Sarah Jessica Parker comes with the IIPA program.

4

SIX-THIRTY THE FOLLOWING MORNING brought a
knock on my door. At least people knock here. I was already dressed; sleep has not come easily. Stiffening in anticipa-
tion, I opened the door.

"I'm Dan Wilson — I'd prefer Dan," said the figure in the
doorway. I've learned names are interchangeable labels within
the CIA. Dan was well dressed, a charcoal pin-stripe suit, blue
shirt with white collar and cuffs. Gold Roman coin cuff-links.
A tie with little American flags. Tall, thin in a runner's way, narrow face, sharp jaw, and comfortable eyes that relaxed my
tenseness. His nearly collar-length brown hair had graying locks
at the temples.

"I'll take you to breakfast where we can talk. It may be your
last meal as Maxwell Hunt."

"*Last meal?* Firing squad at nine?" I asked. He smiled but
didn't answer.

"Do we *have* to go to the cafeteria?" I asked.

"I wouldn't go there if I lost a bet. We're going to a private
dining room. After breakfast we'll talk about your future. By
noon you'll be a different person. I know this is traumatic. I'll
try to help it make sense. You're unique. We don't do this often. We'll try to do it appropriately."

"Not much of the past few days makes sense. My friends think I'm dead. I hurt in a dozen places and look like hell. I stopped counting stitches at fifty-four. I have a great job and plans for the next few months. I keep expecting to wake up from a terrible nightmare."

"The alternative is *more* than a nightmare. We know how dangerous Juan Pablo is when he's angry. *Please* listen to me while we have breakfast."

I ate unconcerned about calories, sodium, or saturated fat — eggs, bacon, ham, sausages, and biscuits. *Very* sweet coffee. We sat in a quiet corner. The few others in the room talked quietly. Probably discussing routine events — assassinations, keeping the Oval Office and Supreme Court at bay, infiltrating Britain's MI6, and dealing with the remnants of the KGB.

"Monday morning a bomb went off in the Francisco Marroquín classroom where you were to lecture. Fourteen students had arrived early: five died. The Chamber of Commerce lecture was canceled, but another bomb went off there at the exact time you were to speak. Several employees stacking chairs were killed. I imagine you'll not be invited back to lecture."

"Probably no honorary degree either," I quipped.

"Probably. But maybe posthumously," Dan countered. "Yesterday, Juan Pablo was stopped at Dulles airport and denied entry. He was carrying two loaded pistols — with illegal silencers. He presented a diplomatic passport. *Our* agents, showing State Department credentials, questioned him. He said he was to visit friends in different parts of the country. He was asked their names. He gave *your* name. Our agents told him you suffered a massive stroke that took your life and that our Justice Department could press murder charges against him because the stroke resulted from the beating he gave you in Guatemala. Juan Pablo was visibly concerned. He's back in

Guatemala. . . . We kept his guns. . . . We've also arranged to have your obituary published in the Guatemalan paper: *La Patria*. We want everyone you know in Guatemala to believe you're dead."

"Dan, Juan Pablo said he'd come to the U.S. and kill me if he discovered I've done *any* work with the CIA. So he's back in Guatemala, having been questioned by U.S. officials he must believe were CIA. He's likely wondering if I'm actually dead. You have his guns. I'll bet he still has his chain saw."

"I think he's convinced you worked for us. Remember, we have a sizeable CIA mission in Guatemala. There are Guatemalan employees at the embassy. Juan Pablo might have coerced information about you from one of them. If he has *any* reason to doubt your death, we think he *will* try again. But we're reasonably confident he thinks you're dead. And if he doesn't believe that, at least he doesn't know where you are."

"So I'm safe? He can't get in here. I can't get out! And I'm not sure what you mean by "reasonably confident.""

"Listen carefully in our sessions, Maxwell, and follow our advice. Or you don't have a future, and you'll waste our time. If all goes well, I'll remain your contact. Over the next two days you'll talk with a dozen people, sign a lot of papers, and begin the transformation to a new life."

"I believe everyone deserves a second chance, Dan. I never imagined this might be the way it happens."

Wilson walked me to a conference room. More soon joined us. Like their names, their dress was about the same. Some of the neckties varied in width as much as a half-inch. Local option. One of the American flag lapel pins had only forty-eight stars — maybe his grandfather had worked for the agency.

What began occasionally sounded like a Socratic debate among themselves over who would give me the poisoned hemlock. I decided I wasn't going down easily. First to speak was a wedge shaped, fiftyish, crew-cut, gray-haired, no-nonsense, posture-perfect, *had-to-be* former Marine. He was introduced as Jim Smith. Of *course* it was Smith.

"Hunt, your *experiences* over the past few days should convince you that you have only one sensible choice about the direction of your future. . . ."

I interrupted, "'one sensible choice' is an oxymoron. If I have to make a *choice* there have to be alternatives. And I think the last few days were less *experiences* than *calamities*. I went to Guatemala to give lectures, not to come home a mess and read my obituary."

Smith continued as though I hadn't uttered a word. "You agreed to talk to us about Juan Pablo Herzog. We didn't force you. Don't complain."

"What I helped you find out is that he's one mean SOB. And he's good at throwing sucker punches. I didn't know he was waiting for me, and had Isfahani with him. I could have talked to you *here* without going to Guatemala and be given a room accessible to homicidal thugs. *You* reserved the room for me."

Smith wasn't impressed. "Your trip paid a *bonus*. We learned about Juan Pablo's intentions. If they hadn't gone to your hotel room, they would have bombed or shot you at one of your lectures. *Forget it!* It's *over!*"

"*My trip paid a bonus?* You learned you can't provide protection. I ended up full of stitches and three square-feet of bruises. Plus there are five dead students at Marroquín and more dead at the Chamber."

Not one person at the table seemed phased. Each *believed* the agency had just completed another well-executed mission. Just like the Bay of Pigs.

Smith changed his attitude from brusque to disdain. He spoke as though I weren't present. Without looking up, like reading a script and inserting the newest names and places, he said, "Maxwell Hunt no longer exists. His death has been reported in the newspapers. We can't stop him from walking away, going back, and surprising friends in Gainesville. Not a very smart choice. Then Juan Pablo — who we *hope* believes Hunt's dead — learns he's very much alive. . . . What we have planned at the minimum gives us, and maybe Hunt, an advantage. If we all do our jobs and," lifting his head and staring directly at me, he continued, "*you* precisely follow our instructions, you may die peacefully in your bed of old age at ninety-five."

Before I could respond, a droll voice from a seriously short but generously fed agent spoke, "Mr. Hunt, let's get to why we're here. There are several *musts*," he said, nodding at me. "The first obviously is your *name*. It has to be changed. Not too much. And you might want to keep your initials."

"My initials are MWH," I said. "They're inscribed on briefcases, suitcases, shirt pockets and cuffs, watch, wallet, a couple of fly rods and reels, several pens, and a golf bag I won as a door prize and use to store garden tools. If other characteristics of my new identity even vaguely hint at my former one, wouldn't using these *same* three initials be foolish?"

"Possibly, Mr. Hunt. But it is your choice," said the droll voice. "In the witness protection and security programs federal marshals have trouble teaching participants to respond quickly and *only* to their new names. If someone in an airport behind you calls out, 'Hey, Maxwell,' you don't want to turn around and say, 'Hi!' But when the gal in Starbucks asks for your name to write on the coffee cup, we *want* you to say, *without* hesitation, your new name, *not* Max. We want you to *quickly* adapt to your new name. We need a name that won't be hard for you to assimilate because it's at such variance with Maxwell Hunt. We want . . ."

Smith interrupted and took over, "Let's *start* with your first name."

"OK. Maybe Mac for Max?" I suggested, toning down my sarcasm.

"That's good — Mac. That's a contraction. For what? Mackenzie? MacDougal?"

"How about Macduff, with Mac for short?"

I didn't tell them my parents had a Shetland Sheepdog named Macduff. His full name was Summerlove Macduff of Inverness. He stopped and peed the first time he was trotting down the runway in the Connecticut equivalent of the Westminster Dog Show. The owners gave him to my parents the next day. If I use Macduff, I'll leave off Summerlove and Inverness. And on my first flight as Macduff, I won't pee on the runway while trotting to the plane.

"Macduff is fine," said Smith, "now what about a last name — I gather you prefer something that doesn't begin with H?"

"I do. . . . A friend named Jim Brooks died a couple of years ago. I never got around to contributing anything in his memory. Maybe I can use Brooks."

"Brooks is good. We don't like using something too common, like Smith. There are too many Smiths already."

"I know," I mumbled. Half of the people I'd met in the past few days were named Smith.

"Middle initial? You want to change the W?"

"Let's drop it. Having one narrows the size of the pool if Juan Pablo starts searching for me."

"Done!" Smith said, cutting off further discussion. "Gentlemen, . . . let me introduce Macduff Brooks!"

He turned to me and said, "We have an arrangement here in D.C. to change a name in the chambers of a judge we trust. There won't be a public record that can be searched. The papers will be kept in our files. You'll get a back-dated birth certificate, and, if ever necessary, we'll see that it's placed in the vital statistics records — anywhere in the country."

In one fell swoop fifty years of Maxwell W. Hunt were erased. He wasn't dead, but he was certainly missing.

I felt drained, but commented, "It isn't easy to wipe out a name or create a fifty-year-old. What happens to my . . . rather *Maxwell Hunt's* . . . bank accounts, car and voter registrations, house deed, a few promises, and bequests? There's a half-completed manuscript on my desk. A will in the drawer. A car at the airport that needs gas. My lawn needs mowing. There's a pile of dirty laundry in my bedroom. You may be able to give me a new identity, but the old one doesn't just disappear."

"We know that. But we *do* make things disappear," Smith answered. "Your coauthors will have to decide what to do with your manuscript. The car's been returned to your house — it still needs gas. We don't do lawns or laundry. I have your will here. It was in the very back of the upper drawer of your desk at the law school."

"How on earth did you . . . ?"

"One of our agent-lawyers has been in Gainesville. He visited the law school Monday and showed Dean Stein powers of attorney. They identified our agent as the attorney who prepared your will, including your request that he be appointed executor. Dean Stein took him to your office where the agent found your will. Incidentally, on the way out of the office, the dean pulled your name-plate off the door and tossed it into the wastebasket. Then our agent met with your friend, Professor Palladio. He wrote your obituary. I apologize for this intrusion, but we needed to work quickly before good-meaning friends stepped in to help, and inadvertently compromised your situation."

Passing across the table a coffee-stained, worn folder that had written on it: "The Last Will and Testament of Maxwell W. Hunt," Smith noted, "Here's your old will. . . . Does anyone else have a copy?"

"No," I answered, "I have no close next-of-kin. I wrote it after El died, leaving everything to the law college and several charities. I assume that as Macduff Brooks I'll be able to have a new will with all the same bequests."

"We've prepared one for you, witnessed, dated, and notarized as of eight years ago. There's no appointment of an executor so you may wish to appoint someone by a codicil, probably an attorney in your new location. And, of course, you have to fill in your name and sign it. Do that now, using your new name — Macduff Brooks — with no middle initial."

Like a punctured balloon — the air gushing out of me — I slumped back in my chair. How could my life have changed so quickly? And how do these government people work, compromising privacy and taking liberties with others' lives? A week ago I was in Gainesville adding some finishing touches to my presentation for the law meeting in Washington, shortly to have lunch with Roy Palladio to plan a trip to Easter Island, and looking forward to hearing Joshua Bell play Tchaikovsky's *Violin Concerto* the following week. . . . I thought, "Life's good" . . . but now it's *past* tense.

After a few deep breaths and a sip of coffee I stood and stretched my arms. Then sat back down. Trying to create a handwriting script that differed from my old, I signed the will. I must have looked mentally, as well as physically, battered.

"Overwhelmed, Mac?" asked Dan Wilson, patiently.

"Yeah, I wonder if I'll ever know who I am."

"Understood. But you *can't* go back to being Maxwell — *ever.*" Dan continued, "You're the first academic we've placed in the protection program. Most of the entrants have been our own full-time agents. They've served years, their identities not even known by many people at Langley. Your case is a first for us in many ways, some of which we haven't fully thought through."

"*Your* agents are different, Dan. They take the job knowing they might be compromised. I never thought about that as a law professor. . . . Is this really necessary? What if Juan Pablo and Abdul Khaliq are killed this year. Then I'm no longer in danger. But it's too late, I'm settled in some Hicksville in West Virginia doing God knows what. I'd rather have my old job back. And I'm happy living in Gainesville."

"We're concerned with *right now*. You're in great danger. We'll worry about the future when it arrives. Remember, Mac, being a law professor didn't get you here — it was your work for us. You *never* said no."

"I know." Dan was right. I never said no when asked. Was it patriotism? Or compulsive behavior?

"Mac," Dan noted with a tone of fatherly comforting, "I sense you're *committed* to making this work. That makes our role easier."

I wasn't committed, just *pragmatic*. There's a difference. Commitment means a little flag waving. That's not what I want to do. If I'm going to be Mac, it's going to be plain Mac, not Mac-formerly-a-law-professor. The diplomas, degrees, memberships, and awards as a professor are probably already in boxes in a closet at the law school. They'll sit there until some new custodian finds them in a few years and files them in the dumpster outside. If anyone asks where Maxwell Hunt is buried, the best answer would be: "in the Gainesville landfill." I wonder if it's being committed or pragmatic to ask that my art be collected from my office and sent to my new location.

"You don't do lawns or laundry, Dan. Do you do art?"

"I understand. Our agent said you had some Japanese woodblock prints in your office. We'll have them removed and stored with your household belongings."

"Thanks, the dean will be pleased to see the 'ugly foreign cartoons' gone." Dan looked at me quizzically.

"We have more to decide," a new voice said from the far end of the table. Except for Dan, he had the longest hair of the group, but it still didn't reach his collar. He had a Slavic accent. Maybe the agency hired some Russians when the KGB downsized.

"Let's do one more thing before lunch," the new voice said. "It's a question Americans seem to toss out at dinner parties — 'If you could live *anywhere*, where would it be?'"

I'd played the game with friends and tried to recall where I'd said I wanted to live. But this time it was for real. They're going to give me a one-way ticket to my choice.

"Do you mean *in* the country — the U.S.?"

"It's *absolutely* your choice, Mac. We don't want to settle you in Topeka or Tulsa, and after a year have you insist we move you."

"If you try to settle me *anywhere* in the Great Plains I'll be demanding a new place before the moving van's left Florida."

The droll voice agent looked upset. In a go-to-hell tone, he interrupted, "I'm from Oklahoma. You have something against the Great Plains?"

"Ever watch *CIS-Topeka*? Or *NCIS-Tulsa*? You want me to spend summers in Oklahoma and winters in North Dakota? I prefer summers in Paris and winters in Marbella."

"OK, you get the point," said the new voice, "but the more places you live, the more people will know you. Our agents are assigned specific areas of the country. *No* agents cover abroad." I thought out loud, hoping someone would interrupt if my reasoning were irrational. "On one trip west, my wife El and I explored Paradise Valley, a fifty- to sixty-mile stretch north of Yellowstone National Park in Montana. We were attracted by a creek near Emigrant that flows into the Yellowstone River. If I had a log cabin along that creek, I'd have the privacy I've sought since El died . . . and that my new life as Macduff encourages." After a pause, I asked, "What do you think? Is Montana OK?"

"Anywhere you like. We have an agent in Bozeman."

"I assume I can have my medical records sent to me?"

"Yes. They'll be reworked to include your new name and a former location that is *not* Florida. . . . Your dental records will be destroyed. Your fingerprints as Max will be altered. Mac, have you ever worn glasses?"

"Never."

"You do now; we'll fit you tomorrow. With frames that don't make you look like a professor."

"Should I grow a moustache? Never had one." I was thinking somewhere between Boston Blackie's pencil-thin one and Sam Elliot's shrubbery.

"Moustache is good," said Dan.

A young, testy agent took over, and we began to talk about what I would *do* in Montana — what kind of work. His shaved head enhanced ears that begged for coverage. A full beard bore some remnants of breakfast. His tone showed he thought the meeting was boring and keeping him from important work. I thought he'd been dozing, slumped down in his chair, maybe to hide his inexperience. "The government isn't going to pay you the rest of your life. You'll have to work."

I answered quickly, "Why does the government pay so many people for not working? Does *having* to work apply here as well?" The day was showing — I was tired and taking it out on the next generation.

Jim Smith winced and took over. "You're still a taxpayer. At some point we expect you to earn your own money."

Another agent, perhaps the group's lawyer, squinting through tortoise-rimmed, Coke-bottle bifocals, added, "It would be difficult for you to teach law — if you're thinking of that. Your credentials — educational background and publications — would be checked."

But that's what I do. I teach law. Even if I stop, I have several books that will be used for years to come. I have contracts to write more. It isn't easy to discard a profession. I'm feeling excommunicated. And I haven't abused any children.

Another agent shuffled papers in front of him. He'd been hunched over a laptop, frenetically tapping throughout the meeting. Apparently the group's CPA. "You hardly need to work. We know about your assets and income. Your retirement plan was TIAA. We'll convert it to your new name. You can start drawing income in a dozen years — normal retirement age. You have a good plan. Also, royalties from your publications will continue for eight to ten years. They'll be paid to your estate, which we can keep open that long, annually transferring the funds to your new account. Open an account in a Montana bank — your choice. You also have a brokerage account started with an inheritance a decade ago. I'll transfer it to a new account in your new name, but run through here. Then forward it to your new broker. Tax free. Find a broker where you decide to live. . . . Any thoughts about what you might like to do?"

"Maybe a fly fishing guide," I tossed out with little thought. "Guiding would give me a very different identity. I once told both Herzog and Isfahani that I'd never fish again after El's death. If they ever look for me, it won't be in the Mountain West. But I won't stay there in the winter. The only sensible Montana creatures between December and May hibernate. I'll find a small, secluded place along the Florida coastal salt marshes. . . . Don't worry. I won't live in Gainesville."

"We'll talk about a second location — *especially* Florida — another time," Smith noted. "Let's get you to Montana for now. What you do for a living is your choice. Be a guide if you wish. Just remember that if you forfeit your cover doing something foolish, all we lose is a lot of tedious paper work and having to spend money on you."

"You could use the money saved to buy new uniforms."

"That may be humorous to you," another agent said, interceding, "but not to me. . . . The witness protection program has problems with too many people relocating in certain places. *Everyone* wants to live in Hollywood. There must be some neighborhoods in Beverly Hills that are half relocated people."

"Half in relocation, the other half in rehab," I quipped, probably close to Beverly Hills demographics.

"It's getting late," noted Dan. "What haven't we covered?"

"I have belongings in Gainesville," I answered, "at both my house and law school office. How do I get my things?"

"We'll sell your car. Vehicles are easily traced. Buy one at your new destination."

"Since my law school days are over, you can tell the dean all the books in my office have been left to the law school library. I have copies of what I've written . . . rather what Maxwell Hunt wrote. I'll want those, even if I have to keep them hidden.

. . . I just thought of something else. I have files of my Guatemalan trips . . . I can't fully recall what's in them."

"*We* know. We went through your files," said the only agent who hadn't spoken. He had sat quietly listening all day. Heavily pock-marked face, like a golf ball. Middle-parted hair. Eyes with horizontal slits like a German gun turret on the beaches at Normandy. I would have been horrified to walk in and find him going through my files. "Everything related to Guatemala has been removed and is in our files now. *Nothing* suggests you ever compromised us. You never mentioned your work for us."

Smith took over again, "Dan Wilson has access to your Gainesville house. We'll move what you want to storage under Dan's name, for later transfer to some storage warehouse in Montana. Once there, you can sell, give away, or keep what you want. I suggest you dispose of most of your clothing. Use the Goodwill facility in Bozeman, but destroy anything *you* might be identified with, specially tailored suits, and *anything* with UF Gator logos."

"What about books inscribed to me, especially some special ones when I was a kid?"

"If they say 'to Max' throw away the page with the inscription. Or get rid of the book."

"And photo albums of trips El and I took?"

"Same answer. They're a dead giveaway."

I was stunned. The photos of El and me stay. So do the books my favorite aunt gave me that were so endearingly inscribed. But I *can* do without my dozen London bought, twin-flap, pin-stripe, charcoal-grey Harrods suits. Not quite "English Bespoke" tailoring, but elegant on any law college scale. Probably made in Harrods' basement by illegal Chinese immigrants. I could donate them to the CIA. Then they'd look like London MI6 agents. I'll keep one suit and a couple of blazers. I won't need a suit and tie if I'm a guide rowing a drift boat! Even if it's a wooden boat with a lot of varnished mahogany. I'll dump scruffy clothes Goodwill won't take. I should leave my old sneaks to the law school dean — he wears sneaks to work. They pair well with his cheap, off-the-rack, polyester suits.

"I think my future is in jeans and Wrangler shirts. I've never worn either. But no rhinestones. When I guide I'll wear a Stetson as a sort of trademark, maybe with a little gold alligator pin on the headband."

"You might be surprised how clothes change one's appearance," interjected Smith, "but leave the gator pin off the hat."

"Anything else we can help you with, Mac?" asked Dan.

I didn't answer. My mind was on overload. But my mute switch was on.

Smith had a final warning. "Don't make contact with *any* former law school associates, co-authors or editors of your books, neighbors, or even distant relatives. If needed, let us do it for you. Max is *dead*. He *must* stay dead. And don't go back to Gainesville — period. People in the program who've followed our advice have *never* been compromised and killed."

That evening I sat in my room, my only companion a soon empty bottle of a full-bodied French Drouhin *Pouilly Fuissé*. Courtesy of Dan, who thought the session went well. I wanted to go out and walk the streets. But if I did, I didn't know who I would be. Dan said I was Macduff Brooks. I feel like Maxwell Hunt.

5

OVER BREAKFAST THE NEXT MORNING Dan told me there was one final change to be made.

"We want to make you *look* like someone else."

"I thought you wanted me *not* to look like Maxwell Hunt."

"It's more challenging for our people if they have a goal in mind."

"I'm not auditioning for a role in a movie. I thought you *hid* people, not created your own versions of Frankenstein."

"We won't do much Mac, just a touch here and there to distract someone who thinks they know you."

"When do you want to do this?"

"Tomorrow morning. Right here. We have our own medical clinic and a D.C. plastic surgeon who comes on call."

"Can I shoot him after he finishes so he can't identify me?"

"I'll tell him you asked."

"What about fixing my bad knees at the same time?"

"No, but he does great frontal lobotomies for us."

Before I went under, I looked to assure myself the surgeon wasn't wearing a dark blue suit, white shirt, and blue tie. But I couldn't see under his scrubs. He performed a couple of facial nips and tucks and smoothed out a little dip and slant on my nose from a soccer game decades ago. He also removed a small but visible and defining birthmark an inch below my right ear, grafting some skin from one of the few places Juan Pablo hadn't bruised. Lastly, he altered my fingerprints.

When the bandages were removed a few days later, my first look in the mirror showed subtle touches that made an overall modest change. I didn't think I would be mistaken for Max. And hopefully not for Frankenstein.

My hair had grown enough for its new trimming. A young man came to my room carrying scissors. His massive hair looked like Liberace's late period. Or early Elvis. But not his dress — that looked like Elton John. All black and red leather. I hope he doesn't need Elton's big glasses to see to cut my hair.

From the chair I asked, "So you're the agency's barber?"

"*No*, I am not a *barber*," he replied, obviously displeased. "I am a hair *stylist*. We need to talk about . . . *style*." He walked around behind me, draped both his bare arms over my shoulders, put his head down close to mine, and whispered in my left ear, "I don't *cut* hair. I *fashion* it."

I could smell lavender. Then I saw his tattoos — shoulder to wrist on each arm. Detailed copies of Picasso's erotic drawings. I wondered if he's in the protection program. If I saw him on the street, I would never guess he's a hair stylist for the CIA. Even if he wore a little American flag lapel pin.

"Make my hair look like it was cut in a Montana *barbershop* and not a Sunset Boulevard hair salon," I said, and shut my eyes and hoped for the best. It came out OK, longer than I usually wore it as Max, not quite as long as one of Ted Turner's Montana bison. I was thankful I didn't smell like lavender. I checked my arms. No erotic tattoos.

The effect of all the work agreeably took off a few years. But a touch of gray hair-coloring put a few back. My moustache was beginning to show; it would soon obscure a scar left by

Juan Pablo. My new glasses could have come from an ad in *GQ*. If El saw me now, she might pass on by. Or make a pass.

With Dan's help over the following week we addressed a few final details. We created a new e-mail address and added special software to a laptop he gave me. Nothing seemed impossible for him when he entered the right access code. We downloaded, executed and returned checking account forms from the Montana Bank of the Rockies in Emigrant, Montana. Dan closed my Gainesville accounts and transferred the funds to Montana. Two days later a checkbook arrived from Emigrant, the balance matching what Dan transferred. My Gainesville account checks had a leaping dolphin on the front; my Montana checks show a serious looking grizzly. A welcoming e-mail from the bank said it had a free toaster I could pick up when I stopped by the Emigrant office. I need to build a house for the toaster.

Dan asked, "who will you use to handle your investments?"

"I have one rule in retaining a broker — *never* use a big New York *broker*. That matches my *never* use a big New York *bank* rule. I'll find local Montana folks who don't take orders from Wall Street. . . . One thing I don't have yet is a Montana driver's license. Any suggestions?"

"Montana is one of those red states that fantasize that the federal Constitution reserved some powers to the states," Dan said. "Montana is *certain* that states are above the federal government in the constitutional hierarchy. Some western state officials aren't very cooperative with federal agencies, and especially dislike the FBI and the CIA. The only acronym that excites them belongs to the NRA. . . . You'll have to stand in line and get your driver's license, like everyone else. Until you can show *Montana residency* the motor vehicle office in Bozeman won't talk to you about a license. Florida residency will get you a polite rejection. Washington, D.C., residency will get you a frown and a lecture on how government *should* function."

"How did I get a new Social Security number — better yet a new financial statement from the Social Security Administration — showing Macduff Brooks has accumulated exactly what Maxwell Hunt had in his account? And how are my bank funds and brokerage accounts being transferred so smoothly without my signature?"

"The Lord works in mysterious ways," said Dan. "We think *we* do even better." He excused himself and left.

Until now I've never known much about what goes on inside that big, cumbersome, contradictory entity called: "The Government." Much less within the myriad of secretive agencies. I'm learning to shut up and adapt. I've adopted a mantra: "I have no choice — Hare Hare." No drums. No free lunches. No saffron robes. Just a little reality.

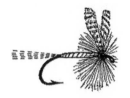

6

PHYSICALLY HEALED but brimming with mental mis-apprehension, two weeks after I arrived I was let out of my confinement for a solo walk. I was where I thought, a military facility on the edge of D.C. It was Macduff Brooks' first day on the loose. A cab dropped me near the White House.

My initial stop was Starbucks. "A Grande coffee latte please, low-fat milk, no whipped cream, no chocolate sprinkles." I automatically reached into my left rear pocket for my wallet. Nothing there. I was flustered.

"What's your name?" the young man asked, holding up an empty cup and black marking pen.

"Max . . . *I mean Mac*, that's with a 'c'!" I was ready to run. If I can't handle Starbucks, what hope is there? Nervously, I tried my right rear pocket. A wallet! It had a Social Security card, a Visa card from the Bozeman Federal Credit Union, an AMEX card, medical and prescription cards, and a ten-dollar D.C. metro card. All the cards had my new name. There were also five brand new ten-dollar bills. The last time I'd looked, my wallet had Guatemalan quetzales. I hope I'll never need them again. Lastly, there was a Starbucks card with fifteen dollars credit. The CIA was buying me coffee!

Walking along the east side of Farragut Square, without a thought I went up two steps toward the entrance of the Army and Navy Club. The bar's on the second floor in front. The Gentleman Jack's on the shelf on the far left. I could almost smell it. Only three weeks ago I stayed here, before I flew to Guatemala. I'll miss the club. My liver won't. The doorman frowned at me and I backed down the steps. I wasn't close to meeting the dress code.

Walking away from the club, West Point's "On Brave Old Army Team" began to bellow from my shirt pocket. A West Pointer, Dan had given me the cell phone.

"Hello . . . General, *sir!*" I said.

"How's your walk going?" Dan asked.

"Fine, but I don't care for the rap music on my ringer."

"It has a D.C. number. Destroy the phone when you get settled and buy a new one."

"I'm already changing the ringer."

On an impulse, I tapped in the phone numbers for my Gainesville home. Maybe not a bright idea. A computer voice said, "This line has been disconnected. Please try again. For a fee of six dollars, we will attempt to connect you every two minutes."

I feel a little disconnected myself. When I returned to the military base, Dan drilled into my memory his personal cell phone number that I can use if I have any questions or any trouble. It's my own special 911. Likely to be a little late if someone shows up on my doorstep in Montana, points a Glock at me, and says, "Buenos días. Adiós Maxwell!"

Tomorrow I leave for Montana. The whole process of getting into this program may soon be a distant, surreal memory. I hope so. Better than a recurring nightmare.

I walked to my room mumbling, "*I have no choice. Hare Hare.*"

7

A GAINST THE FLOW OF MORNING TRAFFIC Dan drove me to Dulles airport. He was unusually relaxed. Either he had a good night's sleep or was ecstatic to see me leave.

At the departures concourse he said, "Macduff, I'm pleased I've been assigned as your main contact in the agency."

"I wouldn't have it any other way," I responded. We shook hands. Firmly and sincere, the way friends do. It helped a lot.

My tickets read Denver with a connection to Bozeman. No government jet this time. No first class. Not even business class. My seat was far back in steerage, which would be as crowded and stale as the hold on a slave ship.

When I was down to number three in a long line at the ticket counter, I realized I didn't have an identifying photo. I opened the ticket envelope Dan had given me in the car. On top of the ticket was a new passport issued to Macduff Brooks. The photo showed traces of yet-to-heal redness on my nose.

Settling into my seat on the plane, I opened a book I'd bought at the airport — Randy Wayne White's latest Southwest Florida set tale about the recent transgressions of Doc Ford and his flaky Harvard-graduate friend Tomlinson. This was the second copy of the book I'd bought in a month. The first was probably in a garbage dump in Guatemala City, along with my notes for the lectures I never gave.

I tried to look preoccupied with the book so I wouldn't be bothered. My seat was by a window, reducing by half my chances of having inquiring seat-mates. As I searched for the page where events in Guatemala disrupted my reading, a couple sat down beside me. Late fifties. Taking the aisle seat, the man sported a tan wrinkled suit that needed one final trip to the cleaners before it went to charity, a pink button-down shirt, and an Art Deco tie that had to have been a gift from a mother-in-law who never thought he was good enough for her daughter. The tie wasn't fully tucked under his shirt collar at the back of his neck. That was OK — his pink shirt wasn't tucked into the back of his pants. He was abundant and needed the aisle for expansion of a third of his bulk. The drink cart will never make it to the last few rows.

His diminutive wife wore a prim, orange-print dress and sat clutching her purse in her lap with gloved hands. Her husband ignored her with his nose in the airline's magazine. She looked primed for three hours of conversation and kept glancing at me. I held White's book closer to my face and tried to look lost in my reading, praying she wouldn't ask questions about me I didn't know how to answer. The takeoff scared her; she closed her eyes and squeezed her purse. After we settled at altitude I made the mistake of breathing. She asked where I was headed.

"Denver," I answered, without turning my head. I turned the page and moved my head a little closer to my book. A few more inches and I would touch. I thought I could smell Doc Ford cutting open a putrid snook's stomach in his research lab.

"Do you *live* in Washington?" She was still there.

"No, I'm heading home — west," was the best I could come up with at the moment.

Her husband opened a plastic bag and pulled out their breakfast. It was what I was smelling, and blaming on Doc Ford. Food that travelers bring on board planes as acts of civil disobedience. Something that drips or spatters and has an offensive, pungent stench, complimenting the plane's stagnant air. She removed her gloves. At least the meal required her attention for a half-hour. Despite the smell, I'd be happy to buy her seconds to keep her occupied.

After finishing, folding her napkin, smoothing her now spotted dress, putting on her gloves, and returning her purse to her lap, she turned slightly toward me and, without taking a breath, said, "*We* live in Falls Church Virginia and my husband works in D.C. at the Commerce Department and he takes the Metro *every* day and we're going to a conference in Denver about how Colorado can increase trade with Mexico because there's some agreement the U.S. has with Mexico that's supposed to help trade but my husband thinks it will shift a lot of American jobs south of the border. He does a really good imitation of Ross Perot when he was a presidential candidate claiming there's a 'giant sucking sound' coming from Mexico. But, of course, my husband can't do that at the program."

She made her own little sucking sound and put her hand to her mouth to thwart a giggle. She was imitating her husband imitating Ross Perot. She could qualify to be on *America's Got Talent!*

Abruptly, she stopped, either for a breath or waiting to hear where I lived. Maybe she forgot she had asked that at the very beginning of her trade soliloquy.

"Where did you say you lived?" She hadn't forgotten.

That *wasn't* her earlier question, which was *if* I lived in Washington. But I had to say something because she stopped with the question and looked directly at me. People on planes usually talk looking straight ahead. I took her turn of the head to mean she was ready to have me answer.

"I live in Montana." It was almost true. At least it might be by this evening.

"Do you own a ranch?"

"You betcha!" That's Montana talk I'll have to learn.

"You *look* like a rancher, except for the glasses. They make you look like a professor."

This lady should be working for Dan Wilson. No one grilled me like this last week. But she's probably right. There go my *GQ* glasses.

"What do you do other than owning a ranch?"

"I'm retired."

"What *did* you do?"

I guess next it will be what church I attend, and after that what I drink. "I inherited," I answered. I wasn't lying, just doing a little creative biography on the early years of a fictional character.

"Oh, how nice! You *never* worked?"

"Not exactly, I worked very hard." And I was working even harder trying to say something that would cause her to retreat.

"You *said* you were retired?" She phrased it as a question and looked directly at me. I was *required* to answer.

"I did, and I am." I was sure Dan had sent her to test me. But she served a purpose. I'd soon be meeting people I didn't know. Some would ask about my past. I needed some personal history that would be easy to remember. This was as good a place as any to practice. So I gave her a dose of improvised, boring family history.

"My brother and I inherited a family business that made metal hinges in Hartford, Connecticut. He was the better businessman. I did the design work. We worked hard, and when he died two years ago in a train wreck, I had to sell the business to pay estate taxes. The government received a substantial tax payment. Thirty-seven people were laid off when the new Dutch owners moved the plant to China. I decided to move to Montana."

When I reached Montana, I would write this down and begin a chronology of the early years of Macduff and the Brooks family, the years before Macduff was created *at the age of fifty-one!* I would make it as uninteresting as possible. Making hinges seemed a good start. Living in Hartford wasn't bad either.

I prayed that what I'd created made sense to my seat mate, and she would direct her attention elsewhere. I hoped she wasn't from Hartford. And her family wasn't in the hinge business. Her husband was no help; he was sound asleep. Probably what her friends do when she starts talking.

Before she could continue, we were thankfully descending into Denver. The stewardess was making announcements. The lady listened to them attentively, staring forward, her gloved hands in her lap, holding onto her purse.

8

THE NEXT FLIGHT INCLUDED THREE HOURS sitting on the tarmac in Denver and one hour in the air to Bozeman. Bozeman's exquisite, visitor friendly airport terminal made me feel welcome and forget about the flights.

The taxi driver asked, "Where to?"

"Into town and stop at the first auto-dealer we see," which proved to be Nissan, where, after a little bargaining, I drove off in a deep-red, X-Terra 4x4 SE SUV, with oversize seventeen-inch tires. I liked the roof rack and built-in steps on the bumpers, the long running-boards, and its mid-size. I would soon learn I didn't like the mileage. The first check on my new Montana bank account immediately cleared.

Passing through the vibrant downtown, I stopped at Powder Horn Outfitters and bought two pairs of jeans and three conservative western shirts. Then I wandered on foot south a few blocks through the campus of Montana State University. Some of the buildings must have been designed by an exiled Soviet architect who'd worked designing the gulag. He must feel at home in Montana in the winter.

After a bison steak and Moose Drool at Ted's Montana Grill, I headed east on Interstate 90 through the frayed edges of the mountains thirty miles to Livingston, where I stopped at the late Dan Bailey's fly shop. A brochure on the counter said

Dan had opened his shop in 1938, after abandoning pursuing a PhD in physics in New York City. Abandoning physics and a life devoted to examining supersymmetry or loop quantum gravity was a smart decision. Abandoning New York City was even smarter. Dan became one of the West's fly fishing notables, especially for work in conservation, including fighting the Allen Spur dam proposal that would have flooded part of Paradise Valley south of Livingston.

Fly shops are to fly fishing folk what Toys R Us stores are to seven-year-olds. After buying an assortment of fly fishing miscellany, for which I had no immediate need, and stopping for food at Albertson's, for which I had more immediate need, I headed south on Route 89 for a night's rest at a place called Chico Springs.

Driving in the hazards of dusk without my lights on, twenty miles south of Livingston, I watched colors metabolize as the sunlight fled over the Gallatin Range to the west. Suddenly a car closed behind me with a rainbow of flashing lights. An escort Dan Wilson arranged? No — a Park County Sheriff's Office deputy. He walked up as I got out of my SUV. No mirror sunglasses. No Smokey-the-Bear hat. No *Semper Fi* posture. His name tag read *Deputy Ken Rangley*. Early to mid-forties. Enough hair to suggest a relaxed department hair code. Clean shirt, but no starch and no creases. Rangley was my height . . . a touch over six feet, and my dress . . . *relaxed* fit. He smiled and said, "Hi."

I smiled back and said, "Hi."

Not especially articulate, but a non-confrontational way to begin. He could have said, "Spread your legs and place your hands on the hood."

I added, "I don't *think* I was speeding, officer."

"*Speeding!* You were going forty! The speed limit's sixty-five. I've *never* seen anyone drive forty here. Especially with Montana plates. The locals drive their John Deere tractors faster. Plus, you don't have your lights on. And your SUV doesn't come up on our vehicle registration?" It was said cordially and turned into a question at the end.

I handed him the papers from the dealer. "I bought this a little after noon today. I've come from Florida. I'm heading for a place called Chico Springs."

"It's Chico *Hot* Springs. Nice place. You're about twenty minutes away. An hour the way you drive. You fly fish?"

He'd seen the Dan Bailey's logo on the bag on the passenger seat. "I do, hopefully a lot more pretty soon."

That led to a forty minute discussion about mutual interests. He also drove an X-Terra, and spent as much time fly fishing in Paradise Valley as his job allowed. A lot of it with his teen-aged daughter Liz. She was about the age my daughter would have been if El — seven months pregnant — hadn't died.

Rangley's a UM-Missoula graduate. He dropped out of the UM law school after one term, worked in D.C. for the FBI for three years, and came home to Montana to settle. A call for Rangley interrupted our conversation for a few minutes. Now it *was* dark.

He returned and said, "I assume your *lights* work."

"I don't even know where the light switch is," I answered. Rangley smiled, reached in, and flipped on the lights.

"My daughter's taking driver ed at her high school. Maybe you could sit in on some of her classes." He smiled again and said he had to check my license because he'd reported the stop. I pulled out my wallet and realized I didn't have a Montana driver's license. My Starbucks card wouldn't help. I had a valid Florida license, tucked away in a file in Washington, issued to a person who no longer existed. But there was a *card* in my wallet I hadn't seen the night before in D.C. A piece of paper was folded around it. It read: "Thought you might need this — do get one in Montana. Dan." It was a Washington, D.C., driver's license issued to Macduff Brooks. I gave it to Rangley. "I'll get a Montana license in the next few days."

Rangley ran the license details through his computer. As he read the response, his jaw dropped and eyes widened, his face showing surprise. I didn't think registration information was that interesting.

"Mr. Brooks, you said you came from Florida. But you have a D.C. license. I'm being shown information I haven't dealt with since I worked for the FBI in D.C. Whatever it means, you can go. But I suggest you drive a little faster than forty or you'll have some local drive right up your back."

Another slip. I'd foolishly mentioned coming from Florida. I may have to weave that into some of my new family history. I can use Miami or maybe Disneyworld. They're pretty much interchangeable.

As Rangley walked back to his car, he turned, "Give me a ring, Macduff. Let's go fishing. And it's *Ken*." He hadn't given me a ticket. He did give me a piece of paper with his home and cell phone numbers.

9

AT CHICO HOT SPRINGS, a comfortable bed was waiting in a North 40 cabin. I was under a down cover by
eleven, windows slightly open to a near freezing night. It was
one in the morning in D.C. and Gainesville. I lay back and
wondered if dreams would come as Max or Mac. I may not
know *who* I am yet. But I do know *where* I am. One out of two
isn't bad, considering the past couple of weeks.

I didn't sleep well. At two a.m. I got up, poured a glass of
Gentleman Jack, and sat by the large window. "How did this all
happen?" I wondered, and began to think of earlier days. One
day a decade ago kept coming back, a day spent on the Snake
River in Jackson Hole, not far south of here — where El died. I
remembered every minute, every thought, and every conversation of that day: It began with a symphony, and concluded with
a funeral march.

*Stan Lee at the Izaak Walton Fly Fishing shop in Jackson had called
me in early June in my law school office and said the stonefly fishing was
the best they'd ever had, a float had just been canceled, and a guide was
available. Since El and I were heading to San Francisco where I was to
give a lecture, we decided to stop over and do a float. I'd never fished stonefly imitations. I'm not an entomologist. If a* lepidoptera *landed on me, I
wouldn't know whether it planned to stick a stinger in me, lay eggs, or
plant some pollen in hope of a new cross. I looked up stonefly on the Web*

and learned about plecoptera, *the Mesozoic origin stonefly. It missed out on Darwin — it still looked Mesozoic. The nymph stage may look prehistoric, but it stimulates the taste buds of the most reticent, modern trout. The trout that listened to Darwin and developed. That's really intelligent design. If you were a stonefly nymph and faced a brown trout swimming toward you, ten times your length and a hundred times heavier, prehistoric or not, you'd be scared into performing heroic maneuvers. Stan Lee promised to set aside some big #4 and #6 stonefly imitations for us.*

A week later El and I were looking out the window at the Grand Teton mountain range as our plane curved onto the final leg into the Jackson Hole airport. Just below us was the Snake River's silvery, serpentine curve, conforming to ancient glacial patterns. Floating the Snake early was intriguing to us. Instead of late summer golden hues of cottonwoods and aspens, we would see a pageant of early wildflowers growing along the river's bank — delicate purple Harebells, white Yarrow and Cowparsnip, yellow members of the Aster and Composite families, and red Spirea and Indian Paintbrush — the Wyoming state flower. And maybe see some newborn — otter, elk, moose, and even bear.

At the airport we took a taxi to lodging at Moose. Early the following morning we bought licenses at Will Dornan's Snake River Angler. We waited for our guide outside the Mangy Moose store. And waited. And waited some more.

"El, our guide was due here at eight a.m. sharp. It's past nine!"

"Are we getting a guide who's experienced in rowing a drift boat in fast water?" she asked.

"Stan Lee assured me we would. The releases at the Jackson Lake Dam have increased the flow to 13,000 or more cubic feet per second, making the river look as though the dam just broke. When we're here in the fall, it's dropped to around 1,500 cfs. That's more like a leak in the dam."

A disheveled, scrawny twenty-something named Steve Brewster, labeled Brew by his drinking buddies, arrived an hour and fifty minutes late. He showed signs of an all-nighter. Brew was about 5'5", pushing 120 pounds. Dirty, jaundice-yellow tendrils of crinkly hair were tied in a pig-tail. His muddy complexion was partly due to a bimonthly shaving schedule. This wasn't the scheduled month. Bowlegged, he wore old cowboy boots that were creased and cracked, causing his legs to slant out to each side from where his knees knocked, making him look like an adolescent girl trying to walk in heels for the first time.

We assumed Brew was merely a little flaky, and we were anxious to get on the water. If I'd had any sense, I would have phoned Stan Lee to recall Brew. We'd always floated this river with real pros — guides who made it look easy. The truth is that Deadman's Bar to Moose isn't easy.

Mumbling nothing more than a groggy "sorry" for being late, Brew drove us north the half-dozen miles and down the steep, narrow access road to the ramp at Deadman's Bar. On a summer day in 1886, the bodies of two mining partners were found at Deadman's Bar and another at Bill Menor's ferry at Moose. Brew didn't tell us he'd never floated the Snake. He was pulling an old plastic drift boat that had seen better days. The anchor was a rusty cast-iron train-wheel he found behind a bar along the tracks of the Burlington Northern line in Livingston, Montana. One plastic seat was cracked. The others had seat padding protruding from splits in the vinyl. One wooden oar had duct tape around a split on the blade.

While we rigged rods, Brew offered, "I moved to Jackson last month. I guided two years, a lotta wade trips into Yellowstone Park for an outfitter in West Yellowstone. I loved the town — the bars were a blast! But I wasn't gettin' much work, so I came here."

El turned to me when Brew went to hang the anchor off the transom of his boat. "Maxwell, we've been to West Yellowstone. I thought it was dreadful — tacky. The town smothers the West Entrance to the park like a big flea market. Except for that neat Bud Lilly's fly shop, the town is little more than a food and fueling stop."

"Yellowstone Park was a bummer last season," Brew commented. "And it don't look better this year. Clients are goin' elsewhere. Firehole

River's warmer than usual because of some pissed-off geysers around Biscuit Basin. They're crackin' asphalt and spewin' hot water in the parkin' area. Plus, the Yellowstone River's lousy. The cutty numbers are way down."

Brew made five attempts before he backed the trailer into the river. Three guides waiting to launch were struggling to contain their laughter.

We finally pushed off at ten-thirty. In the first two hours, El and I were making Brew's day one that guides post on their Websites. I first tied a clunky #4 black rubberlegs on El's tippet, with a light, yellow yarn indicator a couple of feet above the fly.

El asked, "Why the yarn?"

"Unlike the floating hoppers we use in the fall, your rubberlegs sinks," I answered. "Without the yarn, you have to feel a strike. That's not easy. As soon as the fly is touched by a trout, the yellow yarn indicator will twitch. Not much — watch it for the slightest unnatural movement. I'll try the same fly without an indicator — see how good my reflexes are."

El was sitting in front. I like her there because it's the best seat in the house for looking for fish. My rear seat's the best in the house for looking at her.

A trout broke the surface fifteen yards ahead near the west bank. I softly called to El, "Try to drop your fly to your right — three feet off the bank — just below that red wildflower clump."

Even before the rubberlegs had time to sink, the placid surface exploded as a nice brown trout began to perform a pastoral symphony for us — pursing its lips to announce an opening allegro vivace. Pushing a column of water ahead of its mouth, the fly balancing on the bottom lip, the trout closed its mouth around the fly in a single gulp. Then a twisting, show-time back dive, and into an andante within the tranquil, private underwater world we'd interrupted. The trout headed downstream and began a shallow turn that backlighted every dorsal and tail fin vein. Abruptly, El's line went slack. The brown had broken off or stopped, and we were overtaking it. It wasn't gone. Only the line tension was suspended, until it tensed and *cut a wide oval curl across the river, an* allegretto — *spraying droplets in its crescent wake. The brown was tiring, but another run began. This time an illusion. It stopped after twenty feet to begin a final* largo — *a slow, heavy rise only partly rending the surface as it half-twisted and slapped down into the dissonant water. And then — concession.*

Brew slipped the guide net under as the barbless hook fell loose from the cutthroat's mouth. Its eyes looked questioning and troubled at an unfamiliar world where it couldn't long survive. A quick photo and we eased it back into the water, holding it upright with its mouth upstream to direct the current's flow through a quivering body. It deeply drew a few breaths before disappearing in an impulsive display of newfound strength that hopefully foretold a quick recovery. A symphony — deserving of applause. Maybe a standing ovation. But too tiring for an encore.

I was tying on another fly when Brew, noticeably uneasy, turned from his middle guide seat and asked, "Maxwell, you been floatin' this river. What channel ahead you want us to take?"

That's his job. "It's your call, Brew. We haven't been on the Snake this year. You know it's different every spring." At least he should know.

"Yea, but I ain't floated this part. I'm the first of our guides doin' this section this year. All the guides have been fishin' the South Fork."

"You should probably stay left here," I suggested. "You can see strainers down the channel to the right."

He may have seen them, but I began to doubt he understood them.

Sawyers or sweepers are fallen trees unwilling to let go because some of the roots tenaciously remain anchored to the shore. The trunks loom outward from the bank, barely above the surface. Denuded treetop branches drop onto the rushing surface, the current bending the trunk downstream until the tree slashes upward, released from the water's grasp. The process is repeated. Over and over again.

Strainers don't thrust about as dramatically. They're trees and brush pulled from the bank, floating downstream until caught and held, often piling two stories high. Water passes through, but nothing else. Gigantic

61

spider webs waiting patiently for their prey. Favored prey are drift boats. It's what makes this section of the Snake so dangerous. And so appealing because the sweepers and strainers create some good trout habitat.

Brew sought safety in the middle of the river. He was unsure where to go. Turning the bow first one way and then, uncomfortable with his unreasoned choice, swinging the bow the other way. Until his conspicuous doubt set in about that choice as well. At the last second the current sucked the boat into the left channel.

It proved to be the provident channel. No threat ahead was visible, but that's never a good reason to head down a channel you don't know. I was becoming worried. Worried is one stage after being concerned and one stage before scared. I didn't want El to sense my feelings. She's not a strong swimmer. Brew was in the guide's seat, but he wasn't guiding.

A hundred yards further the channel angled right and rejoined the one we hadn't taken. I looked back and saw what we'd avoided — a large strainer that blocked the entire channel. Pure luck. It was another half mile before my heart beat was back down on the chart. Before long, we stopped for lunch near the foot of a gravel bar. We'd face further channel decisions on full stomachs.

To his credit Brew set out a delicious lunch. Stan Lee had told Brew, "If you want happy clients at lunch time, see my friend Cindy Gomez." For going on forty years, Cindy's owned the Reel Food Café in Jackson, one door down the wooden sidewalk east of the Izaak Walton shop. Cindy's boxed-meals have saved countless guides that reach lunch break with disgruntled, fishless clients.

Four miles of river to fish remained before Moose. Soon after we pushed off we approached another braid and a choice of four channels. Brew was visibly nervous about choosing a channel. I was behind him in the rear seat and couldn't see his face. El was in front glancing back at me with an expression of growing fear.

"You talk to Stan about these channels?" I asked Brew. "This section has good water, but it flattens out up ahead."

"I know how to row, dammit! There's plenty of water," Brew replied. There was an edge to his voice — a bravado masking indecision. *"The worst this channel is gonna do is braid again. Then I think we'll rejoin the channels off to the left."*

We were close to stage three — scared. I didn't want to think about what was stage four. Over Brew's blowing hair, wind-loosened from its pigtail, I saw what I didn't want to see. The winter snow melt, as moderate as the snow pack had been, had carried piles of debris down our channel. Not a few branches, but whole trees that forty yards ahead were piled one atop another. Only the river's flow could pass through its maze of limbs and branches. A drift boat didn't have a chance. It was a strainer about which guides tell horror stories. We were heading straight at it.

One narrow side channel doglegged sharply to the left about ten yards before the strainer, sucking off part of the channel's water. Maybe enough to float our drift boat.

I yelled at Brew, *"Take the left side channel! We can't make it through the strainer straight ahead."* He didn't hear or he didn't understand or he was just frozen in fear and didn't have a clue what to do.

"Brew, left!" No response. I grabbed the back of his collar and yanked him out of the guide's seat. He landed on the floor and covered his head with his hands. The way you're told to act when a grizzly's heading toward you. I needed to do something, and bear mace wouldn't help. I stepped over an oar, dropped into the guide seat, and started back-rowing. I'd never rowed a drift boat. El was looking at me, afraid to watch the fast approaching strainer.

I yelled, *"El! Get down below the sides of the boat!"*

"Max, I'm scared!"

I struggled with unfamiliar nine-foot oars, but was beginning to work the boat left toward the side channel. I could only slow us a little. Our previous guides always seemed to keep their drift boats floating at an angle. I did the same. But what angle? Bow left? Stern left? Maybe if my bow were *pointing left at the side channel, I could row hard forward with the right oar as we got even with it, and try to turn us into that last safe passage.*

I was wrong. I had no more business being in the guide's seat of a drift boat than in the pilot's seat of a 747. My stern should have been left, and I should have been back-rowing hard, letting the part of the current rushing into the side channel suck our stern away from the deadly main channel. We were going too fast. Ten feet before the side channel there was a boulder showing a few inches of its top that we couldn't hit without swamping the boat. Brew was cowering on the floor. Head down. Whimpering. Useless. I was beyond any hope of using the side channel. Back eddies off the downstream side of the boulder pulled at the bow as we surged past. The duct tape on the cracked oar gave way and the blade broke off. We swung broadside. I lost control.

The first branches of the strainer met us sideways and the boat's hull snapped. We flipped up against the maze of jagged reaching arms. A sharp branch pierced through my jacket, waders, and the flesh of my right side. I was yanked out of the boat as its broken parts became embedded in the tentacles of the trees. Suspended in the strainer a foot above the water, I swung around scarcely in time to see El fall off the bow of the dismembered boat. She fell silently, blood pouring from an ugly gash in her cheek. Years ago, when I first saw her emerge from shadows descending a staircase for a blind date, I had fallen in love with that face. I'd never seen it so contorted with terror. Her soft, pleading mouth was soundlessly calling for help against the hush of death.

Brew had fallen out and was gone from sight, likely in a death-grip in the dark waters beneath the maze of grasping limbs. I struggled to reach El, captured by branches an arm's length away. I managed to pull away from the limb, slip out of my jacket, and yank down my wader top, releasing a surge of blood-stained water. The added freedom let me work through some branches. The half-turned remnants of the boat behind me momentarily slowed the water's flow. I reached El's hand and could feel the squeeze of a thousand touches of this small hand that never failed to send warm messages. But the current overwhelmed the boat's fragmented remains. It flipped up, wedged in its own set of the strainer's limbs, and the water's onrush lodged me deeper within the lower branches. I was again losing blood from my side. A massive, sweeping branch was caught in the new surge, and I watched it dip into the water and be pulled away from me downstream. The force of the current was fighting against the strength of the bending branch. In an instant the branch could bend no more and flew up, smashing through lesser branches. As I felt El's hand slip from mine, the branch struck me on the temple and I was gone, lapsed into a mute world from which I didn't return for days, when I awoke in the bleached sterility of a hospital room in Salt Lake City. The tiny, two-person, star-filled galaxy that El and I had carved out from this vast universe was over. And, as Shakespeare noted: "The rest is silence."

My head jerked abruptly. My empty glass crashed to the floor of my Chico Hot Springs room. It was 4:30 in the morning. I was Maxwell Hunt, and I wanted El back. I drifted off for two hours and woke with a thick head and dry throat. Plus a heavy heart and large dose of self-pity.

10

A FTER BREAKFAST a Livingston realtor named Zelda arrived with a stack of elaborate color brochures with photos of Paradise Valley homes — starting at $2.4 million. She must have spent half that much on plastic surgery and makeup, a protection program against aging that wasn't working.

"Zelda," I said, "I don't want a McMansion on a flood plain knoll along the river. Some of those owners have demanded the government build barriers from flooding. The river is *supposed* to rise, but as those owners insist: 'not in my back yard.'"

"Macduff *darling,* these homes are *fabulous* investments. And you'll have several *gorgeous* movie stars as neighbors! Just think of it!"

"If I want to see movie stars, I'll use HBO."

I let Zelda go home early and asked around about an agent who wasn't auditioning for a job at Sotheby's or Christie's. I met an eighty-year-old lady, Miss Bess, who'd lived near Emigrant most of her life, and knew every land owner within twenty miles.

"Miss Bess, I want a wooded lot where I can build a small log cabin. Fifteen hundred square feet max and maybe near a stream or creek."

"I'll make some calls." She spent fifteen minutes on her cell phone, and we began our search along Mill Creek. After a few days scouting every mile of the creek, Miss Bess calling owners, and some negotiating, I bought a half-dozen acres, including 200 feet of the creek. The purchase wouldn't have been possible without her.

During my flight delay in Denver, I'd looked at log cabin plans and found one I liked. The interior will be unfinished so I can tailor it to the uncertain habits of a new-born, fiftyish, single, defrocked law professor, would-be fishing guide.

I moved into a rental condo in Emigrant. Then came surveying, permitting skirmishes with Park County's building department, laying in a long gravel drive, and pouring the basement and slab. The cabin arrived as a pile of logs and beams on an eighteen-wheeler flatbed. I hired a couple of energetic and financially anxious young fishing guides, both guiding for Angler's West in Emigrant. Both named Jim, they were looking for almost any form of extra work during a summer when the fishing season hadn't been kind to guides. When they showed up the first day, I explained my work rules. They were in addition to the generous hourly wage I offered.

"My main rule, guys, is you call me if you're not going to show up to work with me. And a second rule is that you're *not* to show up if a chance arises to guide a paying client fishing. That's you're *real* job."

"What if I get a call early in the morning for a trip that day?" asked the taller of the Jims.

"Call me and tell me — and go guide. If you have a friend who can sub for you here, fine."

"Man! You aren't gonna finish the cabin at that rate," said the second Jim.

"I will. . . . There's a bonus. Stay working with me until I move in and you get free access to my section of Mill Creek, alone or with your clients — as long as I own the place."

"Rumor says you want to guide in another year or two. True?" asked the taller Jim.

"Yeah. My next project is a drift boat. And then learning to guide. I'll be picking your brains about guiding."

"Guiding hints are trade secrets," he joked.

"Are they less secret if I take you both to Emigrant and buy lunch every day you work here?"

"We get a brew with lunch?" asked the second Jim.

"Nope, you get a beer at the cabin — at the *end* of the day. If you want, you can stay after work and fish the creek."

Fair rules brought tenacious effort. We worked long days raising the outer walls, adding the front and rear porches and the roof, and finally fitting specially made doors and windows. I moved into the cabin in early November, on a day the weather reports showed snow over Oregon rushing to get to Paradise Valley. On their last work day, I gave each Jim a key to my gate.

11

THE CABIN'S 1,500 SQUARE FEET is spacious for my needs. It sits about three feet above the highest water mark anyone around here can recall. The front door opens to a vaulted ceiling living room. In the middle of the cabin is a central fireplace made of stones we gathered from Mill Creek. The building inspector never asked where they came from. When we gathered them, we rearranged the creek's flow, creating pools that hopefully will encourage trout to join me living along this section.

My living room is lined with low bookshelves leaving room above for art. Two leather armchairs face the fireplace, which also opens to a less formal room to the rear, where a two-seat sofa faces the fireplace. A small dining table and four chairs are behind the sofa at the very rear, in front of a large window overlooking Mill Creek. A door leads to a long rear porch.

Off the front living room to the right when entering the front door are my bedroom and bath, taking up one full cabin side — front to back, about a quarter of the cabin's total square footage. In one corner is a small fly-tying table. There's a king-size bed for my six-foot plus frame. By the bed are tables with reading lamps. Only one burns every night, while I read until exhaustion takes over. My bathroom has a jet tub to ease the wear my intended young man's job of guiding will inflict on my already battered body. Maybe the job will keep me young. Or delude me into thinking so. A smaller second bedroom and bath are to the left off the main living room.

Kitchens scare me. Food preparation is a menacing venture. My kitchen is small so it can't be intimidating by mere size. It's at the rear in the far left corner, an open design for a non-cook, not for resale to some gourmet chef. I have a small oven and a large microwave. A large oven *would* be intimidating. For my skills it would be a food crematorium. I can heat water, but only to pour into something else, like a coffee cup — not to have anything immersed in the water, whether to simmer, steam, stew, boil, or in some other way ruin good ingredients. Now and then I cook eggs. The score is 8 to 4 — eight cooked eggs to four charred frying pans. The owner of the Howlin' Hounds Café in Emigrant told me I need to put some oil in the pan first. Oh! . . . It's on my shopping list. Mostly, if it can't be done in the microwave, it just isn't done. I frequent two kinds of sanctuaries, one a church and the other *any* restaurant that cooks better than I do. I have a lot of choices.

Along the wall between the door to the second bedroom and the beginning of the kitchen are bookcases from floor to ceiling. One section swings open to show an otherwise hidden staircase that leads below. That part of the bookcase serves as storage for mystery novels. What's behind is part of my own mystery.

Next to the fireplace in the rear sitting room is a small, wall mounted, flat screen TV. There are three satellite dishes on an outer corner of the cabin. One provides standard fare. The two others do not.

Completing the main floor are large windows with special glass that should rebuff at the least an errant hunter's .30-30. The thick, heavy front and rear doors both have two oversize locks and deadbolts. Almost as large as Manhattan dwellers use in tiny apartments.

That's the main floor, the only floor the Park County building inspector and tax assessor know about. But below my living room is a basement room. A tour of the main floor wouldn't show any stairs or provide any suggestion that there *is* a basement. Even looking in all the closets. The latch to the swinging bookcase door is *in* the bookcase, behind *The Hidden Staircase*, one of Carolyn Keene's Nancy Drew mystery novels. The basement room wasn't on the plans I filed, and the building inspector never knew it was there when he stood in my sitting room, two feet from the room's hidden entrance, and said it all checked out and I could have my certificate of occupancy.

I think of the basement as my "music room." In it are my oboe, English Horn, music stand, and a chair, all on a small Oriental rug. My parents decided I should learn piano. I switched to the oboe, that "ill wind that nobody blows good." At least not for the first few years. After a dozen years, I'd managed to take most of the ill out of the wind. My teacher now plays with the New York Philharmonic before thousands. I play in my basement alone.

My music room also has two computers, plus a printer, fax, scanner, decoding device, phone hookup, and safe. A wall mounted screen connected to a second outside satellite dish provides special communications with Dan Wilson's office in D.C. It currently includes a relay of the main TV channel in Guatemala City. Another wall screen connected to a third satellite dish provides a computer link with Dan.

Finally, the music room is where I keep weapons I'd prefer visitors not see. That doesn't include several upstairs, including an octagonal-barrel, brass-receiver, lever-action, loaded Henry Big Boy .44 magnum — over the front door for quick access.

Plus an old, large-loop, lever-action, Winchester Model 73, .30-30 — over the living room mantel for decoration. And the first gun my dad gave me when I turned sixteen, a lever-action Marlin 39A .22, which I use for plinking — beside the back door in a rack. I have a thing about lever actions. It goes back to growing up with western movies and TV. Beside my bed are a Super Blackhawk Hunter .44 magnum Ruger revolver and a short-barrel Coach 12 gauge shotgun. Both are loaded. I don't shoot skeet. The shotgun has number nine birdshot in the left barrel and double ought buckshot in the right. If someone breaks in, I'll lead with the left and land the knockout blow with the right.

Hidden in the music room downstairs are a couple of Glocks and a P229 Sig Sauer .357 magnum. There are also two more rifles. One is for target practice — a Model 54 Anschutz 5+1 .22 long-rifle with an Olympic match-grade, target-barrel. It has a folding, rear adjustable sight and a walnut, Monte Carlo stock. Next to it is my favorite — a CheyTac, Intervention M-200, Long-Range-Rifle-System. It includes a tactical ballistic computer, a Kestral 4000 Pocket Weather Tracker, a Vector IV laser rangefinder linked to the ballistic computer, and a NXS, 5.5, 22x56 telescopic-sight, with a muzzle brake and suppressor. It fires .408 or .375 caliber rounds. They travel up to 2,500 yards. That's nearly a mile and a half!

Some of the guns I owned before I encountered Juan Pablo in Guatemala. The others are Montana purchases. It's not hard to buy guns in Montana. Some folks here think ownership should be mandatory.

One small cabin. Ten guns. I don't hunt. And I don't want to be hunted.

12

TWO RIVERS DEFINE MY FISHING LIFE — the Yellowstone and the Snake. Both begin not far apart in the high country near the southern boundary of Yellowstone National Park. The difference is that the Snake begins a little to the west of the Continental Divide, while the Yellowstone begins a little to the east. If I stood on the divide and tipped two water bottles out from my opposite sides, the water from one would join the Pacific, and from the other would join the Atlantic by way of the Gulf.

The Snake journeys south past the Teton Range in Grand Teton National Park, through Jackson Hole, turns west, and twists through Idaho to join the Columbia River, which flows into the Pacific.

The Yellowstone, on the other hand, journeys north through the park — dropping over two magnificent falls — exits the park and meanders through Paradise Valley, passing a couple of miles from my cabin. It makes an easterly bend at Livingston, joins the Missouri River near the North Dakota border, turns south through Mid-West states, and adds to the Mississippi River at St. Louis, eventually flowing into the Gulf of Mexico.

From my favorite locations on these two rivers, I view waters that struggle to reach their final oceans. At Moose in Wyoming the Snake is rimmed to the west by the Teton Range, around which it must pass to reach the Pacific. At Emigrant in Montana the Yellowstone is rimmed to the east by the Absaroka Range, around which it must pass to reach the Atlantic. The Snake runs south until it can turn west. The Yellowstone runs north until it can turn east. That's the magic of the American West.

The closest thing to a hometown for me is Emigrant, Montana. It's eight miles from my cabin — a good place to launch a drift boat on the Yellowstone River. For a lot of drivers passing through Emigrant on Route 89, it's little more than the place with the blinking light. It's the only light along 89 between Gardiner and Livingston. To Montanans this doesn't qualify as a *traffic* light; it's a *reference* point. Drivers on 89 slow from eighty to seventy-five; those entering slow down, glance left and right, and without stopping roll onto 89. Emigrant suits me fine. I'm happy to see so many folks stop at Emigrant, gas up, have a meal, buy a few fishing supplies, and pass on. Mainly I like to see them pass on.

In addition to the fly fishing shop, there are a gas station, a branch of my bank, a general store, the Old Saloon, and the best place for breakfast I've found along the Yellowstone — the Howlin' Hounds Café. There's also a car wash. Cleaning a boat and trailer after drifting fights trout-killing pests, such as the New Zealand mud snail.

Emigrant takes its name from the nearly 11,000-foot mountain peak that tries to dominate the eastern sky. Gold was discovered in Emigrant Gulch in 1862, luring prospectors who flooded in following the trappers who'd worked the valley for several decades, including the most famous of them all — Jim Bridger. Trappers and prospectors in the valley had to be the cleanest in the American West. They bathed in large, wooden tubs at hot springs where the Chico Hot Springs resort now caters to a noticeably more upscale group. The newer folk smell a lot different.

If some of the Paradise Valley agricultural interests had their way a century ago, there'd be a dam on the Yellowstone River just south of Livingston, where the Absaroka and Gallatin mountains pinch-in to provide an easy span for a dam at the northern entrance to the valley. The reservoir created by a dam would have backed up to Emigrant, maybe making my cabin lakefront property. There might not even be an Emigrant — just a Montana lost city of Atlantis.

13

K EN RANGLEY DROPPED BY the Howlin' Hounds
Café in Emigrant one morning where I was sipping
freshly brewed coffee. A half-dozen locals were having breakfast, hunched over in groups of two to four at the few tables
closely spaced in the small room. I'd been sitting quietly alone
overhearing four different conversations. When Ken sat down,
I knew whatever we said would be absorbed by more than the
two of us.

"Got time to fish late today?" Ken asked.

"Sure, any thoughts about *where?*" I responded. Five heads
turned to listen.

Ken noticed. "How about that section of East Mill Creek
near the forestry sign where we must have released a dozen last
week?"

There's no such sign on East Mill Creek, but a few guys are
going to be looking for it no later than this afternoon.

"Ever get a Montana driver's license and give up the D.C.
one?" Ken asked.

I winced. I've never mentioned D.C. to anyone; Ken saw it
on my temporary driver's license the day I arrived. "Yeah, I'm
now a Montana driver. I even drove seventy-five coming home
with the new license."

"Who'd you work for in D.C.?"

I wasn't prepared for this. . . . "Ken, I just remembered. I forgot to leave my gate unlocked for an electrician. He's due in about five minutes. I promise I won't do more than eighty on East River Road." I left the table with my coffee barely touched.

"I'll be by your place around 5:30 with my fly rod," Ken called as I went out the door.

When we headed for a spot along the Yellowstone to fish that evening, Ken asked, "You a little touchy about D.C.?"

"Ken, I didn't *live* in D.C. I did some consulting for the government, but I lived elsewhere. I'm not sure folks around here take kindly to people from D.C."

"Sorry I raised it. . . . Where's 'elsewhere'?"

I wanted to be more open with Ken, but I didn't want to lie. As a policeman he has access to records to trace people. If he searches Macduff Brooks, he'll run into some dead ends. That might make him even more curious.

"I grew up in Connecticut," I answered. "Practiced . . . I mean *worked* . . . in Hartford." Fortunately we were soon fishing, and the inquiry ended.

Dan Wilson and I talked by phone the following evening. He's become a reliable and comforting friend. I was sitting on my porch, watching the sunset and sipping from a long-stem wine glass half-filled with an unpretentious red Spanish *Ribera del Duero*. I told Dan about my conversation with Ken, especially my referring to "practice."

"It gets easier with time," Dan offered. "I know you're wary, not only with other folks' questions, but also about what you *might* say that doesn't fit with what you've *already* said."

"Could Ken access anything connecting me to Maxwell Hunt?"

"Not a chance. What he *will* find is that Macduff Brooks doesn't have a history. If you told him you were in the Navy, he might be able to learn there's no record of service for a Macduff Brooks."

"I told him I was raised in Connecticut and worked in Hartford."

"That's OK. He might do a search, but he won't find anything. He would if he searched Maxwell Hunt, but not Macduff Brooks."

"That'll make him doubt *anything* I tell him."

"Is he becoming a good friend?"

"I like to think so."

"Then he may understand you have a history you don't want to talk about. Maybe a bad marriage or a job loss. Maybe a terminal illness."

"I've survived one terminal illness . . . meeting up with your group in D.C. . . . Dan, I trust Ken. I hope it's based on good reason as much as a need to have a friend."

"We'll keep talking about it. What I called about is Juan Pablo. Guatemala isn't getting any better. President Colom visited Castro in Havana. Colom *apologized* for allowing Guatemala to be used for training the Bay of Pigs invasion! He awarded Castro the highest honor Guatemala can bestow, the Great Collar of the Order of the Quetzal. The same award Juan Pablo's grandfather received years ago. Next it may go to Chávez in Venezuela or Ortega in Nicaragua or Morales in Bolivia. It can't be pleasing to the conservative elites who control most of Guatemala's business interests. It's exactly the kind of act that fuels Juan Pablo's determination to be president. He hates Colom. Our CIA mission staff in Guatemala City has been increased. There could be a coup d'état, with Juan Pablo taking the presidency. Meanwhile, our ambassador seems content with cutting ribbons. Can you believe that?"

"Our ambassador doesn't interest me," I responded, "Juan Pablo does. As for Castro, I hope the award has a choke collar. I suspect you've backed off sanctioning Juan Pablo because he may be useful to rid Guatemala of Colom."

"That's partly why I called. We *have* backed off. But I don't imagine that changes his intentions about *you*. We don't even know where he *is* right now. We were planning to take him out in September when information about the possible coup reached us. We don't want Herzog to be president. We have *some* scruples. Be careful! *Stay* in Montana for the winter. We can't help you if you're on the move. Put off looking for a place in Florida for another year."

"If I stay here for the winter, can you arrange to shovel my driveway? At least send in a Saint Bernard with a case of Gentleman Jack. Or better, a Christmas air drop of a whole cask. I assume you know where I am."

"I have your location on the screen in front of me so exact I can drop the Gentleman Jack in your lap. Or pour it in your glass. Right in the empty wine glass — the one that's on the table next to you on your right."

Isn't it nice to have a friend in case of an emergency? Dan hung up. I took my glass and went inside. And checked my window and door locks. Twice.

14

ON THE KIND OF FALL DAY that falsely told me a
Montana winter can't be all that bad — bright sun and
sixties — I drove to Bozeman and came home with four bottles
of Gentleman Jack and a two-year-old rescued Shetland sheepdog. After a few months the Gentleman Jack will be gone. I
worry the sheltie may stay forever.

Two days earlier I had a call from the courthouse in Bozeman — the chambers of Judge Amalia C. Becker.

"Macduff Brooks? This is Amy Becker in Bozeman. I'm
Ken Rangley's second cousin." It was the voice of a singer. So-
prano. Precise diction. Natural. Not forced. Unwearying.

"This is Macduff. Have you ever sung the role of Violetta in
Traviata?"

"I have! I studied voice at Indiana U a century ago."

"If it was a century ago, you must have sung *Un di felice,
eterea*, with Caruso playing Alfredo?"

"Maybe it wasn't really a *century* ago. Anyway, I'm a trial
court judge in Bozeman. Ken said you might be interested in a
proposition I have for you." She stuttered, embarrassed. "Mr.
Brooks, I mean a *proposal.*"

"That sounds better than a proposition. Could we meet and
talk about your proposal? I usually don't agree to marry over

the phone. Not even on leap year. And no one has ever proposed to me calling me *Mr. Brooks.*"

She laughed. Laughter was better that a contempt of court order. "Ken said I might have difficulty with you. But I do have a *serious* proposal. It involves a beautiful young lady. Interested in hearing more?"

"Of course."

"One of my cases involves a sheltie. She was head shepherd of a flock of two she devotedly guarded for more than a year. Then the flock divorced. Both spouses fought over the dog so combatively it's the first time I've appointed a veterinarian as a *guardian ad litem* for a dog. I asked the local rescue center to find an owner less belligerent. Ken thought you might like a dog."

"I'll be in town tomorrow. If the dog doesn't bite me I'll take it."

"Thanks. If this sheltie bites you, you probably deserve it. If I didn't have asthma, I would have kept the dog. I'll even buy you lunch, Macduff. Meet me at Martha's, a good cafe with an outdoor patio that takes dogs . . . two doors from the vet's."

I arrived first. Judge Becker arrived a few minutes later, with the sheltie prancing along behind as though it had won the Westminster Dog Show.

"You must be Mr. Brooks," she said. She was a bright, mid-forties lady, with an appearance as pleasant as her voice.

"You must be your honor," I answered. "Or your ladyship. What do you prefer?"

"I prefer Amy, unless you're up on charges before my bench."

"*Vae victis.*"

"Woe to the vanquished? Are you giving up already?"

"Depends on your proposal."

"The proposal is sitting next to you. This is Jane Doe, what we've called her because she cowered whenever we used her real name. You can give her a new name."

"I was thinking of Virginia Wuff."

"What!"

"After you called me, I forgot what sex you mentioned the sheltie was. I've been thinking of it as 'the dog' or 'it.' I've been reading a biography about Virginia Woolf, the English author who struggled to resolve her gender preference. Since I was confused about the dog's gender, I thought I'd call it Virginia Wuff."

"If you're going to call her Virginia Wuff, you can't have her."

"If I drop the 'Virginia'?"

"OK."

"And you agree to stop propositioning me?"

She turned red, which gave her a radiance lost in some past disappointments. "And withdraw the proposal?" she asked.

"Can I have a rain check on that?"

I dropped the Virginia. Wuff spent the drive home sitting on the passenger seat, leaning toward me with her head on the divider. Her head stayed down, but her eyes looked up at me. Deep, dark eyes that had me hypnotized by the time we arrived at the cabin. I'd brought home a twenty-five pound control freak! I knew I'd keep her when I came out of my bathroom heading for bed, and she was already sound asleep with her head on my pillow. The bed's a king size, and she left me a corner of my own. But no pillow. I soon learned Wuff brings a presence to the house I've missed — knowing there's another breathing life around and we have to take some time exchanging affection. I hope she'll want to stay.

15

ONE ADVANTAGE TO LIVING ALONE is that when critical, essential, life-altering questions arise — like: "*Should I buy a new boat?*" — you can engage in a dialogue with yourself that reaches the conclusion you wanted in the first place. No one says: "*What, another boat! We can't afford it!*" Or worse: "*That's fine, and I want a new car!*" Wuff is my sounding board; when I ask her questions, she tilts her head to one side, stares at me, and I'm sure I hear a little whimper that means: "*Yeah, go for it!*"

By such consensus I decided to acquire a drift boat. The next question was like the grocery check-out clerk asks: Plastic or paper? Most drift boats are plastic, sarcastically called Clorox bottles. That's unfair. Many are exceptionally durable, making them the choice for guides who are on a river nearly every day. Like alligators, plastic drift boats win no awards for style, but they've evolved over the years to be exemplars of function. I'm a throwback. I like wooden furniture, not plastic. Wooden houses, not Hardy-board. And Morgan 4 plus 4s, not Corvettes. I hope I'm never asked to read plastic newspapers.

One day in early fall, as the cottonwoods were coloring the river banks a golden saffron, I saw a *different* wooden drift boat. Having walked down from a late lunch at the Howlin' Hounds Café to the center of the bridge at Emigrant, to indulge in the fall color, I saw a wooden drift boat emerge from beneath the bridge that took my breath away. The inside okoumé mahogany plywood, and various parts made from different hardwoods, glistened under layers of varnish. I ran to my SUV and followed the boat as best I could, keeping it in view when the river came close to the road. It floated only another couple of miles to Grey Owl Ramp. I was waiting when it came ashore and the owner proudly showed me the boat after his fishing friends left. My accolades were welcome, but I suspect this boat soaks-up praise *whenever* it's on the rivers.

"If you're interested, the guy that designs and builds them has a small company a few hundred yards from the river. Not far from here."

On my drive home, I detoured and stopped at the boat shop: Montana Boat Builders. The young owner, Jason Cajun, came out when I drove up.

"I just saw one of your boats at the Grey Owl takeout. It's beautiful. They're works of art, Jason. I can't start building a boat at my cabin, unless I like working in the snow. My garage-boat house won't be built 'til next summer."

"I've got enough room for you to rent space. Build it here."

Before I fully realized what I'd done, I left owning plans for a sixteen-foot Freestone Guide. I laid out the floor and sides the first week in December. Soon, seven- to eight-hour days in the shop became common. Jason's help was invaluable; he had a sensible answer for every bothersome question. Working long hours through the holidays, I listened to the New Year's celebration at Manhattan's Times Square on the shop radio, two hours before the New Year reached Montana.

By early February, the floors, seat pedestals, and side guide boxes were roughed in. While snow piled up outside, I consumed coffee and sandpaper in equally vast quantities.

Weekly additions to the snow stacking up in the valley threatened to continue throughout the winter. It was too late to consider driving to Florida. And I wanted to finish the boat and some cabin projects. I hope I can plan better next year. Dan Wilson is pleased I'm staying in Montana. Wuff has never experienced a Florida winter, and I'm afraid to tell her how nice it is.

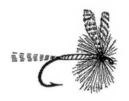

16

MAY DROPPED THE CURTAIN on Macduff Brooks' first year. Wuff and I had a party. No one else was invited. I ordered a half-size coconut cake, with a scriptural "Tight Loops" in frosting across the top. When I got it home I added a single candle, poured a flute of Champagne, and consumed the entire cake, except for the share that Wuff begged.

Our next party was to christen *Osprey*. The name's reflected in osprey heads carved in the bow ends of the gunnels, complete with inset black and yellow glass eyes from a local taxidermist. When everyone had left, I sat in *Osprey's* guide seat admiring the results. Then I thought out loud, "I've *never* rowed one of these boats. I rowed sailing dinghies as a kid, but I never sat *facing* the bow. I faced the stern and pulled on the oars to go where the bow behind me was facing. In a drift boat I row facing the bow. I still mostly pull rather than push on the oars, and I want to go where the bow is facing, downstream. But often not quite as fast as the current. So I row *backwards* to keep control while the current floats the boat downstream. The current does a lot of the work. After all, the boat *is* called a *drift* boat. Another difference is that when I rowed a dinghy I always looked *behind* over my shoulder for anchored sailboats, buoys, ducks, and swimmers, but in the drift boat I'll be looking *ahead* for large, unyielding boulders, and collections of various size rocks threateningly known as rapids. Also for sawyers, strainers, and sweepers, those unfriendly floral arrangements made from large trees. And, if I'm really having a bad day, an unexpected waterfall."

During the months building *Osprey*, I discovered a website for a guide school — World Cast Anglers at the Orvis fly shop in Jackson. The course mixes classroom work, ranging from entomology to safety, with five days rowing drift boats on different sections of Henry's Fork and the South Fork of the Snake. The instructors *assume* you know how to fish. Another check written and I was enrolled.

Hours on a jury-rigged rowing machine in my cabin helped me prep. Almost a dozen twenty- or thirty-somethings completed the class. My roommate Mike was 25. I was two years older than his father. By the end of the program, I was ready to adopt him. He made me feel like a teeny-bopper. Maybe not quite that. My hair remains sparsely speckled with gray — Mike *tried* to turn it white.

Driving home from guide school, diploma in hand, I chose Teton Pass and then through Jackson. A dozen miles north of town, passing the Deadman's Bar to Moose section of the Snake reminded me that at some point I'll have to face floating the Snake River again. But El's death hangs heavy. At Schwabacher's Landing, I walked out to the riverbank and threw in some wildflowers. I didn't know exactly where to throw them. El's body was never found.

When I think about that, I can't avoid wondering why. Searches continued downstream all the way to Wilson. If I carry my thoughts further, I start to imagine her struggling to survive on the river's shore, only to encounter a hungry grizzly and her cubs. But that would have left human bones. That's when emotion takes over, and I lose further rational thoughts about her death.

I knew I had to spend a couple of months in a self-imposed boot camp getting in shape to start guiding. I began by rowing a section of the Yellowstone five days a week, even before the river was fully self-cleansed of spring run-off debris and mud. My dress rehearsal launch at the Emigrant ramp thankfully appeared to be without spectators. Backing the trailer into the water was easy. Only then did I realize that the anchor was in my SUV, and the tie-down strap was holding the boat securely to the trailer. When I finally pushed off and rowed toward the center of the river, as the current started me downstream, absorbed in self-praise, I remembered my lunch and drinks were on the back seat of my SUV. And my sunglasses and trademark-to-be Stetson hat were on the bed in my cabin.

Next morning, having breakfast at the Howlin' Hounds Café, wearing my Stetson I thought I looked like a seasoned guide. An older fellow sitting at the table next to me looked up from his paper and said, "Nice boat you got. Kinda hard to launch a boat that's strapped down to the trailer, ain't it?"

"It is," I admitted, wondering where he'd been watching from. "And it helps to have the anchor rigged," I noted, wanting to preempt what he might next say.

"Yup. . . . I see you brung a hat today." As I walked out he called, "Might want to take sunglasses."

Each day on the river brought more upper-body strength and less evening fatigue. Each week of my two months boot camp I sipped my way through a bottle of Gentleman Jack. I consider it a self-prescribed, medicinal-liniment, distilled strictly to suppress fatigue.

On some rowing days my urge to fish became unbearable, and I did some casting after anchoring. I'm not comfortable with rowing and fishing at the same time. It's like text messaging while driving. When I wasn't rowing alone, I conned some lessons from one of the two Jims who'd helped build the cabin, in exchange for a drift on *Osprey*. It was a fair trade when I consider the advice I received on positioning the boat to help clients fish.

By season's end *Osprey* had logged some 800 miles on the river. And I'd consumed twelve bottles of my special *liniment*.

17

WORD HAD GOTTEN OUT there was a private, quirky, *older* new guy in town who lived alone and had built a beautiful wooden boat he was using for *some* guide trips.

But I wasn't going to use *Osprey* for most floats. I bought a used plastic boat. *Osprey*'s reserved for clients I know respect wood. I began to have calls from outfitters and agreed to take a few clients. The demand especially increased in August after some of the guides returned to college.

After guiding three to four days a week for most of the early fall, I saved the waning days of a golden October to tow *Osprey* south through Yellowstone Park to stay in Jackson Hole. I planned to float alone on the Pacific Creek to Deadman's Bar section. Deadman's Bar to Moose remains an enigma. It's my favorite float — but one I can't yet bring myself to attempt. Images I want exorcised remain vivid in frequent nightmares. But each day I increasingly think I might be able to face that section again. At least I'm beginning to call it by its name; for a decade I could refer to it only as "*that* section."

I awoke at seven the morning after arriving late at Signal Mountain Lodge in Grand Teton National Park and decided I *would* float Deadman's Bar to Moose, if I did it with someone who knows that tortuous section of the river better than I do. I called John Kirby in Jackson. I'd met him and hired him as a guide for a couple of floats after guide school. "John, Macduff Brooks. I've brought my wooden boat down from Montana and thought maybe . . ."

He interrupted, "I *wondered* if you'd call. I said I'd take a day off if we could use *Osprey*. I've never rowed a wooden drift boat, but I hear they're great. When are we going?"

"When are you free?" I asked. "I'm at Signal Mountain Lodge."

"I had a client call an hour ago and cancel. Can we float today?"

"I can be at Deadman's Bar within an hour," I said. "We can do Deadman's to Moose. Can you pick up lunch?"

"OK. See you at Deadman's."

John knew *where* I wanted to float, but not *why*. He wanted to row a wooden boat and catch some fish; I wanted to put-to-rest my persistent torment. John never knew El and Maxwell. But he was questioned by the police and press after her death because he was scheduled to be their guide, until illness of his dad called him east to Georgia and Steve Brewster substituted. Brew wasn't John's choice and proved a tragic replacement.

We pushed off in *Osprey* at Deadman's Bar as some high cirrus clouds began to capture a clear blue sky, warning of a weather change by midnight. John rowed the first couple of miles, watching me throw casts to the bank.

"Try to get that fly closer to the bank, almost on the rocks," he suggested.

I was watching two adolescent otters tumble off the bank ahead when John yelled, "*Lift the rod!* Tip up, *not sideways.*"

A cutthroat broke the surface curtain, absorbed the fly, rolled to flash us its namesake crimson throat, and vanished into the depths. I reeled in line that had piled on the casting deck and then used the open palm of my left hand against the reel to control the drag. The cutthroat headed downstream straight along the bank, twisting left and right like a submarine eluding a destroyer, never more than two feet off the refuge under the bank, searching for anything to wrap the tippet around to break the line. Trout aren't too smart, but they know how to react instinctively to survive.

John was rowing hard forward, trying to match the pace of the desperate trout and reduce the stress on my light tippet.

"Damn! The line's gone slack. It's off," I said.

"No, it's not. Reel in fast." John back-rowed to help. "It's turned a half-circle, heading back toward us, gaining slack to throw off the barbless hook."

I got the slack in. The small hook, a #18 encased within an imitation of something more tempting than familiar to trout, maintained the tenuous link between the boat and the fish that was unable to seek the safety of the depths. John and I flashed smiles at the trout's abrupt turning splash and its final thrust across the river, where it surprisingly stopped two feet short of refuge within the underwater limbs of a fallen tree on the opposite bank.

"I think it's surrendered," John proclaimed. "It's swimming around slowly without direction." He turned the boat to work the long-handled guide net close under the fish. But the prospect of capture or a second wind changed its mind, like *Rigoletto's* dying Gilda rising for a few final lines of the closing aria. The trout showed another burst of adrenalin, thrusting thirty-feet downstream. Then it stopped again and, after we floated to close the gap, accepted the net.

"Great cutthroat. Beautiful color. Lucky catch!" he said.

"Luck? Perfect fly choice. Perfect presentation. Perfect set. All followed by a perfect play to the boat. And you were OK with the net. I may ask you to fish with me again. . . . How come everything I catch is luck and everything you catch is skill?"

"Except for when you catch whitefish . . . then it's your skill."

We kept the trout only a few seconds, to admire its complexion and praise its competitiveness. John easily slid the barbless hook free and held the fish under the surface, facing upstream. We watched it breathe deeply to regain energy. And then, without our sensing any movement, it wasn't there.

As our float progressed, both the river and John's humor proved cathartic. He has reason for self-deprecation. He's a Bulldog. One of those unenviable individuals who, in their late teens, when their judgment is still to be forgiven, somehow find themselves studying in Athens. Not in Greece, but at Georgia's major institution of more-or-less higher education. Since I was determined to become a wintertime resident of Florida, it wasn't a compromise of identity to favor the Florida Gators in playing my role of Macduff.

"John," I asked, "why did Georgia choose the planet's ugliest creature — the bulldog — for its mascot?"

"The Florida gator's uglier."

"But gators eat dogs," I responded. "That's survival of the fittest. It's only natural that Florida beats Georgia. Darwin would agree."

"What's *Darwin* got to do with it? He was a running back for Alabama in the late 1950s."

Even with so much baggage to carry from four years in Athens, John makes any day on the river pure joy.

We anchored for a late lunch alongside the ruins of the Bar B-C dude ranch. It's spread along a terraced bank that extends west until it reaches a brief, steep slope in the moraine, rising to a second higher terrace, and then a third even steeper.

After lunch, back on the river, despite John's good intentions, he brought back some demons for me. "I'm pretty sure this is near where a drift boat crashed into a strainer about eight years ago. I was scheduled to guide but had to go to Georgia for an emergency. A guy named Brewster took the float. He was a disaster. He was killed. The clients were a couple from Florida. I think the guy was also killed. It's a dangerous place, Mac. We're taking a safer channel a bit to the east."

I was relieved at his choice. I didn't want to see whether the channel El and I floated that day was still as threatening. And I didn't want to correct him. It was *eleven* years ago, and it wasn't the *guy* who was killed.

18

O N THE FIRST OF NOVEMBER I learned that some men really are from Mars — I floated with a Martian.

As a favor to John, I agreed to one final float of the season. He called me at Mill Creek the week after our float.

"Mac, come back down to Jackson and do a float for me the day after tomorrow?"

"Do I owe you any favors?"

"Always. I let you catch more fish than I did last week."

"I thought *I* intentionally caught more than you did. Not that *you* intentionally caught fewer than I did?"

"Same thing. Can you do the float?"

"Big tipper?"

"From California. Probably yes."

"From California? Probably over-extended."

"Yes or no, Mac? I've got a couple of people on the line."

"I've got a fish on the line."

"I thought you were at your cabin."

"I am. Behind my cabin. Standing in Mill Creek. A little cutty just took a #18 Hare's Ear nymph."

"Nymph? I thought I trained you not to use *bait!*"

John passionately prefers dry flies. "Sorry I told you. Yes, I'll do the float. Plastic or paper?"

"Leave *Osprey* at home. I don't know them. A guide friend who's fully booked needs me to help. I'm booked that day."

"So, I'm really doing your *friend* a favor?"

"Right."

"*And* you. Do I get credit for two favors?"

"Are you always this difficult?"

"I am when I'm interrupted with a fish on the line."

The couple want to do the Deadman's Bar to Moose float. They're Kath and Parkington Salisbury. From Newport Beach, California. California is a warning. Newport Beach is a warning twice told. But I owe John for helping me exorcize some demons on that float last week.

The Salisburys arrived at Moose on schedule. He was wedded to his cell phone, acknowledging me with a dismissive nod. At the Deadman's Bar launch area thirty minutes later, every guide and client in the area overheard that Salisbury liked to be called Park and that he was about to make a killing in some obscure .com start-up. I haven't yet worked out how to deal with cell phones on floats. I've had clients whose phone lines were busier than their fly lines. But emergencies arise, and my conscience keeps me from adopting a *no cell phone* rule. I usually talk about it before we float. It's surprising how many prefer to turn off their cell phones and take a chance on emergencies.

When *Park* finished, he turned, looked at me with a virile, macho grin, and said, "Mick, I can't wait to catch one of those Snake River cutthroats. Last month, I cooked a Yellowstone Park cutthroat I caught at Buffalo Ford. Baked it in paper, like they do pompano in New Orleans. It was real tasty. So were the Bear River and Colorado River cutthroats I've caught this year. Now I'll complete the grand slam — eat one caught here."

"Park, it's Mac — not Mick. And you're not going to eat a fish caught from this boat. First, you're in the Grand Teton National Park and the park rules say *only* catch and release starting the first of November. That's today. Second, I talked to John early this morning. He said he made it clear to you when you booked, and again this morning, that his and *my* rules were catch and release, whenever and wherever. Period. Clear?"

"Yea, sure . . . Mick."

"Another thing, if you ate a Yellowstone Park cutthroat you ate a trout you were *required* to release. The invasive Yellowstone *Lake Trout* are wiping out the cutthroats. They don't need a two-legged predator killing them."

I don't like arguing with clients. Park's a six-footer just over the edge of being out-of-shape. A little puffy here and there, his belt showing old marks from tighter clasping. His jaw's beginning to lose definition; little folds of skin fluttered as he talked. Details hard to describe, but suggesting rich food and a lot of drink. No time to exercise because he must spend hours managing his glossy, lampblack hairpiece — a two-inch thick carpet with a permanent wave that crests in front and reaches ebb tide in back. Not a touch of gray, and none of the life or body of natural hair. I wondered how much wind it would take to blow off the whole sculptured mass. Park's tanned face also had a gloss that had to come from a bottle. His head looked so artificial he was ready to mount in a wax museum.

Kath was a head shorter, shoulder-length auburn hair. A stunning beauty, with a quiet voice and soft nervous features that spoke of stress. She had habits of wringing her hands and twisting strands of her hair. She's likely a dozen years younger than Park, and I placed him around my age — fiftyish. Park had arrived dressed in expensive waders, boots, and jacket — the best of Simms, North Face, and Patagonia. He had an English House of Hardy special-edition bamboo rod. Kath's gear was out of Cabela's catalogue, the cheapest they offer. A seven-foot fiberglass rod that was old and too short. I loaned her a Sage nine-foot five-weight, a better choice for this river.

Park said he was *"in* investments." That can mean a lot of things. Art, antiques, real estate, or maybe high-risk hedge funds. He spoke the language of money and self-professed success. He had Newport Beach written all over him. Maybe he's in training to move to Jackson. The vehicle Park and Kath left in Moose was a huge metallic-gold, California vanity-plated SUV. Big money — bad taste. His watch was large, heavy, and gold. One of those half-kilo, twenty-carat, Rolex-like wrist-weights that tell time around the world. A watch I usually associate with a twenty-year-old inner-city kid who just signed a big deal with the Knicks. More gold hung around Park's neck.

Kath didn't reflect the same glitz. No big watch, no gold chains. She wore a tiny, attractive, gold lobster pin on the collar of her burgundy turtleneck sweater. She didn't have the "look at me" appearance Park tried to project. Her voice had a trace of accent I didn't recognize until later. It was Maine, where she grew up. I should have guessed from her lobster pin.

Maybe it's another of my personal quirks, but when I guide a couple, I often like the gal more than the guy. Not that I've tried to cut one out from the herd, but women seem more genuine in their appreciation of the floats then men do. Women take instruction in casting better, and are usually more appreciative of the beauty of the river. Kath was quickly reaffirming this. I didn't know anything about either of them, but assumed that a lot would unfold during the hours ahead.

When we launched at Deadman's Bar, I said, "Park, you might want to let Kath have the front seat. It's easier to fish from. I can give her better instruction since I face the front."

"Mick, you just want her there because she's a good lookin' babe. *I* sit there. Kath — get in the back."

Park took the front seat. On his first back cast he looped his line on Kath's shoulder, lodging the fly in the anchor line."

"*Damn it*, Kath. You snagged my line. *Watch* it!" Park yelled. He finally got his fly on the water, but wasn't interested in what a guide can do — improve a client's *chances* to catch fish. He *expected* the money he paid for the day's float *entitled* him to so many trout. California's big on entitlements. Jackson's Albertsons would be happy to sell him trout by the pound. Not me.

About half-way into our day's drift we anchored for lunch along a gravel bar. Park dropped into one of the two folding seats I set up next to my small roll-up table. "Gimmie a beer, Mick. Make it two while you're there. Kath, I got three fish so far. You didn't catch a damn thing."

Park had caught two nice cutthroats. Kath had hooked and lost a good size cutthroat, but seemed content with the day. She ignored Park's rudeness, and said, "Macduff, what a morning this has been! I loved seeing those two bald eagles skim alongside not more than five feet above the water. And that bull elk in midstream crossing the river was really exciting, bounding off when he saw our boat approaching."

"That elk was a *trophy!*" said Park. "I'd like to come back and bust him when the season opens."

"Park, there's *no* hunting in the national park."

"Hell, I got a .44 magnum rifle — with a silencer. Elk's great eatin'."

I wasn't prepared for Park. Maybe a good lunch would help. Although guides fix lunch for their clients, I have a culinary impairment. I'm more scared to be in a kitchen than in my workshop with the saws, planer; and drill press all running at once. But I know a gal named Sue in Jackson who dislikes fishing as much as I like it and who likes cooking as much as I avoid it. She owns a small restaurant, the Reel Food Café, just off the main square. She inherited it when cancer took her mom Cindy a few years ago. Cindy had made the lunches for us the day El died. Sue knows if I made the lunches it would cast a pall over the day's float. So she makes gourmet lunches for my full-day floats, and even keeps a list of my repeat clients' and friends' likes and dislikes.

"That was a wonderful meal," Kath said as we finished.

"It *was* good Mick," added Park. "Kath, toss me another couple of beers."

After we ate, I rigged two #16 dry flies. There was no hatch to match, so I matched the clients. A Lime Trude for Kath that likened her sad green eyes, and a Parachute Hare's Ear for Park, who after four beers had a kind of ruffled feather look.

"This gravel bar we're anchored on is a favorite for fishing, as well as lunch." I said. "We'll stay a bit and try it. Park, work downstream from the boat, one of the best holes for trout is about twenty-yards from here. I'll walk Kath up to that bend upstream, there's a good bar for her to practice casting," I suggested, pointing north to where the river turned slightly west.

"Dammit. You keep her in my sight. I'll be watchin'. Leave me a couple of beers, Mick."

Before we started out in the morning I had given Kath some brief casting lessons on land. Despite all her nervous hand movements, she was pretty good — listened and quickly corrected common mistakes. Like dropping the rod tip too soon on the forward cast and dumping the line in a pile short of the target. I didn't tell her *not* to break her wrist. I told her that for short casts from a drift boat she can keep her elbow against her side, letting her rod be an extension of her forearm. I think it's better to say what to do than what not to do. That can be corrected later. I wondered how Park would react if she started to out-fish him in the afternoon. It was clear their marriage was fragile and she was scared of him. You could tell a lot by her body language, her hands, and the way her brow wrinkled and mouth tightened when he raised his voice to her even slightly. I think my brow was wrinkling too. But it's none of my business if married clients are unhappy with each other. Working a drift boat, often sitting between spouses all day, is turning me into an amateur psychologist. I'm trying not to let it get to the active social-worker stage.

Comfortable that Kath was producing good drifts of the trude, I went back to see how Park was doing. I thought he was on one knee working on his rig — maybe undoing a wind knot — but as I got closer I saw he was clubbing a trout with a piece of driftwood, the slow rigid curl of the tail unveiling an ebbing life. By the time I got there a beautiful eighteen-inch cutthroat was bloodied and dead. Park was trying to slip it into a plastic bag.

"I *told* you there's no keeping fish! You don't deserve to be on this river."

"One dead trout won't empty the goddamn river, Mick. Just pretend it died from swallowing the hook." There was a discomforting, hostile edge to his voice. No hint of contrition. It wasn't the time to again correct his calling me Mick.

"It didn't die swallowing a hook. You planned all along to kill one. Don't you understand?"

"So what are you going to do? . . . Arrest me? Report me to the park pansies?"

"No, but I'm pretty creative at dealing with clients who don't listen."

Kath returned from around the bend, drawn by the louder parts of our discussion. She was shivering and it wasn't from the cold. She hopped into the stern seat of the boat, never looking at Park, knowing he needs anger management. I kept my distance from him, walked to the drift boat, climbed in, pulled in the anchor, and backed off the bar, quickly putting us out into the five- to six-foot depth of mid-stream.

"Hey, where in hell you think you're going? Bring that boat back," Park demanded. As I rowed to keep us away from his reach he lunged a couple of steps and tripped. Six cans of beer didn't help his balance. His hairpiece fell off and floated off with the current.

What Park heard next he didn't welcome. "You'll never float with me again, Salisbury. You can *walk* out. It's a few miles downstream to Moose. It's hard, slow going along the rocky shore because the water's low this time of the fall. I suggest you stay close to the water. Most of the brush by the river is huckleberry, and this is the time of the year the grizzlies are stocking up. They're in what's called *hyperphagia*. Gorging themselves — getting ready for hibernation. One of them might enjoy a change in diet if it sees you. When you finish your walk, I'll be gone. Kath will be waiting in the bar at Moose. Maybe she'll find someone there who won't scare her like you do." I took a small tube from my bag and tossed it to Park. It landed at his feet. "Put some sunscreen on that bald head!"

Park's expletive-laced screams were echoing off the moraine slopes as Kath and I rounded a bend out of his sight.

I made three calls on my cell phone. Two to other guides I knew were floating behind us. I told them the story and suggested they not pick up any hitchhikers. They agreed and would pass on the word.

Pushing hard downstream at first, I realized this was my favorite part of the river, and it was a beautiful day. We were free of Park, drifting through spectacular country alongside the Grand Teton range. And I was alone with a pretty lady in my boat. But Kath was a troubled woman, silent and occasionally trembling in the seat behind me. As I was thinking how to help, she asked quietly, "Macduff, is it all right if I fish?"

Fly fishing is good therapy. I moved her to the front, the seat Park had kept for himself. In another hour she gained a rhythm to her casting that was wonderful to watch, throwing an occasional tight loop out of *A River Runs Through It*. In the final miles she landed four cutthroats.

"Kath, that last fish was the best cutthroat from my boat this season. You belong on the cover of *Fly Fishing*. It's the longest and best hued cutthroat I've seen in a good while." It was even better for its impression on a gal I suspect is going to see some solo time ahead. And maybe come back and fish with me. I know Park's from Mars. Maybe Kath's from Venus.

When we set foot on the bank at Moose, there was a slight trace of a smile as Kath hugged me. I hoped it was for me, but maybe it was relief seeing a park ranger heading toward us. The third call I'd made as we drifted out-of-sight of Park was to a ranger acquaintance, Clyde King. When we reached Moose he was waiting. I told him the story.

"That's exactly what happened, Mr. King," Kath affirmed.

"There's no reason for either of you to wait. Mrs. Salisbury, it's your call whether you want to be here when I confront your husband. And Mac, we haven't seen a bear along the river this entire season, but I'll bet the guy's looking. He should get here in two to three hours. He has a couple of difficult places to get around where a few trees piled up during the spring runoff. I'll be here waiting."

I'm still a pretty inexperienced guide. But a *younger* guide might have had a difficult time dealing with Park. He's closer to my age than to a twenty-year-old rookie-guide trying to avoid trouble with an outfitter who's taking a chance on him as a guide. I've never suffered fools gladly. Park is a fool's fool.

The *client from hell* story didn't end with my leaving Kath at the bar in Moose. Two weeks later I received a hand-written letter from her. A strange but welcome arrival in this age of e-mail. Beautifully written in real ink on small, beige note paper, with her maiden name, Kathleen Macintosh, in Old-English script. Probably stationery she had from the days before she married Park. One of the postage stamps on the envelope was a drawing of a Royal Wulff. The letter was sent to me by way of the fly shop in Moose:

Dear Macduff,

I learned from the fly fishing shop at Moose that good guides usually get about $100 for a tip. I couldn't possible pay you what I really owe you for teaching me a lot more than how to cast. I hope the $200 check will buy you a bunch of Lime Trudes. I'll always remember that fly — I have it here on my desk. At first, there was some irony in the bitterness of a lime and the episode with Park. But after that fly began to attract trout, and floating downstream with you placed some miles between Park and me, the bitterness diminished.

I went into the bar in the restaurant at Moose where you dropped me. I wasn't waiting for Park. The owner of the bar gave me a couple of glasses of Pinot Noir and some tissues for a few tears. The last I'll shed over Park. You remember I picked up his hairpiece as we floated. It was expensive; I knew he'd want it back. It was a mess. I left it at the bar draped over a bottle of Snake River ale, with a note that said only, "Bye." Fortified by the wine, I went to the Jackson Hole airport and caught a plane east to a safe haven here at my folks' place in Bar Harbor, Maine. It's a long way from where Park and I lived near L.A. I learned a lot on the river with you, about fly fishing and about me. I am worried that Park might search for me, like the husband did in that Julia Roberts movie, Sleeping With the Enemy. *But I guess he saw the end coming. The lawyers have begun to sort out the rules of engagement for my hopefully soon-to-be-granted divorce.*

The news you will enjoy best . . . your patient ranger friend Clyde sent me a note . . . is that when Park arrived at the take-out at Moose, hours after we left him, he was full of scratches from the brush, and his expensive bamboo rod was broken in more places than his angry spirit. Clyde arrested Park. He resisted and was taken away in hand-cuffs. He won't be fishing again soon.

I would like to fly fish again. The part without him was as good as a day can be. There's a certain peace to the rhythm of casting I won't forget. And I won't forget the view of the Grand Tetons from the deck of the restaurant at Moose. Maybe one day you'll take me floating again. Next time I promise there won't be any fish-clubbing baggage.

Oh! There's a little gold lobster pin enclosed. My grandmother left me two. Just a little memento — a conversation piece for your hat band. People may ask if there are lobsters in the Snake River.

Best, Kath.

I didn't write back. I'm not good at letters, especially to women. But I did send flowers, with a brief note that said thanks for the pin. I *would* like to float with her again. She's the best kind of client — eager to learn, athletic — and a very pretty lady sitting only a few feet in front of me. The little gold lobster pin is in my Stetson hatband. It's a story that gets better with each telling.

19

BEFORE DEPARTING FOR FLORIDA Wuff and I took a final mid-November walk up Mill Creek Road, after *weather.com* speculated that we might have one more week before the sun, above freezing temperatures, and the bears all disappeared until spring.

Two miles beyond my cabin, a strip of private land follows Mill Creek Road for two miles upstream. Between the road and the creek the strip ranges from a few dozen to a few hundred feet wide. It's graded down from the road, along which is split-rail fencing. Every fifty feet a sign warns: "No Trespassing — Arrogate Ranch." At the creek's far side the property rises abruptly in levels. The lowermost are dotted with ranch buildings, including a modest size architecturally impressive lodge. Beyond, the slope increases, rising gradually toward Emigrant Peak.

The ranch owner has created a finely appointed property. And protected Mill Creek — the jewel of the ranch. Mill Creek meanders through the property, tumbling down the last stages of Paradise Valley's eastern mountains on its westward flow that takes it past my cabin to join the Yellowstone River.

When I asked about the ranch at the general store in Emigrant, the clerk said, "It's owned by an investment broker from New York. You'd think someone that smart and rich could spell the name of his own ranch correctly, and add the 'w' to make it *Arrowgate*. After all, there *are* two crossed arrows at the top of the gate."

I'd passed the ranch often to fish high, small, mountain streams, pulling ten- to eleven-inchers from what appeared far too shallow pools to hide cutthroats that size. The ranch has its own prime fishing stretch along Mill Creek. Some promising pools are temptingly visible along the road. One afternoon, out for a walk on the road, I watched a version of *obesis americanis* park his car next to one of the many "No Trespassing" signs, rig his rod, and climb over the fence, breaking a rail and heading for the creek as nonchalantly as though he owned the place. I shouldn't have said anything, but I did.

"I'm pretty new to understanding Montana access laws. Do they allow climbing fences to get to creeks or streams?"

He turned, squinted into a late, bright afternoon sun and replied, "This creeks *public*."

"The creek *bottom* is, but can you cross *private* property to get into a creek?"

"I can — and I did. The New York bastard who bought this place fenced it off. I been fishin' this piece of the creek for twenty-five years. I got *rights*."

"Do they include breaking the guy's fence?" I got a multiple four-letter-word answer, which was little more than an expression of the frustration repeated throughout the West as hunting and fishing land ownership changes and new fences and signs go up, emblazoned with a lot of "No's." The part of Mill Creek within the ranch is technically accessible under Montana's stream access law, but not by climbing the fence and trespassing across the land. Where Mill Creek leaves the ranch's property, it's possible to enter the creek on public land and wade upstream and fish right in front of and past the ranch's lodgings. I've never tried that. I don't like to see people wade past my log cabin when I'm sitting quietly on my porch, access rights or not.

Maybe someday I'll meet the ranch owner and offer a float on the Yellowstone for a day wade-fishing on the ranch's section of Mill Creek. But only if I'm allowed to walk in the main gate, not climb over his fence.

My section of Mill Creek is also accessible by wading upstream from the west. The week after my encounter with the fence buster, a spin-caster fishing worms came splashing up the middle of the creek while I was sitting on my rear porch. His puffy cheeks echoed a bulging stomach that obscured his belt. He stopped and stared at me. I stared back. Neither said a word. He finished a beer, tossed the glass bottle into the water and started to pee in the creek. But his *microphallia* and obesity compounded his distraction staring at me, and caused him to miss his target.

I called out, "Thanks for not polluting the creek; you're peeing into your right hip-boot!"

I'd been cleaning my double-barreled Coach shotgun which was on the deck next to me. I picked it up, looked at him through the open barrels, and slammed the gun shut. He turned away so fast he dropped his rod. From his fishing-vest pockets three more beer bottles fell out, cascaded over his stomach and shattered on the creek's boulders. He lost his balance trying to catch the falling bottles, fell into the glass and cut his hands and one leg. Not too badly, but enough blood that I wondered whether or not trout have the instincts of sharks and would soon be circling him. Swearing like a sailor, he got up and did an ungainly hop, skip, and splash downstream and around the bend. I haven't seen him again. All that and my shotgun was empty. All the shells were locked in my cabin.

20

ON A SULLEN, CHILLED NOVEMBER DAY a week before Thanksgiving, I found a note tucked under the clasp of my gate. Handwritten on *Arrogate Ranch* paper, the envelope flap was adorned with an intertwined *LLL* stamped in a red-wax seal. The note said:

We haven't met, but I read in the Bozeman News *that you moved to Montana from the East, becoming a fly fishing guide a little later in life than usual, and built a beautiful wooden drift boat. It said you lived on Mill Creek in Paradise Valley, somewhere along "our" creek. I asked one of the ranch hands to find out where you lived and drop off this invitation. Please come and join us for Thanksgiving dinner. About four p.m. Western casual. RSVP. LLL*

I assumed the signed initials LLL at the end were the ranch owner's. That afternoon, I left my RSVP speared on one of the arrowheads on the Arrogate Ranch main gate:

Your invitation came as I was wondering which can of soup I might open for Thanksgiving dinner. I'll be there at four, through the main gate, not from the west up along "our" creek. It's too cold for that. And maybe it's too "late in my life" to try that route. Thanks, Macduff Brooks.

At least LLL will know the *name* of the person he's dining with. All I know about him is local rumor, that he earned a ton of money in the East and has spent a lot of it here. No one I've talked to has met him. He apparently values his privacy.

Osprey was the focus of the *Bozeman News* article. My intentionally evasive movements assured my face wouldn't appear in paper. I *was* in one photo, screwing in guide seat footrests, hanging over a side, butt up and head down, face hidden under my Montana Boat Builders cap.

The dinner invitation said: "Western casual," whatever that means. Probably intended for his eastern guests, who must be flying here for the holiday. They're likely to arrive looking like they're heading for a costume party if they buy their western wear in Manhattan.

Thanksgiving afternoon I pulled on new jeans that fit like tailored trousers. No embroidery. The belt was cowhide with subtle, braided horsehair inlay — my shirt a tawny brown plaid, with single-point front yokes, three points in back, and pearl snaps. I debated about footwear. Narrow toe boots don't accommodate my feet, so I chose a pair of brown, plain toe, marbled-leather shoes. The hat was easy — a bison-skin Stetson. Not the trademark one I use for guiding, one saved for dress. Because it was cold I added a tanned leather vest. And for the walk to the ranch, an ankle-length, brown, oilskin, duster coat. I looked like Kevin Costner playing Wyatt Earp. But I don't own Colt 45s. And a pair of Glocks in shoulder holsters didn't seem "Western."

Trudging through new snow to the ranch lodge front door, I realized it was my first holiday meal in more than a decade that I wouldn't eat alone. There'd been invitations, but I used successive excuses to say no until the invitations stopped. The first few years after El died I was too grieved to accept — the last few years too scared. I hope I'm a passable guest this time. I'm curious about who owns the ranch. And his guests. The invitation did say: "join *us*." A compelling reason for going is I don't have to prepare the meal. That alone justifies the risks.

The large, double, wooden front doors of the ranch were decorated with intricately woven wreaths of twigs and fall leaves. I knocked and stepped back to admire the lodge's façade. Onto black ice. My feet went out and I went down. Hard on my rear. Sitting facing the door, feeling unusually foolish, in that second before I started to get up the door opened. A woman stood in the doorframe. From my position she looked threateningly tall. Probably the owner's trophy wife. Probably *not* the butler. Certainly not the scullery maid. She wore jeans that were not struggling to make a statement. A pleated, cranberry, collarless tunic extended a foot below her waist. Around her neck a single strand of tiny hollow metal, egg-shaped beads hung to just above her waist. Her earrings had similar but even smaller beads. Light brown hair cut just at the point it touched her shoulders. A mature face with a classic straight nose that could have been sculpted. It was the first part of her face that drew my attention. The second was the grin.

I didn't move, but uttered a weak, "Oh! Hi."

Looking down she paused, then said, "Howdy cowboy. Fall off your horse? May I bring you a drink? How 'bout a chair?"

It wasn't a good start. I tried to correct it, "Please close the door and open it again."

She did.

This time I was on my feet. She was outlined by the glow from the fireplace beyond. About five-six tall. She stared at me with an angelic grin, which was kinder than saying anything. It was my turn to speak.

"I'm Macduff Brooks. I was so taken with you that you knocked me off my feet?"

"Before I opened the door? I *know* you're Macduff. I'm Lucinda. Lucinda L. Lang. The LLL on the invitation."

Was it *her* house? Now I was really confused. I suggested, "Would you like to close the door and try again?"

"If I did, you'd be a three time loser, and I couldn't take you in and feed you."

"Maybe if your husband answered the door I'd do better."

"No."

"No, he doesn't answer doors? Or no, I wouldn't do better?"

"A bit of both," she said. "There's *no* husband here."

"Did he slip on the front stoop and kill himself?"

"No."

"Will he be back soon?"

"No."

I was getting cold. My questions as well as the temperature. The sun had set and it was below freezing. "I'm cold. Are you going to ask me in?"

"I intended to — when you knocked. Now I don't know whether I should." Another grin. "Come in. I'll get you a drink. Why don't you sit in the living room? There's a fire going. I'm having a Roughstock Montana Whiskey with a little soda. What would you like?"

"Anything Jack Daniels makes. With soda."

"Single Barrel OK?"

"Even better." It's a touch smoother than Gentleman Jack.

We sat in the living room before the crackling fire, talking mostly about our mutual captivation with Mill Creek. Maybe I mistook the time, but two hours passed, and we were still the only ones in the room. I didn't mind. She didn't seem to either.

"I know I'm not going to meet your husband. Am I going to meet anyone else? Or do you have me all to yourself?"

"I have you all to myself," she responded. "There's no husband here because there's no husband anywhere. I'm a spinster, an old maid."

I should have known. No ring. Nor an indentation around the ring finger where a ring might have recently rested. Her only jewelry was a watch and the necklace and earrings. The watch wasn't a status emblem. It all made me admire her even more.

"There are *no* other guests. I invited seven. You're the *only* one who accepted."

"Maybe they were here another time and are recovering from falling down in front of your door."

"I invited three Manhattan business colleagues and their spouses to come for the holiday weekend. After accepting months ago, last week they received what they apparently thought was a better offer — a private Lear jet to Peter Island in the British Virgins. They sent me collective regrets in a brief e-mail four days ago."

A slight quiver in her lower lip caused her to pause. Then she continued, "I decided to have the dinner anyway and take pot luck at your being an interesting guest. The *Bozeman News* writer thought you're interesting. And I don't cancel dinner invitations four days before the event. *Especially* I don't write personal, social event notes . . . on *e-mail*."

Her colleagues had been rude, and she was visibly hurt. I had a role to play. I liked playing it as duet instead of an octet.

While Lucinda fixed us refills, I surveyed the room. Elegant. Reserved. Smart. The kind of room *Architectural Digest* tries to place in its magazine but can't because the owners value their privacy and choices. The room had three Remington bronzes and two of his night paintings.

When Lucinda returned with the drinks I asked about the night scenes.

"They're *grisaille* oils . . . a difficult method that fills the canvas with moonlight, candlelight, and firelight. They're wonderful in the evening with the fireplace going."

"Your mantel has attractive ceramic jars. I think I've seen some . . . in New Mexico?" There were three off-white with red and black geometric decoration, and one with birds' heads.

"They're from Acoma, an 11th- or 12th-century Navajo pueblo west of Albuquerque, on top of a mesa. Called 'Sky City.'"

Lucinda's rooms weren't especially large. I commented, "I like your lodge. It's scale and it's comfort."

"I'm so tired of seeing the grotesque, enormous houses my colleagues have been building in South Hampton and Vail, even in Tuscany! It's overkill by the overpaid."

"Something I've wondered when I've driven by your ranch entrance. Why *Arrogate*? I don't think you left out a "w."

"Arrogate's correct. Claiming *ownership* of this piece of land seemed wrong. I'm determined to leave it better than I found it. I've placed most of the land in a conservation easement."

As I talked to her, the clarity and motion of her eyes were transfixing. Lots of people have eyes that reflect light. But more provoking was the way hers communicated and *moved* as she expressed herself. And how they followed me when *I* moved, like when I'd walked the few steps to see the detail on her bronzes and jars.

I tried to limit the conversation to questions *she* had to answer. The ranch lodge made it easy. It was a combination of her creative mind and enthusiasm. There was an addictive Midwest, down-home ethic and determinism to her. By a series of questions I learned how she'd crashed through the glass ceiling of the brokerage firm she works for in New York City. But unlike many of her colleagues, she appreciates her success less for what it's given her, than for what she hopes it will allow her to do in the future.

Beyond the living room the walls of the lodge were lined with art, mostly depicting the natural beauty of the West. The centerpiece is a magnificent Bierstadt painting of the Grand Tetons, the mountains dwarfing a small Indian on a pony at one lower corner.

"Lucinda, I'm not upset that the discourteous six are in the Caribbean. This is the *first* time in a dozen years I've been alone talking to a cultured, articulate, and attractive woman."

"Are you *that* private?" she inquired, only partly diverting a blush.

"I lost my wife twelve years ago. Our close friends asked me to dinner. At first I went. They were all couples, I was the first to lose a spouse. I thought many of the dinners would never end. There were some smiles. And sometimes a few laughs. Invitations began to come from single women. Some were widows. Some divorced. Even a few spinsters, like you!"

Lucinda spilled her drink. "No wonder spinsters don't get anywhere with you. They can't hold their liquor!" Her grin turned into a laugh. "I'm sorry. Go on."

"I'd seen this happen before when a colleague lost his spouse. He ended up marrying the former wife of another colleague. I turned down all those invitations. A few were persistent, invitations to meet at a secluded restaurant where we wouldn't encounter any of the woman's friends, especially ones who might tell her husband. I hope they enjoyed their meals. I never showed up." I wasn't sure why I was telling her all this?

"I'm sorry about your wife. I have problems with dinner invitations, but not because of the same tragic history. If I invite eight, after the dinner I think maybe four would have been enough. . . . *Sometimes* two is even better."

115

She maintained the grin I was learning was her trademark. It comes with a slight tilt of the head and an unblinking focus on you with her clear, green eyes.

She continued, "At a table for eight or ten, often one person dominates the conversation. Sometimes about politics. Or the economy. But more often their own purported accomplishments. You can't imagine how bad that can be in Manhattan. These dinners become less interesting social occasions than entrapments. It's difficult to get up and leave. When I have left early, the invitations abruptly, but blessedly, ended."

One hesitation about having dinner alone with Lucinda had been whether I could avoid answering the kind of questions about my life — past and present — that inevitably enter a dinner table conversation. Talking about the past for me is like writing a novel, working back in time to create a character, without knowing exactly how that previous life is going to develop in reverse. Some of that had started while we sat in front of her fireplace before the dinner. When we went to the dining room, I hoped she'd forget where we were in our conversation.

We dined at a table that sat ten. Lucinda had set two places across from each other at one end. She'd made a statement by turning plates upside down at each of the other six places.

"If all eight had arrived, would I have been seated opposite you?" I asked as I held her chair.

"No."

"You mean as the sole unknown guest, I would have been seated at the foot of the table, with you at the head, hidden from each other by the centerpiece?"

"No."

"In the kitchen eating with the help?"

"*No.* There's no kitchen-help. Because you were to be the only unknown guest, I would have put you right next to me."

"And now I'm across from you. I'm losing ground," I said.

"But I can see you better, and there's no one on my other side to distract me."

Another touch of blush spread on her cheeks, and she changed the subject by tilting her head down and saying grace. I tried to listen, but she'd reached across the table to hold hands.

The dinner was a delicate *trout amandine*. She served the same *pouilly fouisé* wine that Dan Wilson had given me when we finished my conversion from Max to Mac in D.C. I wondered if Lucinda had some kind of conversion on her mind.

I held up my wine glass: "To Lucinda, for giving shelter and food to a fallen stranger."

Lucinda responded: "To the stranger — who sent flowers."

The flowers were on the table. I hadn't included a note.

Some inevitable first-meeting questions returned after dinner. Sipping coffee, she set her cup down, lifted her eyes, looked at me intensely, and asked, "From what our mutually shared housekeeper Mavis told me, I'm not sitting across from a serial killer. She wouldn't tell me much. Apparently, we both like this part of the country. What brought *you* here?"

It was an opening I could take as far as I wanted, maybe defusing her questions. Not prevent her from asking them, but answering on my own terms. There was something I couldn't decipher about the time of day, the drinks, the ambience of this house, and mostly her eyes, that made me take a step further than dictated by my earlier intentions.

"I moved here a year and a half ago," I answered. "Like a lot of people who bump hard into something around fifty, I needed a change. My wife . . . El . . . the most wonderful human being I'd ever met . . . was expecting our first child. They died in an accident. I might have saved them. . . . It was a decade before I moved here, from the house we'd shared in Florida." It was all true. It didn't mesh with what I'd told the lady on the flight to Denver, but the odds were in my favor that I'd seen the last of her.

"I'm sorry. I shouldn't have led you back to your loss. Everything I've heard about you has been complimentary. You must know you're a mystery to your neighbors. Not many obviously well-educated men arrive in Montana, throw themselves into building a cabin and a drift boat, take a guide course, and become a fly fishing guide."

"You mean at my age — a 'little later in life than usual'?"

"I had that coming. Guiding's strenuous from what I hear. And that comes from two young guides at the fly fishing shop in Emigrant. I didn't ask about *you*, but when I mentioned I lived on Mill Creek, they asked if I knew you and said they helped you build your cabin. I said I didn't know you and they told me what I've repeated. They said your boat's the nicest they've seen on the river. The photos in the Bozeman paper were beautiful. *Your* photo suggests you were trying to hide everything but your butt. Anyone who read the article knows a lot more about the boat than about you. You *are* a mysterious guy."

"Lucinda, I've told you more than anyone else in Montana. *No* one knows about my wife and expected child. I want to keep it that way. When I think back to times shortly before I arrived here, I confront some days I can't explain. Trying to doesn't help – not yet. You're right about the article. I *was* trying to hide. I don't have a face that's ready to smile for the public."

Somehow I hoped she wasn't thinking that she was asking questions that were too personal. I have to face my loss better than I have for nearly a dozen years. It was a lost decade for me after El's death. I want this next decade to be better.

"Macduff, may I hire you for a day on the Yellowstone?"

"No."

"*No! Aren't you a guide?* Guides take people fishing. Are you this hard to hire with everyone?"

"For *some* people. But not for *you*. I don't guide for fees when it's a neighbor. I decided I'd do *some* guiding professionally for paying clients — it helps pay bills. I prefer to take friends out with all the payment I could hope for introducing them to new experiences on moving water. . . . The season's over. If you're here next summer, we'll do a float together. Or maybe walk and fish the creeks upstream from here, especially when the spring wildflowers are starting to bloom."

"I've been developing this ranch for a couple of years, Macduff. I come out at holiday time and a short week in the summer. The furthest I've been is a trailhead a few miles up the road that looks like a good place to start some scenic hikes. I envy you being here to see the seasons change. But not in January and February. How do you survive a Montana winter?"

"I try not to. When I arrived last year, I started building the cabin. Then my drift boat. I couldn't leave them unfinished for the winter. So I stayed. The weather was abominable. Next week, I'm heading east to look for a small, winter place along the marshes on the northeast Florida coast. I'd be there now except for your invitation. My companion — the new love of my life — and I were about to leave for Florida. We'll leave in a day or two; she'll love the Florida beaches."

"Companion?" Lucinda interrupted. She'd been sitting with her elbows on the table, her chin on her clenched hands, leaning forward toward me. Completely absorbed, as though we were the only people in the world. And then I mention a companion! My comment disquieted her. Disappointment was em-

119

bedded in her expression. She began to say more, but couldn't get out her words. She sat back stiffly.

"Oh! . . . Macduff . . . well . . . you could have brought her to dinner. I didn't know when I sent the invita. . . ."

I interrupted, realizing the confusion. "I couldn't impose her on you, Lucinda. She has terrible table manners. She eats much too fast. And she whines a lot."

"That's no way to talk about a lady you love!"

"It's true. She sleeps with me, until she wakes me up a little before six, with her incessant, annoying whine."

"Why?"

"So I'll take her out to pee!" I couldn't hold back a smile that turned into laughter.

Lucinda's eyes widened, she was back leaning toward me. "You're *awful*. What is she?"

"A Shetland sheepdog or, as the kids who see her call out, 'a little Lassie!'" Her name's Wuff."

"Next time Wuff gets her own invitation. Likely the *only* invitation."

We went back and sat among the Remingtons. I added some split logs to the fire and told Lucinda about my client from hell experience with the Salisburys. She approved the way I dealt with Park. Maybe because I stepped in and separated Park from Kath. I thought her manner signaled she'd experienced a comparable, unhappy relationship. Lucinda was certain to tell the Park story back in Manhattan.

Kath's letter and Lucinda's dinner were a couple of unexpected nudges leading me somewhere. I surprised myself imagining being paired off with either one. But when I walked into my cabin later that evening, I patted Wuff and said, "Wuff, I *know* I've just been to Venus."

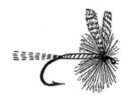

21

WUFF AND I LEFT MILL CREEK two days later to face the long drive to Florida. At least I was unlikely to encounter Juan Pablo. Two summers and one wintering over were history. How successful my guiding was is better told by my clients, but most departed saying they wanted to fish again next year. They liked being in a drift boat, even though it usually wasn't *Osprey*. On the few times I took Wuff along, most clients wanted to adopt her. Not one asked to adopt me.

We headed north, Yellowstone Park had closed most of its roads for the winter. But going north through Livingston wasn't without its rewards. I stopped at Dan Bailey's for fly tying materials and Sax and Fryer for a pile of books. I hadn't tied many flies during the summer. I'll tie a bunch in Florida.

The drive east seemed interminable. We slanted down through eastern Wyoming and Colorado, staying west of Denver, turning east in Pueblo and crossing into America's Sahara — Kansas.

On the fifth day, we drove straight for Florida's eastern coast. Wuff's been a good traveler and friend I needed for the trip, to retain what part of my sanity wasn't left in one of the Great Plains states. I hope I've given Wuff some of the same peace. Beginning with the day I brought her home, she's taught me I needed a companion.

22

MAXWELL HUNT DEPARTED FLORIDA on the flight to D.C. a year-and-a-half ago. He never returned. As *Macduff Brooks*, I didn't know how I would conduct myself back in the state where I'd lived for twenty years. Where El and I expected to remain the rest of our lives. We dreamed of retiring south of St. Augustine somewhere along the salt-marshes, exactly where I'd now arrived. I was looking for a place to hide from both Juan Pablo and the Montana winters. And maybe from myself.

I met with a real estate agent named Janet. El had talked to her briefly more than a decade ago, when our coastal property aspirations vastly exceeded our financial resources.

"Any interesting listings?" I asked.

"Most everyone wants beach front. But I have one listing that might interest you. It's about where St. John's County and Flagler County meet along Pellicer Creek. New England sportsman Henry Cutting bought the land in 1887, to create an Adirondack style camp and private hunting preserve. His workers fashioned his fireplace from coquina-stone from Flagler County beaches. A porch wrapped around the lodge, its roof supported by palm and cedar trunks. He added riding stables, a tennis court, and a unique first-in-Florida swimming pool that's continuously replenished from an artesian well."

"I can't afford that kind of property, Janet."

"That was sold to Flagler County. But he also secretly built a much smaller 'cottage' of some 1,400 square feet, using similar palm and cedar columns on the porch. It's north of the main lodge, across Pellicer Creek in St. John's County, in the pine woods on the banks of the salt-marshes that border to the east. Cutting built the cottage to escape his wife's too-frequent lavish parties. He died soon after from a heart attack on his boat. The cottage was sold to a reclusive mystery-novel writer who used it to craft his books. When he died, his five estranged children battled over his estate for a dozen years. They were finally ordered to sell the property by a local judge."

"Is it listed?"

"Not like most properties. I knew the owner and was the only local realtor all the children knew. By their unanimous decision, only last week, I'm to be the *only* person allowed to sell the property. It's not to be listed in the newspapers, and there's to be no general publicity. It's the way many unique pieces of property are sold, avoiding the masses of would-be buyers with inadequate funds who spend weekends touring homes where they'd otherwise never be admitted."

"May I see it?"

"Certainly, right now."

The narrow, sand entry road to the cottage twisted and turned beneath towering pines and mushrooming oaks, discouraging wayfaring strangers. When the cottage came into sight, I turned to Janet and said, "I'll buy it!" As impulsively as I had bought my Montana land. I used most of the remaining proceeds from the sale of my Gainesville house and closed within a week.

Soon after I moved in, sitting on the small dock and planning how I'd improve the lighting, Dan Wilson called and said,

"Mac, you know we don't like you buying a place in Florida. . . . At least, *please* don't go to Gainesville. Abdul Khaliq Isfahani was in Gainesville at an alumni reunion a couple of days ago. We know he wandered around the law college. He entered the country a month ago; we've been tailing him."

"Thanks for the warning." I wasn't too worried about Isfahani, unless he was with Juan Pablo. Isfahani has good reason to attend an alumni function at the *university*, but why would he go to the law college at the edge of the campus — well away from where he took classes? When Dan called, I *was* about to leave for Gainesville. The UF women's soccer team was in the NCAA tournament. Despite Dan's concern, I went — wearing sunglasses and a floppy, wide-brimmed Gator hat.

Parking a block away from the law school, I sat in the car for an embarrassing moment of self-pity. I'd come to work here for twenty years and never once entered without thinking how fortunate I was to be a UF law professor. Few people were around, at least until the library opened. The last students I'd taught had graduated. Current students were nearly finished with exams, some would be graduating in a week. I shouldn't know *anyone*, except for a faculty or staff member. But it was Sunday and they were unlikely to be at work.

Seated on one of the low brick walls, I picked up a discarded copy of the Friday *Alligator* — the student newspaper. It mentioned the appointment of a new law school dean. My old nemesis had left after only three years. Four students carrying law books sat down next to me, waiting for the library to open. They were talking about the new dean.

One student, who said he'd been a member of the dean selection committee, spoke in glowing terms about their success. "He's an insurance law guy. Wrote *the* books on the subject. . . . Any of you know what happened to Dean Stein?

Another said, "No one seems to know. He was here one morning, but an hour after the president called him to his office in Tigert, we had a new interim dean."

"Whatever," said a third. "Right now, I have to worry about our last final exam, and clerking for the summer."

He turned to the fourth student. "Did you understand what Professor Gross said about Souter's opinion in the Supreme Court's *Sosa v. Alvarez-Machain* decision?"

She was opening her International Law text, written by Maxwell Hunt. I interrupted . . . "What did Professor Gross say about the decision? I know the opinion fairly well."

They looked at me curiously. I kept on my sunglasses. One said, "Are you a professor here?"

"No. I don't teach here," I responded. "But I've taught the subject in Europe and the U.K." That much was true. "I was a consultant for the Justice Department and helped defend the case for Sosa." I didn't mention that Sosa was in the Witness Protection Program.

We had an interesting discussion of the case. As is likely with any complex decision, I agreed with some of Professor Gross' views on the decision and disagreed with others. The students had a good grasp of the Court's reasoning.

"I have to be off. I think you'll all pass — with ease. Good luck on the exam."

One of them commented as I left, "He seems to know the case better than Gross. He *did* work on it. I wonder who he *is*?"

Another said, "I talked to Gross after class Friday. He said it was a shame that Hunt, the UF law professor who wrote our casebook, died unexpectedly of a stroke in D.C. a couple of years ago. Gross said Hunt worked on the case with the Justice Department. I wonder if this guy and Hunt worked together. It's a small world."

"One professor," commented the young woman, "told me she believes Hunt never died; that he was working for the CIA and they have him hidden. . . . Could that have been him?" With open-mouth, wide-eyed stares, all looked to where I had disappeared around a corner and stood waiting for the elevator . . . listening to their conversation.

I played my hiding game a little longer, walking quietly through the halls of the nearly deserted third floor that houses faculty offices. Mine was at the end of a corridor and apparently hadn't been reassigned. My office keys were in my pocket; I never threw them out. And I didn't want to mail them in from Montana like a hotel room key I forgot to drop at the desk.

I unlocked and opened the office door to an empty room. There were tiny holes in the walls from my picture hooks. On the credenza behind my desk was my old name plate the now departed dean had excitedly removed when he heard about my death. He'd tossed it into the trash. I suspect my secretary Marilyn fished it out. I slipped it into my pocket and left.

My occasional depressions about not being able to arrive every morning and teach were self-imposed. No one forced me to say yes to work I assumed would be short of risk-taking. That assumption proved wrong. I'm paying a high price for my choices. I have a new bed to sleep in, along with a new house and a new identity. I'd give them all up in a second. But I kind of like my new moustache.

Driving back to St. Augustine after the soccer game, I realized it's easy to do something stupid to satisfy selfish personal interests, and risk what a lot of people have done for me. At the cottage, I poured some Gentleman Jack and took it down to the dock. It was dark and getting cold, but I'm from Montana and have to bear it. In the chill air I dozed, and my thoughts drifted to those earlier events that changed my life.

A decade of languishing years dragged by after El's death. If time cures grief, someone forgot to start the clock running. While my life had been defined by her presence, it became twice defined by her loss. If there's truth to the proverb: "All work and no play makes Jack a dull boy," I went beyond dull — into apathetic, blunt, colorless, and through the rest of the alphabet to — with the aid of Gentleman Jack —zonked.

Work became my catharsis. After El died, impelled by sleeplessness and escorted by the dark of night, I often arrived at the law school hours before my eight a.m. classes. My resume swelled by lectures, books, visiting professorships, and consulting. On the other hand, my half-page personal data had a decade-long black hole.

What I hadn't done over the decade was eat sensibly, have annual physicals, or exercise. And I hadn't sought female companionship. What I had done was gain twenty unwelcome pounds, and increase the value of Jack Daniel's stock. Most of all, I had rebuffed females seeking my companionship. I hadn't met a woman at a dinner, a concert, or around the campus whose physical presence compared with El's spiritual presence. I kept fulfilling two clichés — plodding along and nose to the grind. Pretty dull boy. Maybe I should have changed my name to Jack.

One day at my dentist's office in Gainesville, I'd glanced at a magazine on the table: Fly Fishing. *There was a smiling kid on the cover holding up a small trout that took me back decades to my teen years and a small stream I fly fished for brookies in Northwest Connecticut. As a teen I also spent hours at a gun club and began competitive shooting. My scores were good. Truthfully . . . better than good. But fishing and shooting wouldn't support me. I had to find a job.*

One weekend at a university jobs fair during my senior year, a man came up to me. He was wearing a dark blue, poorly fitted wool suit . . . creases on the jacket but not on the pants. Off-white shirt, dulled from too many conflicts with starch. A narrow, plain blue tie that was decades out of fashion. And a little metal American flag pin, crooked in his lapel. His dated, clear plastic-framed eye-glasses had spotted lenses. Short hair — no

127

sideburns. The man said he was David Smith, and he had a career proposal.

"You'd work for a federal agency."

"Which one?"

"It's in D.C."

"What would the work be?"

"Classified."

"Where would I work?"

"Here and there."

"I've never been to either of those places."

"The survivors' benefits are great."

"That means I'd be dead."

"If you're killed, we put a gold star in your honor on the wall at the entrance to the agency's headquarters."

He left, but he didn't seem discouraged. He never told me what he meant by "the agency."

I ultimately chose military service — Navy OCS. Then I met El. A blind date. Blindsided. The date was magical. I proposed on our second date. We were married and moved to Newport, Rhode Island. I went to sea. First to the Caribbean and Cuba's Guantanamo Bay. I spent time off the base in towns in Oriente Province, gathering information on Castro's popularity. On what public reaction would be if he were to have a fatal accident. I didn't know the "agency" I'd been recruited by was thinking about arranging such an accident.

After service came law school. In my last year another government recruiter showed up. Same uniform, different recruiter. His sideburns were a half-inch longer, and his American flag pin was straight. The agency must have hired a fashion consultant.

"I've taken a job with a law firm," I told him. "I'm married, and I don't aspire to having a gold star in my honor placed on the wall in Langley."

"I'd prefer you call it the agency. I don't know what you mean by Langley."

"How about the Company."

"NO!"

*"The **CIA**?"*

He nearly fainted. Then he smiled and went away. He never mentioned his name — part of it had to be Faust.

I spent a few boring years in general law practice, where I was the very lowest lawyer on a very high totem pole. The partners said I could be one of them in four years. I wasn't strong enough to climb that far that fast. But at least my pole wasn't greased. The firm used that one for women.

After a couple of years, El and I moved to Gainesville, Florida, home town of the NFL minor league Fightin' Gators Football Team. It's putatively a part of the University of Florida, which coincidentally happens to be in Gainesville. I taught at the law school, located on the far edge of the campus, beyond the athletic fields. The university president knew a lot about the football team. I don't think he knew the university had a law college. We encouraged that.

El and I lived a life to dream about. But I'd heard the best dreams last only a fraction of a second. It seemed like that when El died in Wyoming. She died because I didn't know how to row a drift boat and save her. Her absence ended my joy in teaching and in most everything else. But I hung around the law school for ten more years feeling sorry for myself.

The State Department often sends professors abroad. A few are induced by seductive pleas of patriotism to gather information for the local mission of the "Agency," our CIA. Aka the "Company." Or sometimes just "Langley." The CIA calls them "agents of convenience." They help direct public opinion toward U.S. positions on current issues. Sometimes they're convinced to do more than influence public opinion. Agents of convenience possess another benefit; they don't look CIA. CIA agents tend to exhibit a dramatic homogeneity in dress and manner, a persona easily picked out in a crowd.

Two years after El died, I agreed to meet with some people at the U.S. embassy while lecturing in Asunción, Paraguay. We gathered in a limited access area of the embassy. No windows. Big table. Metal chairs. No refreshments. The men in ill-fitted suits were back. I hoped they were interested in my ideas on conflicts between U.S. foreign policy in Latin America and rules of international law, but they didn't show much interest in the rules part. They wanted me to travel up the Río Pilcomayo to a small town, Pedro P. Peña, near where Paraguay meets Bolivia and Argentina. Three leftist cells in that area were merging with the Peruvian Shining Path terrorist group. I was to meet with one Tomás Ortega, a disillusioned member of one cell who was willing to work with the U.S. Just a simple meeting. Ortega would give me a list of names. Nothing more.

I asked the apparent leader at the embassy meeting, "Why me?"

"We need an unfamiliar face. Most of us have been in that area."

"What's the risk?"

"If they think you're with our mission here — big risk."

"Do I get to carry a weapon — an Uzi?"

"Not a chance," replied another of the agents.

"How about a concealed Glock?"

"No!"

"Bear mace?"

"Jeez, Hunt, be serious! This is essential to national security."

"Do I carry a cyanide pill?"

"I'll give you a dozen. Listen! You're only going to meet with Ortega and bring back information."

"Can't he fax it? But a fax wouldn't appear clandestine, and I know you're trained to act suspiciously."

"Fax isn't secure, Maxwell. Will you do it?"

"I don't know the name of even one of you. What if I need to call?"

"Why?"

"I can think of a dozen reasons, mainly if I have trouble."

"We couldn't help you."

"Why not?"

"You're officially a tourist. Tourism comes under the consular section of the embassy. We're CIA."

"I thought the CIA called me an agent of convenience?"

"Only when it's convenient."

My tour to Pedro P. Peña proved to be more than a tour. Tomás Ortega gave me a list of forty-three cell member names. Back home a month later, I read in the Miami Herald *about fourteen "terrorists" in northern Paraguay who were killed by unknown assailants. Ten of those killed had names I remembered from the list.*

A huge splash off the dock brought me abruptly out of my macabre thoughts. A redfish had been spooked by the dock light. My glass was empty. I wished my memory were as well.

23

M Y SOCIAL LIFE DURING THE WINTER in Florida was Lucinda's voice. I first called her the week before Christmas at her office.

"How are things on Venus?" I asked.

"Are you calling from Mars?" she answered.

"Going to invite me to New York for Christmas dinner?"

"I'm afraid you might slip and fall in my hallway. My building's full of legal vultures waiting to represent you." Her voice softened. "Macduff, I started to call you a dozen times. I never got past the first few numbers. Thanksgiving was *so* good."

"Thanks, my butt's still bruised."

"I didn't mean that part . . . I'm on overload at work. Or I seem to feel more and more that work here is always an overload. . . . Please call me Tuesday . . . Christmas Day. That would be the best present. My boss is waiting outside my office with an armload of files. We're trying to finish some investment planning before the holiday."

Christmas morning we talked for two hours. I described my Florida cottage to her. It made the cottage even more comfortable. It was missing one thing.

"Would you send me a photograph, Lucinda?"

"Forgot what I look like?"

"No. About five feet. Crew cut. Heavy metal in the nose, ears, and tongue. Anorexic. Typical New Yorker."

"How much have you been drinking?"

"One glass of eggnog. One part egg — five parts nog."

"Is anyone with you, Macduff., other than Gentleman Jack?"

"He's all bottled up. But Wuff's here."

"How does she put up with you?"

"I know when to feed her, where to scratch her, and when to let her out to pee. The same things I'm trying to learn about you."

"I prefer to pee inside."

"I'm willing to make concessions."

"Why don't you call me in another decade or two . . . the pictures will be on their way tomorrow."

The pictures came and the cabin is twice as nice.

I'm now the owner of a Montana *cabin* and a Florida *cottage*. A cabin on the edge of Mill Creek that flows into the Yellowstone a couple of miles away, gerrymanders north, east and finally south to the Gulf of Mexico, and ultimately mixes with the Atlantic. And a cottage close to Pellicer Creek that flows into the Matanzas River a mile away, and empties into the Atlantic. I wonder if my two waters ever meet. Maybe somewhere off Margaritaville in the Florida Keys.

The cottage is on a slight rise at the edge of the salt marsh. Cypress walls, heart-pine floors, and a metal roof. The single floor is raised on pilings ten feet off the ground. The heart-pine radiates a dark red, grainy elegance to the main living room. The tiny kitchen retains original cypress cabinets. Connected to the house by a wooden walkway is a small dock where I keep an old Hewes flats boat. There's an alarm system on the boat and another at the house. It's possible at half-tide and higher for someone fishing to get back through the tidal marsh as far as the dock. But few come this way. That's one reason I bought the place.

A small gun closet I added hides a couple of Glocks, a .22 rifle, and a shotgun. No Chey-Tac. I don't like carrying guns across state borders.

I spend many hours reading during the coldest of Florida's winter days, when the temperature occasionally plummets to near freezing. When it does, I turn on my computer and look up the weather in Montana. The St. Augustine low is usually above the Montana high. It makes me warmer knowing that.

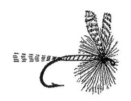

24

O N A LATE MARCH DAY, while I was hoping that Juan
Pablo was so involved with his dirty tricks in Guatemala
that his hatred for me had been pushed to a back burner, an
unexpected call came from D.C. Not from Dan Wilson, but
another agent I knew only by name — Bruce Rogero. He works
at Langley on Guatemalan issues. His comments supported
Dan Wilson's.

"There are disagreeable rumblings in Guatemala," Rogero
related. "Juan Pablo has consolidated his power since 'the inci-
dent,'" a term we used to avoid mentioning my identity change.
"The Supreme Court of Guatemala isn't able to function. One
member was murdered last month in the Parque Minerva in
Guatemala City, her body mutilated and impaled on one of the
volcanoes that rises on the large relief map of the country. Two
other members of the court immediately resigned. Their re-
placements are Juan Pablo lackeys.

"There's a federal warrant out for Juan Pablo's arrest in the
U.S. We believe he was here last week using false diplomatic
credentials and was part of a group that murdered a CIA agent
in Virginia. The agent was one of the three who saved Maxwell
Hunt at the Camino Real. We have no reason to believe you've
been compromised, but I think you need to be aware of Juan
Pablo's activities."

"If you're trying to scare me, you've succeeded. Any suggestions?"

"We don't want you to go *anywhere*. It's trouble enough that you have two houses. And we want you to be alert."

"If the protection plan *is* working, and Juan Pablo believes I'm dead, should I be worrying?"

"If he *doubts* your death, Mac, he probably wouldn't have shown his hand by going after one of the agents who rescued you. But he hasn't dropped the matter."

"Juan Pablo's activities in the U.S. can't have been well thought through if he's serious about running for Guatemala's presidency."

"He's compulsive. His actions aren't very consistent. That makes him all the more dangerous. But the career ambassadorship seekers in our State Department believe he should be supported, as long as he speaks favorably about the U.S. and protects U.S. business interests in Guatemala. . . . One more thing — Dan Wilson asked me to tell you that we've lost track of Isfahani."

Rogero hung up.

25

DEPARTURE FOR MY THIRD SUMMER in Montana wasn't determined by when I felt like leaving. I'd booked a few days of spring fishing with clients that started the middle of April. *If* the water temperature and weather conditions mesh, there should be some good *baetis* hatches. On April Fools' Day Wuff and I packed the SUV, closed the cottage, and pointed ourselves generally northwest.

It took a week of long days to settle in at my Mill Creek cabin and get *Osprey* ready. The spring fishing proved to be short of average. Once the snow melt started in earnest, the Yellowstone flowed too fast and too cloudy to fish, not clearing until the end of July. In addition to some wade trips, I took a few clients floating on the Madison. Twice I went to Jackson for a few days to help John Kirby on the Snake. Mostly, I used the time to fish small creeks by myself. And talk to Lucinda on the phone. Her brother, seriously ill with hepatitis, was taking a lot of her time; she wasn't likely to get to Montana until fall.

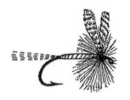

26

THE FISHING SEASON WAS TRANQUIL until a final float on the Snake on a chilly, sparkling, early November day. A float that engulfed my life and made my client from hell story insignificant. Maybe I should avoid floating in November and be in Florida by Halloween. But this float proved more than spooky. I was glad Lucinda wasn't here.

I'd been watching a glorious fall unfold in October. Maybe I delayed leaving hoping Lucinda would call and say she'd be here for Thanksgiving and wanted me for dinner. But I received a different call one morning. On the eve of Halloween, Ander Eckstrum called from Jackson Hole, and said, "Mac, *please* stay into November and take Kris and me on a couple of final floats for the year. We don't care if it's cold and snowy."

Ander and Kris are the best of clients. I knew *about* Ander when Kris was born. We were both at a reception in Havana at the residence of the head of the U.S. Interests Section. Ander was political affairs officer and was passing out Cuban Cohiba cigars in celebration of Kris' birth. As Maxwell Hunt, I'd given the closing luncheon address at the first meeting of U.S. and Cuban lawyers since Castro took power. I never talked face-to-face with Ander in Havana, so I was comfortable guiding for him as Macduff Brooks.

Ander had later become our ambassador to the Sudan, at a time when America was becoming engaged in further hard-to-justify, undeclared, costly, high body-count wars — this time in two places at once, Iraq and Afghanistan. He became outspokenly discouraged with our foreign policy. One evening at an embassy dinner he was hosting in Khartoum, Ander undiplomatically failed to distinguish between good and bad Muslims. He predicted long and bloody terrorism-induced conflicts against the "Nation of Islam," initiated by the United States allied with a diminishing number of European nations. His comments unleashed the usual outrage among Islamists and demands for his immediate recall to Washington. He soon announced his "voluntary" early retirement from the Foreign Service.

From some of our mendacious friends in Kabul, Ander began receiving death threats, offering the killer the same promised rewards of money and a nearly unlimited supply of vestal virgins as earlier apparently had been promised for the head of author Salmon Rushdie. It's never been clear to me why Muslims are allegedly each offered 72 virgins for killing Westerners. *Vestal* virgins were Roman priestesses, named after the goddess of chaste women, Vesta. *Catholic?* That's a *reward?* I guess in the afterlife Muslims aren't choosy.

Ander sought retirement refuge in a gated community in Jackson Hole, choosing the West over his native New England. I first guided him last summer, after his neighbor and former Vice-President, Richard Cheney, introduced him to fly fishing. According to Ander, Cheney fishes pretty good, but he has a distracting habit of speaking from the side of his mouth, and you can tell he's unhappy with the day when he appears to keep his temper barely under control. Ander won't hunt with Cheney, whose friends confirm that he does a lot better fishing with a nine-foot, five-weight fly rod than he does hunting with a twelve gauge side-by-side shotgun.

I knew Ander missed the Foreign Service. But his family has enjoyed the attention he's given them since he retired. And his daughter Kris has become his best fishing buddy. Kris is fifteen and usually out-fishes her dad. They hug a lot and joke a lot. I think of Kris as the daughter El and I lost. I wish *I* could hand *Ander* a Cohiba cigar.

Four generations of *male* Eckstrums, including Ander, were Yalies who were members of Skull & Bones and spent their working lives in the State Department. Ander hoped Kris would extend the same experiences to a fifth generation, aware that some of those earlier Eckstrums would roll over in their graves if they knew the next Eckstrum to invade their male bastions would be a female.

But the West was grabbing hold of Kris. She was thinking about pursuing a degree in biology at the University of Wyoming and maybe even spending a few years as a struggling fly fishing guide. To her dad's delight I tried to talk reality to Kris, with some emphasis on the perils and economics of being a guide, long hours and short pay, an occasional fly embedded in one's ear, and dealing with the "three-percenters." Those are the more-or-less three of every hundred clients who make a day afloat seem like Taddeo di Bartolo's *Inferno*. Three-percenters include Park Salisbury, the husband of the couple who floated with me last year, bent on eating a Snake River cutthroat. That story is often told on drifts by Jackson guides. Marrying someone with a steadier income or having the kind of uncle everyone dreams of — rich — might help with the finances of guiding. And maybe guides should carry some mace, or a Taser, to deal with three-percenters like Park Salisbury.

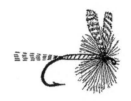

27

O N THE PORCH OF MY CABIN at Dornan's, twenty
minutes north of Jackson, at dusk the evening before the
float, I watched in a deafening silence an early-season, Idaho-
born snowstorm spoil the prospects of a spectacular sunset as
the storm slipped through the canyons and across the folds of
the Tetons. By sunrise six inches of minute snowflakes clung to
every surface throughout Jackson Hole. The firs and spruces
along the Snake were draped with a glossy-white that reflected
all the morning sunlight this primal November day struggled to
produce.

Ander and Kris met me at 8:30. I was using *Osprey* for the
float. I knew Ander and Kris wouldn't arrive with metal cleated
boots, a half-dozen cigars, and a couple of six-packs of Bud.

Launching at Pacific Creek was simplified by the season. I
pushed *Osprey* off the trailer and slid it through the snow the
last thirty feet to the water. That's kinder to the bottom than
sliding over gravel, although *Osprey's* bottom is formidable:
Plascore, Kevlar, fiberglass, and, lastly, sprayed with a hot coat-
ing of black Linex, more commonly used as truck-bed lining.
The bottom should be boulder proof, and even bullet proof.
Within reason.

Pacific Creek, where some scenes in *The Big Sky* were filmed,
flows into the Snake River a few hundred feet upstream from

the boat ramp. A half-mile downstream is another tributary, Buffalo Fork. During the spring snowmelt, and even in the summer after a heavy rain, Buffalo Fork takes its name less from the animal than from its color. The fork churns a chocolate flow of silt and sand that bleeds into and consumes the clarity of the Snake. But the Eckstrums and I weren't threatened with the prospect of muddied water. The snow melt was months behind us, and no rain had fallen since the last full moon weeks earlier.

The Snake's confluence with Buffalo Fork has created a trout-favored hangout around a gravel bar. It's *always* my first place to anchor and wade along the bar. Kris quickly landed a fourteen-inch cutthroat on a #18 Parachute Adams.

Ander followed with a brown and called, "I think mine is *at least* an eighth-of-an-inch longer, Kris."

"Maybe so dad, but yours is *at least* a half-pound lighter, another of your habitually caught *skinny* trout."

After a dozen more cutthroats between them, I suggested we move on. "Let's leave scraps for the next boat — *noblesse oblige.*"

"Ander, you lost your cap landing that brown. I'll loan you my Stetson. Don't lose this hat, it has the little gold lobster pin you asked about," I said, handing the hat to him as I put on an old ball cap from the extra gear in my dry bag.

The downstream drift of the boat and the brisk wind from the south made conditions colder than I'd expected. Both Ander and Kris welcomed my offer of light but warm microfiber headwear that kept the neck warm and could be pulled up over the nose like a balaclava. Along with sunglasses and hats we were an ominous looking trio.

I anticipated an easy day, but we had miles to go, and sunny November mornings often breed nasty afternoons when weather surprises reveal themselves over the Tetons. We moved off downstream again, Ander in the front seat. As Kris put it, where I could better keep an eye on her dad's infallibly unpredictable back casts.

Despite the cold the hours passed quickly. We consumed lunch sitting in the boat anchored on another bar, rather than stopping and setting up a table. It remained cold into the afternoon, but the fishing was excellent. We expected to finish about four, a little earlier than usual for this float.

28

A BOUT THE SAME TIME that we began our afternoon
drift a VW Beetle convertible pulled off Route 89 at the
Deadman's Bar turnout. Its grime matched the beige paint and
obscured California plates. Descending carefully down the
steep snow-covered road, the car turned off after the last gravel
portion before the launching area and parked behind some
trees. It wouldn't be seen because it was behind high piles of
sand deposited for winter road use.

A solitary man stepped out, dressed in white painters' pants
and a white ski parka. The bronze lenses of aviator style reflec-
tive sunglasses set off the rest of his face, which was covered
with white zinc-oxide. If he were trying to avoid overexposure
to the sun, he was a poster child. But it went beyond sun protection when he pulled on white boots and snowshoes, white
gloves, and fitted the parka's white hood over his head.

From the VW's rear seat he extracted a white, canvas-
covered case about three feet long. Head down, he began a determined, methodical lope toward the Snake River across new
snow that covered the small, open field. From an eagle's view
the white figure could be noticed only because it left a long,
slanting, black shadow that moved in a straight line across the
snow from the car to the woods that flanked the river.

Nearing the river's bank, the man disappeared amidst thick, covering brush. He found a spot where he had an unobstructed view of a long, straight run on the river, just before the final turn to the Deadman's Bar takeout. Careful not to disturb the snow-covered brush that hid him from the river, he smoothed the ground, spread out a white pad, sat and pulled a thermos from his bag, and poured steaming coffee. Glancing up-river he saw only a cold Wyoming day quieted by the quilt of new-fallen snow.

A bald eagle glided past, a dozen feet above the river's surface, head down searching the riffles. The man watched its royal flight, sipping his coffee, holding the cup's rim against his lips for its warmth. He was shivering, partly from the cold and partly from the excitement of his task. The shrubbery blocked the wind, but he wished he'd worn a sweater beneath his white parka. He hoped the wait wouldn't be long.

Carefully opening the case, the man removed a white-painted rifle, and then fitted a scope and silencer. A lodgepole pine, fallen amidst the thick brush, provided a secure resting place for the barrel. His numb fingers carefully adjusted the large scope. It would be an easy, close shot. Estimating that the drift boat would float past less than 150 feet away, he inserted three cartridges into the magazine. And then sat on a pad to finish his coffee and wait.

The bald eagle returned, clasping a struggling cutthroat in its talons. Blood spread from around the talons and merged with the trademark red stripe on the fish's throat. *A perfect kill.* The man smiled. He enjoyed watching the way the eagle stalked its prey, dropping down on the unsuspecting fish, which in an instant was torn from the comfort but hollow safety of the depths, and lifted high into the eagle's world.

After a considerable wait, the man saw the first glimpse of a tiny drift boat approaching from the north, entering a long, straight run that would bring it directly by him. Through the scope he could see three figures, none clearly identifiable. They wore parkas, sunglasses, and dark-colored neck wraps that were pulled up to cover their mouths and protect their lips from the chill and dryness of the cold. Both the person rowing from the middle seat and the one in the rear wore baseball caps. The person in front wore a Stetson-like western hat. As the boat drifted closer, the man sensed that both the person fishing from the front seat and the guide in the middle seat rowing were older than the person fishing from the rear. The latter had a ponytail sticking out of the rear of the cap and could well be female.

29

O *SPREY* DRIFTED ELEGANTLY DOWNSTREAM, the sun gleaming off the intense green sides and richly varnished wood trim interior. The boat's dory-like fore and aft curved bottom was side-slipping at a slight angle.

I pulled on the twin nine-foot oars with an easy, repetitive stroke, facing downstream and rowing back against the current to slow us, holding *Osprey* forty feet off the west bank. I slowed further along a section where I had lost a couple of big cut-throats last year. They broke off because of impatience. Not a client's impatience — mine. I'm still impulsively jerky on the set and either have to learn to be gentler or start using 0X leaders. But 0X leaders, some sixteen-pound test, look like ships' hawsers to trout.

Along this stretch the offspring of German emigrant brown trout seek out deep holes that have formed under the high banks. By noon the banks have shaded the feeding line along the western edge of the river. On Ander's tippet was a Lime Trude I favored along this stretch. I like trudes, not only the Lime version Ander was using, but the Adams and Royal Wulff as well. The white wing-tuft makes a good indicator.

Kris was flipping a streamer from the rear seat, letting it sink along the bank and stripping in the line. Ander and I were engaged in discussion — about reported Wall Street incompetence and corruption. I turned my head to the rear to watch Kris' line suddenly tighten, just as Ander said, "If we would have kept the merger and acquisition race . . ." He never finished his sentence.

30

THE MAN IN WHITE had watched the drift boat slowly close from the north, floating with a slight rocker motion through some riffles along the opposite bank. He removed his gloves, rubbed his hands for warmth, sat on the folded pad, and positioned the rifle, supporting the end of the barrel on a firm branch. His right cheek barely touched the rifle's stock, his shivering had stopped, and his breathing showed neither excitement nor remorse. He didn't want his slightest pulse to be transmitted to the rifle. The man's eyes never left the drift boat as it grew larger in the scope. The cross-hairs were focused on the middle of the hat of his target. When the boat turned a hair, he saw a flash of gold from something attached above the hat brim. It was an easy shot that he could make from several hundred yards. But he was only 150 to 200 feet from his target.

The man took a deep breath and held still. With an irreversible half-inch move of one finger, he squeezed the trigger. The drift boat had begun to turn fractionally to the left, to pass a large tree the spring runoff had deposited along the far bank. Only a quiet *pfft* and a slight pulsing kick came from the rifle as the bullet sped on its Machiavellian journey. The fisherman's head jerked in a crimson spray, an arch of blood rising above his head and then falling, separating into hundreds of drops that staccatoed on the river's surface, each drop spreading a tiny red circle until the river dissipated the color. The man's body spilled forward against the front casting-deck. The Stetson fell to the boat's floor on the edge of the brim and rolled a full circle until it too was spent.

The job was finished. The shooter sat up, disassembled the rifle, and returned the parts to the case. There wasn't the slightest tremble in his hands. His most noticeable movement was the smile that began at the corners of his mouth and spread out to complement the illumination from his eyes. Rising from the weeping ground, he gathered his tools of death and quietly walked back to his car, keeping on a line that was not visible from the boat.

At the car the man stopped. He poured and sipped the last of the coffee.

A cry from above made him turn his head. The eagle was climbing. The man gave it a salute — and smiled. Both had made good kills today.

31

I WAS GLANCING BACK AT KRIS in the rear seat when something nicked my ear. I thought I might have caught an errant cast from Ander that left me with a Lime Trude earring. I heard a gurgle and turned forward to see Ander slump forward as a spray of blood, shards of bone, and shreds of brain tissue splattered my face and chest. Other than an eagle climbing away to the north screaming, there was silence on the river. There had been no sound of a shot that would have echoed along the corridors of the canyons to the west.

A stunned Kris screamed, "Dad!" as she jumped past me to catch Ander. He *had* to be dead, the bullet splintered his forehead just below the Stetson's brim, expanding as it ruptured tissue, blowing out a quarter-size hole emerging from the back of his head, carrying with it his life. The bullet had enough killing power to take out one more of us, but Ander's skull had deflected the bullet enough that it penetrated only the soft lobe of my left ear and passed on. Shaking and worried about another shot, I pushed Kris to the floor. But there's no place to hide on a drift boat.

I beached *Osprey*, kicked the anchor line loose, pulled my headwear over my bleeding ear, grabbed my cell phone from my dry bag, and called 911.

32

A DISTANT WHOP, WHOP, of helicopter blades turned my head to follow the copter coming up the river flying low. It spun half-way around to set down softly no more than twenty feet from the river's edge. An emergency crew quickly attended to Ander's body and tried to comfort a terrified daughter who was in no condition to be comforted. Kris needed to hang on to a part of her dad before he was taken away. Ander's covered body and Kris were lifted into the copter. Both the copter's and Kris' throbbing faded as the helicopter disappeared in a straight line south to the Jackson morgue.

The river was again pastoral. The three fishing friends were minutes ago relaxed and bantering about a dozen matters ranging from irrelevant trivia to critical decisions that would contour the world that Kris and her generation would inherit. Now that world had slumped in death for Ander, in uncontrolled grief for Kris, and in disbelief and growing anger for me. Blood had spattered *Osprey* and dotted the gray panels of my jacket. My impulses told me I had to act, but my brain was blocked from a single coherent idea of what I should do. My life had encountered more than its share of dislocations the past dozen years from tragedies staged in a drift boat. First El and Brew. Now Ander.

33

THE THIRD PERSON the helicopter had dropped off was in his late forties, a lean six-footer if lying down and stretched. Clean shaven, but collar-long brown hair that might have been cut by a non-barber spouse. Huntly Byng is the Teton County Sheriff's Office detective in charge of homicide investigations. He didn't arrive in uniform. He'd dropped by his office just as the 911 call came in, directly from removing tree stumps on some new land donated to the Girls' Club of Jackson. Byng was dirty from pulling stubborn tree stumps in the melting snow, his clothes spotted with mud as much as mine were with Ander's blood. He was wearing a Notre Dame sweatshirt as ragged as their football program, but it wasn't the time to talk sports.

A second copter soon dropped off a couple of Byng's investigating deputies. We could hear sirens across the river from more police cars rushing north on 89 and down to Deadman's Bar. As my head began to clear I wondered if either Kris or I were still at risk. Byng had similar thoughts.

"Nearly forty minutes have passed since the shot," he said. "If the shooter were after another person in your boat, he would have taken more shots right after the first. It looks like a selective shooting. And the shooter was satisfied he hit his target. By now he's probably miles away . . . I need you to stay right here, Brooks."

As if I were going anywhere. I was still in the guide seat, still looking bewildered, and still covered with blood that had dried dark. Byng excused himself and gave directions to the deputies. One began to shoot video and stills.

Another deputy slipped on rubber gloves, took a bandage and tweezers from a first-aid kit, opened a zip-lock bag, and said, "I'm going to put a compression bandage on your ear. Have it looked at. You need stitches." After my ear was band-aged he said, "Shut your eyes please, Mr. Brooks."

I closed my eyes and began to feel light touches to my face. I closed my eyes tighter. I didn't ask, but I knew he was picking off traces of Ander for lab testing.

"You have any other clothes on the boat you can use?" the deputy asked. "I'd like to bag your outerwear for the lab."

"Yeah. I keep a dry bag with a full change."

He put my soiled clothes in a large, labeled bag in the cop-ter. My clothes weren't all they wanted.

"We need to keep your boat for about a week," said Byng.

"I understand. I can row it the last couple of hundred yards. The shuttle service left my SUV and trailer at Deadman's Bar. I don't have any more floats scheduled. In any event, my plastic boat's in my garage in Montana."

Byng was noticeably concerned about keeping the most im-portant part of my "work tools" in custody. "I'll take good care of it — it won't be for long, and it won't be damaged. It's a beautiful boat. I'll float with you to the ramp."

When Byng sat in front, he turned facing me and said, "Let's use first names. I'm Huntly, or Hunt," I knew he was softening me for an interrogation. A brief time later, at Deadman's Bar, we loaded *Osprey* onto the trailer. Byng was ready to talk about the shooting. Repeating that I not call him Byng, and especially not Detective Investigator Byng, he said, "If you don't mind, I'll record our conversation."

"Go ahead."

"Thanks. Well, I want you to start with when you first met any member of the Eckstrum family."

"There isn't much to tell." I told him everything I could recall about Ander and his family, but only my knowledge of him *after* I became Macduff. I wasn't lying — I just didn't start at the very beginning, when I met Ander in Cuba. Truthfully, I didn't know much about Ander. You can *know* people, but not know much *about* them.

"You've told me about *parts* of the float, Macduff. Now start at the beginning — booking the float and every detail and every conversation you had during the float."

That was easier. Forty minutes later, I thought I'd done a complete job. But after I finished, Byng had specific questions.

"Did Ander show *any* worry during the float? *Any* indication he thought the earlier threats to his life placed him in danger?"

"No. He apparently shrugged off any concerns. He's never talked about his past on a float. Possibly because he didn't want Kris to worry. But I truly believe he wasn't anticipating any attempt on his life being made on the river."

"Did Kris show any concern?"

"Not a bit. She's sixteen. The world's her oyster. She's deciding on college. Kris is a fine student — an attractive and popular girl with a lot of self-discipline. I'm not sure she even knew about the threats to her dad by Islamists. She may simply have been told he wanted to retire to Jackson."

"Could *she* have been the target?"

"I can't imagine why. Any more than I might have been." I immediately regretted saying that.

"*Could* you have been the target?"

"Huntly, I don't know *anyone* who'd want to shoot Macduff Brooks." I didn't add that I know two people who want to kill Maxwell Hunt. *Technically*, I *was* telling the truth.

I don't like lying. Not because I might have to take a lie detector test later, if Byng develops any suspicion that I might have placed Ander in the line of fire. I simply don't like lying. But there are rare times when severely bending the truth becomes a choice that has to be considered. In this case I couldn't jeopardize my identity. I might have thought differently a couple of years ago. But now there's Lucinda. And Wuff.

Sometimes our conversation worked along the edges of Ander's death. I knew Byng had a lot of blank spaces to complete the puzzle. Murders often are puzzles, and like puzzles, homicide investigations sometimes get shelved and never completed.

"Mac, I know you'd like to get home. But this time is important. Don't rush your answers."

"I'm bushed, Huntly. It's as much the tragedy of the day as being a fifty-plus-year-old guide trying to run with the kids."

Byng turned the conversation to our occupations, I think to suppress my exhaustion talking about the shooting. I learned he's curious about why and how people do what they do. But without prying. Most people have a variety of faces, from dour frown to clown-like smile. Byng only has smiles, a whole range of them. They're infectious and had a welcome calming effect.

I began to learn about Byng's current life. When he's not working for the county, he takes kids with disabilities on nature hikes and overnights into the canyons of the Grand Tetons. He's developed a form of Special Olympics for camping and climbing.

"I don't live in Jackson, Huntly, but I read the online *jhnews and guide*. I recall an article about a policeman in Jackson who'd worked with two Exum guides who teach climbing in the summer out of their base at Jenny Lake. Led by a gifted and popular young guide named — I think — Horn, they had guided three Down Syndrome teens to the summit of Grand Teton. Weren't you on that climb."

"Don't remind me, Mac. I'm not a climber, and I'm not happy with heights. I had to go along. It scared the daylights out of me. But I wouldn't trade standing on that summit with those kids for anything."

Ander's family will be pleased to know Byng will head the investigation. But they *will* expect to hear that Ander's assassin is quickly apprehended and put to endless sleep under Wyoming's lethal injection or gas death penalty. Maybe it's time to bring back public hangings or firing squads. With no hoods. And no special last meals. But it doesn't work that way. Under our purportedly highly civilized and developed legal system, a killer caught in the act will likely still be alive and filing petitions with state and federal courts for another two decades.

Talking to Byng didn't convince me the murder would be quickly solved. I learned from him that murder investigations have a lot of forks in the road. Many can't be approached any better than, as when Yogi Berra said: "When you come to a fork in the road, *take* it."

Sensing I was ready to continue, Byng said, "Mac, there were three people in the boat. Any one of them could have been the target. Ander. You. Even Kris. Stretch it further and maybe it didn't matter who got shot. The shooter just didn't like *drift boats*. Or people who fish."

I hadn't thought of that. Someone who didn't like *Osprey* or fly fishermen or people in boats — and took it out on Ander. That was thinking *way* outside the box.

"Huntly, if the killer didn't like drift boats, that might mean he, or she, didn't like people who fish, or at least who fish from drift boats. Wouldn't the target be the guide in the middle rather than a person fishing?"

"Well, maybe, but you weren't shot," said Byng. "Obviously the main focus was Ander. The shot was fired from fairly close. Maybe the person in front *was* the target. But was it the specific person who sat in front or *whoever* was sitting in front? Maybe the person wearing the Stetson was the target."

"Huntly, do you think the shooter could see the faces of the three of us in the drift boat, partly obscured as we were by the headgear? Or could the shooter identify the target only by where they were sitting? Or by something they were wearing? If I remember correctly, I was turning slightly when Ander was shot."

"I can't tell Mac . . . yet. It's likely you were all facing downstream or a little to one side. The bullet entered Ander in the *middle* of the forehead. The shooter may have waited until Ander turned his head, or you turned the boat. For a better shot. Or to identify him. The bullet nicked you, so the trajectory sent it from the front toward the back of your boat. That suggests a shot straight at the boat coming toward the shooter."

"How do you keep all this sorted out?"

"I'll start a chart on my office wall. The names of the three people in the boat will be across the top. My main questioning follows a line extending down from *Ander*. For now, there's nothing much to put under Kris' name. Not much more below yours. I like to be able to sit back with a cup of coffee in the morning and look at the chart — trying to come up with something to follow that I hadn't thought about."

I would like to know *exactly* what he puts below my name on his chart. I don't want to learn he's had any discussions with the CIA. I suspect he'll contact the FBI because of Ander's past, and because the shooting was in a national park. If my name's raised, hopefully it will be passed by the same as was Kris' name. That leaves Ander the center of concentration.

Finished with our conversation, I drove Byng to Jackson, where I parted from both Byng and *Osprey*, and headed for the local hospital for a little ear lobe repair.

I craved one thing — *privacy* — to sort out matters. While Byng had asked questions, I realized my thoughts repeatedly had turned to: "Could the shot have been intended for me?" If so: "Were either Juan Pablo Herzog or Abdul Khaliq Isfahani behind the shooting?"

Staying at Dornan's the night after Ander's death wasn't appealing — it's too close to the shooting. I drove over Teton Pass to the Sleepy J Cabins in Swan Valley. I wished Wuff, who stayed with Mavis, had been with me; she would have felt at home in the cabin named Sheep Creek, where I spent the night alone. I had a comfortable bed in a comfortable room. I didn't have a comfortable sleep.

Byng expected to talk by phone or meet with me the next day. I called him on my cell phone at eight a.m. A cell phone usually masks the location of the caller. As far as Byng knew, I was still in Moose.

"Hi Mac, glad you called. Where're you staying?"

"I'm in Idaho, at some cabins in Swan Valley owned by a couple I know from guide school. I thought it would be nice to be among friends after yesterday."

"I thought you were at Dornan's. They said you'd checked out and hadn't left any messages." His voice carried a trace of annoyance.

"Huntly, I'm sorry I didn't call you before I left. Anything new about the shooting you can share?"

"My investigators scoured the shooting site late yesterday. The shot came from brush on the eastern edge of the river, only a few dozen yards north of Deadman's Bar. A car had been parked behind some trees. We're trying to trace the tire marks, but that won't help much. A couple reported following a small car south to Jackson that almost hit them coming out the Deadman's Bar road onto Route 89. The car was mostly covered with snow and ice. It was a little after the time of the shooting. The husband thought it was a dirty white Toyota, but his wife said she saw where snow had blown off a rear fender and thought it looked more beige. Maybe a convertible, one of those newer VW Beetles. She thought the plates might have been California. One of my deputies looked at Deadman's again last night but hasn't reported yet. Late last night a small, white Toyota was found alongside a trailer in Pinedale, in Sublette County south of Jackson. The trailer and car both had burned, and there was a charred body in the car. We can't explain why the body was in the car and not in the trailer. Maybe the person was trying to get out and save the car. But it's strange. Some of our people are in Pinedale now. I'm headed there soon. One other thing. A man reported his license plates were stolen from his car in a Jackson parking lot early yesterday morning. They're California plates."

"Any other leads?"

"Well, not yet. We're examining evidence we collected at the site. The Jackson airport's being watched. There was no scheduled airline departure flight from the time of the killing until after we had police checking. We're monitoring private plane departures. We suspect the person left the area by car. We've been in contact with the Grand Teton law enforcement people and town and county police departments outside Jackson. I don't think we found anything of help at the shooting site. The snow's thawing and it's muddy. We'll try to recreate the shooting in a couple of days and might like you there, but we can do it as long as you're available to talk on your cell phone."

"Let me know. I may drive home to Montana today. If that's OK with you."

"I've got your cell phone number. I'll call when I need you. I'm tied up with the Pinedale lead today. Don't get out of touch."

"I won't. You've got my drift boat."

Within a minute of Byng's hanging up, my cell phone rang.

"Mac, Dan Wilson in D.C. We know about the shooting of Ander. A good man. I'm familiar with his problems in the Sudan. I was assigned to our Khartoum agency mission when he made the comments at the dinner. We talked with him about using the protection program and changing his identity, but he thought he was safe, since the *jihadists* had never followed up on their threats to kill Salmon Rushdie. He assumed that if they didn't try to kill Rushdie they wouldn't bother with him. What's your version of what happened on the river?"

I did my best to retell the day afloat. And I told him everything Byng had told me. Talking to Dan I could be more detailed. "I think the shot was accurate and the shooter, assuming he was using a scope, recognized faces. But only if he could see faces. We had on scarves that pulled up like balaclavas, and caps with brims."

I was increasingly troubled about who the target was. "The thought of Juan Pablo on the loose and knowing about my identity frankly scares the hell out of me."

"I understand. We're trying to find out where Juan Pablo's been the past few days. We're investigating the shooting. The FBI is as well, dealing with someone you've talked to — Huntly Byng, the head county police investigation honcho in Jackson.

We have excellent reports on Byng. Cheney met him when he was Vice-President. Cheney had a lot of flights from D.C. to Jackson and Byng was often involved with his security. Byng doesn't have *any* thought that you might have been the target, according to a friend at the FBI. We want to keep it that way. To the extent there has to be any public disclosure, I suspect the FBI will choose their words carefully, as though the shot was *obviously* intended for Ander Eckstrum. At the same time, *we'll* be looking at it as though it were meant for you. If so, we have some work to do to keep you out of harm's way. For the next week stay away from your cabin. Our Montana agent, Paula Pajioli, is at your cabin now. She'll stay there for a couple of days, just in case there's a follow-up attempt on you. Ray Fisk, the new CIA agent covering Florida, is keeping an eye on your Florida place. You gave us keys. We don't really watch second homes, as you know, but we'd like to catch Juan Pablo."

I understood the only reason they were going to watch the Florida house was to trap Juan Pablo. Protecting me was ancillary. They've made a big investment in me, but when investments become too costly, it's time to cut losses. I hope I'm not yet in the loss column.

"I'm going to drive up through Idaho to Montana, and stay around Missoula a week or so. No risk, I know only one person in Missoula. He's on the law faculty at the UM. We've never met face-to-face, so he has no image of me as Max that he might see through. Our friendship developed over the years solely by telephone conversations. We taught the same subjects. I'd recognize his voice anywhere and I assume he'd recognize mine. My voice is the same as it was as Max; it's only my appearance that you changed. Wintering over again in Montana isn't what I expected, but Ander's death has scrambled those plans. . . . Another question . . . any thoughts on how I should deal with Huntly Byng in Jackson? He wants to see me again."

"Keep Byng focused on the theory that the killer hit his target. After all, the distance was short for a sniper. All his questions should be answered with one unassailable assumption . . . *Ander* was the target. Byng's good, and ultimately he's going to explore deeper to see if there's *any* possibility that either you or Kris could have been the intended victim. When he asks be surprised, and a little irked that he would pursue that avenue of questioning. You *must* play the role of an innocent fishing guide and nothing more. Or Juan Pablo will find you and we'll be fishing you out of the Snake or the Yellowstone or the creek in front of your cabin."

I have to be careful the next time I talk to Byng. When I talk to him, it's as Mac. *Never* as Max. When I talk to CIA contacts, mainly Dan and Malcolm, I'm talking as Max being Mac. *My* focus is on Mac but with Max being the target. I don't want to risk saying anything about the CIA investigation, or that I know about Byng working with the FBI on Ander's death. As a kid playing sandlot baseball, I could run through the Abbott and Costello "Who's on first?" dialogue without a slip. Now it's Mac on first, Max on second. I wonder who's on third. I didn't know Dan and his colleagues were soon to plan a third identity for me.

34

MISSOULA IS A CONTENTED western university town blessed with frigid winters that moderate the inflow of newcomers seeking refuge from eastern cities of discontent. About 14,000 University of Montana students race around in pick-ups and Jeeps, compared with the 50,000 UF students who terrorize the streets of Gainesville with their BMWs and Benzes.

Early to bed and late to rise dominated my first three days in Missoula. I woke abruptly sometime in the middle of the first night realizing that all my guns . . . even my bear mace . . . were in my Mill Creek cabin or my Florida cottage.

After breakfast, at a Missoula gun shop I bought a used Saiga shotgun with a short nineteen-inch barrel. It's an autoloader that holds six twelve-gauge shells. I added a box of twenty-five double-ought shells. When I reached my SUV I loaded six shells and placed the gun under a UM "Grizzlies" sweatshirt on the rear seat. My car's fully insured. Now my life's at least better insured than earlier this morning.

The third night was the first I slept through without waking suddenly with images of Ander's killing. That morning I wandered the halls of UM's law school. It felt good to be back in a law school environment. As expected, I didn't see a face I knew. I stopped by the law library and checked Maxwell W.

Hunt in the book directory. A dozen of *his* books were listed. That felt good, too.

After an hour I left and sought out the local coffee shop, ordered an *expresso,* and picked up a copy of the *Missoula Post Gazette.* One of the stories was about Ander's shooting. Nothing I didn't know about. While I was reading, two casually dressed men about my age bought coffee and scones and sat down at the table next to me. They *looked* "university." If this had been Gainesville, they'd have opened their conversation with something about football. But one asked the other about the legal implications surrounding the administrative bungling at the Yellowstone Club at Big Sky. About mishandling *big* money. Intertwined with even bigger greed. When the second man responded, I hid my face in my newspaper. The man's voice was Roger Spenser, the professor I'd spent many hours talking with on the phone over the years. A few minutes later he saw me looking his way, noticed that I was alone, and asked, "Would you like to join us?"

Fortunately, I *was* looking at him. I stared at his mouth, opened my eyes wider, and said nothing. He spoke again, "My colleague and I would welcome your company."

Continuing to stare at his lips, in a struggling voice trying to emulate a deaf person who's mastered lip reading, but isn't yet speaking comfortably in a world of silence, I drew out the words to excessive length, forcing them, and slowly, carefully saying, "I haave to leeave, but thaank you." Walking out my hands didn't stop trembling until I was ten miles south of Missoula. Another blunder — Maxwell Hunt is proving not easy to discard.

Driving south along the Bitterroot, I crossed the Anaconda Range and stayed in Twin Bridges for three nights in a comfortable cabin at the Stonefly Inn. The fishing was pretty good and the weather surprisingly moderate along the Beaverhead and Ruby rivers.

Waking early the next morning I longed to go home. An hour later Paula Pajioli called and said I could. Dodging a snowfall, I hit eighty-five on the interstate. I was becoming acclimated to Montana culture.

Wuff was ready to go home as well when I picked her up at Mavis', who said, "Macduff, I have some mail for you. I'll give it to you if I can have Wuff."

"*I'll* keep Wuff and *you* can answer my mail," I suggested. I went home with both Wuff and the mail.

35

TRYING TO DEAL RATIONALLY with the aftermath of Ander's death kept me in Montana beyond my best intentions. Spending *every other* winter in Montana isn't what I planned when I bought the Florida cottage last year.

Byng brought *Osprey* to me from Jackson. Maybe he wanted to see how I live in isolation, without a companion or spouse. He lived up to his promise — *Osprey* was in good shape. No visible blood stains or body tissue. I asked about the investigation.

"We found the bullet, lodged in some driftwood," he said.

"Could you tell the caliber?"

"Yes, .30-30."

"That's no sniper rifle caliber, more likely to hunt game, not people."

"You're right. If this had been a *professional* assassination, we think the shooter would have used something like a .408 or NATO's 7.62. We can think of no reason Ander would be targeted for killing by some crank hunter."

"Where to now?"

"Well, frankly, we're at a standstill. We're tracing every possible threat to Ander. And we have some other ideas we're pursuing."

Apparently they weren't ideas he wished to share. But he did share some details about his own background. Perhaps he sensed my tenseness and wanted to change the subject. I liked what I heard.

Byng's a former National Park ranger, appropriately educated for a long career in the park service with a bachelor's degree in geology and both a master's and a PhD in wildlife sciences. He told me about his falling out with the park service. After a three-year assignment in Yellowstone and four more in Grand Teton, Byng was transferred to head Acadia National Park on the coast of Maine. He was young and on the fast track. Byng, his wife Sarah, and their two kids moved across country to Maine and settled in. About three months later, Sarah and the kids sat him down one evening.

Byng told me he knew something was up when almost in unison they said, "We want to go back to the Tetons."

Byng had answered, "I've thought about that since the first day here. The vote's unanimous . . . four to zero."

He told the park service he wanted to return to the West. They didn't welcome his rejection of the promotion. They assigned him to be an assistant at the Alibates Flint Quarries National Monument in Texas. He wrote back and said, "I'm too old to spend eight hours a day knapping arrowheads for tourists. Please consider this letter my resignation."

Two days later he received an e-mail that said, "We have reconsidered and assigned you to your former position at Grand Teton."

Byng responded, "I'm not pleased with the way my family and I have been treated. My resignation stands."

They e-mailed again, "You could become a seasonal ranger in Grand Teton and be assured that you won't be transferred."

Byng e-mailed back, "My family isn't seasonal. They like to eat all year."

Good people are hard to keep in the park service. There're two kinds of park rangers. One is career-track people like Byng. They have to move around to move up. If they become attached to one park and don't want to move, they can usually shift to a seasonal position. But seasonal rangers aren't well treated. Payment in "sunsets" doesn't buy food, and housing often means small, old buildings the rangers disparagingly call "dog trailers." I doubt that Wuff would want to live in one.

It was back again across the country, this time at the Byngs' expense. Byng applied for an opening with the Teton County Sheriff's Office in Jackson. That was more than a decade ago. He was hired and is now the head detective — officially Detective Investigator Huntly Byng.

36

LUCINDA CALLED ME FROM NEW YORK early
Thanksgiving afternoon. The annual Macy's parade was
over. Montana families were already sitting down together for
their meal.

"Lucinda! I hope you're at Kennedy, boarding a flight to
Bozeman, and want me to throw a turkey into the microwave
and pick you up at five."

"Turkeys don't fit in microwaves, and you don't know how
to use your oven. Unfortunately, I'm stuck at work!"

We hadn't been together since dinner on the same day a year
ago. We talked on the phone with increasing frequency until
four months ago. But she never made it to Montana during the
year. I wasn't sure work was the full story.

"I'm in my office . . . fifty-five stories high. On Thanksgiving! The building's nearly empty. I had to call you. I wish I *were*
in Montana."

Her building's my favorite New York City skyscraper . . . the
Art Deco, chrome decorated Chrysler Building.

"I used to see the Twin Trade Towers from here. No longer
. . . I'm lonely."

If she were lonely, she isn't focused on her work. If she isn't
focused on her work, she could have flown to Montana for a
few days. I'm sure she thought of that, but I didn't need to re-

visit her reasons. Shifting the subject, I said, "Some of my favorite photos are Margaret Bourke-White's images of the ornate top of the Chrysler Building."

Lucinda said, "I have three Bourke-White 1930 prints on my office wall." Then the frustrations and loneliness came out. I could tell there were tears.

"Macduff, *my dad died*. For the last four months I've been flying back and forth between Manhattan and Indiana. Dad was eighty-seven. Six months ago he was diagnosed with brain cancer and given a year at best. He didn't make half that. Each day he lost a little of what was a weakened body. We buried him Monday — three days before Thanksgiving. A hard way to begin the holiday week. My mother's faring as well as we can expect. My brother and sister have helped but he hasn't been well. . . . I'm sorry we haven't talked very much the past few months. I could have used your good humor and judgment. I didn't want to bother you with my problems. I *was* planning on surprising *you* at your cabin door. With a big turkey — and a big hug."

"I'll take a rain check, but only on the turkey. I need the hug now. . . . I thought you might have gone to Peter Island in the Caribbean with some of your colleagues."

"Can you believe they asked me *Monday* if they could go to Montana with me for Thanksgiving? I'll bet someone canceled on *them*. . . . I'm in my office feeling lousy. Tears all over my desk blotter. Everyone's gone for the holiday. I'm pretending I'm catching up on work. My Thanksgiving dinner is in front of me on my desk. Two Nathan's hotdogs from a stand by the building's entry, and a bottle of water from our office coffee room. *What* a holiday! I hope someone's cooking for you."

"Dining at Nathan's! *Bon appétit!* . . . I planned to join my friends Kim and Pete in Bozeman for dinner. But I'm snowed in. When I rummaged through my refrigerator this morning, I had to throw out a few things. There was a bowl with the remnants of turkey soup. That would be seasonal and I wouldn't have to carve. But it was a gift from a neighbor — last *July*. At least nothing was living in it. There *was* something living in the last bit of another gift — banana bread. Something with a small head that stuck out and looked up at me. If there had been more, I'd soak them in Gentleman Jack and fry them."

"My hotdogs are beginning to sound gourmet," she said.

"I finally settled for one of two dozen cans of soup I keep in stock. I chose the one with turkey on the label. That was my Thanksgiving turkey dinner. Plus a couple of glasses of my best *pouilly fumé*."

"That sounds better than bottled water," she commented. "Neither of us seems to be doing as well as last year. What I really *wanted* to ask, Mac, I *didn't*. Because I thought I might get the wrong answer. But I'll ask it. Are you . . ."

I interrupted, "What's the *right* answer?"

She said, "The right answer is 'yes,' that you're going to Florida and would love to have me visit you."

"Sorry, no invitation."

"You mean you're going to be in Florida, but you won't invite me?" It was said in a softly spoken sadness.

"No, and yes. You're invited. But not to Florida. I can't go this winter. . . . Have you read anything about a shooting on the Snake River near Jackson? It happened three weeks ago."

"I read a one paragraph item about the killing of a former ambassador while he was fishing in Wyoming. It didn't say much, and it didn't happen in Montana, so I never thought of looking for more news. Have any of your guide friends in Jackson told you about it? Has it been solved?"

"The killing is the reason I'm staying over this winter. The ambassador was a friend — Ander Eckstrum. He was fishing with his daughter Kris. In a drift boat — *my* drift boat. I was sitting in the middle rowing when Ander was shot."

"My God, Mac!" Lucinda said, her voice quivering. "Were you or his daughter hurt?"

"The bullet was deflected when it hit Ander and caught the lobe of my left ear. Kris wasn't hurt, at least physically. The bullet could have been meant for Kris or me. Or it could have been some crank who doesn't like people who fish."

"Macduff, here I am in Manhattan feeling sorry for myself. You're snow bound in freezing Montana, with a bullet-pierced ear, and maybe someone is thinking about trying again to kill you. But why would *anyone* want to kill *you*?"

That question couldn't be answered in the time before our cell phones batteries went dead. And I couldn't answer it truthfully without bringing Lucinda into my unruly world. Plus — *I didn't know the answer.*

"I hope no one wants to kill me," I truthfully, though evasively, replied. "Lucinda, can I talk you into coming to Montana over the Christmas holiday? I can tell you more then. It's going to be a lonely holiday here."

"I thought you'd be in *Florida* for Christmas, Macduff. If you were and invited me, I was going to cancel tickets I *already* bought for Montana. I wasn't looking forward to a Christmas alone in Montana. How do ten days starting Christmas Eve work for you?"

"I'll be at the airport to pick you up. And Lucinda . . . no Christmas gifts, please. Except for Wuff. She likes those soft, small soccer balls. There's one somewhere in my yard under a two-foot snow drift."

It wasn't a lonely Thanksgiving after all. I called a florist. When Lucinda tires of working and arrives home at her apartment, a bouquet of fall wildflowers, like those that grow in Montana, will be at her door.

I was reconciled to staying the winter. My cabin's warm. I've added heat to the garage. Wuff has learned to make yellow snow. And Lucinda is coming.

37

ON DECEMBER 7th of my third year as Macduff, as the TV stations showed replays of *Tora, Tora, Tora* and *Pearl Harbor* in memory of that tragic Sunday morning more than a half-century ago, a meeting of eight high-level officials of the Clandestine Operations Section of the CIA was commencing in the headquarters building in Langley, Virginia. The room was secure, located where listening devices were searched for daily and discussions routinely held with neither cell phones nor recording devices permitted. Meeting participants were searched and screened more carefully than commercial airline passengers.

Malcolm Whitney, respected and feared head of the section, unhappy because he was soon to reach mandatory retirement, carefully lowered his worn, sixty-four-year-old listing frame into a leather chair at the head of the table. His red hair had never grayed; his gray eyes had never reddened. Round, metal-framed bifocals, a perfectly trimmed moustache and two prominent hearing aids completed a head that turned heads throughout the CIA. His tailored, deep blue, pin-stripe, double-breasted suit, which none of his associates dared to copy in their dress, covered a body decorated with scars that made him a legend. None of the episodes that had left him with a limp and caused his movements to be made with deliberation diminished his distinguished appearance. Once he was seated he appeared fitter than he truthfully was, which would become all the more apparent when the meeting was over and he began to rise, a process made incrementally longer with each advancing hour of the meeting. Despite his condition, his gentle voice drew the absolute attention of every person in the room.

"Gentlemen, I assume all of you have read the document I circulated. That is the only copy except for my original. Each of you signed for its delivery at the top and again at the bottom after reading. We are convinced that Abdul Khaliq Isfahani is a key participant in an al-Qaeda terrorist training camp located at an old coffee plantation called El Molino Alemania, eighty to ninety miles northwest of Guatemala City. It's the very same plantation where we trained Cubans for the Bay of Pigs invasion in the early 1960s. An invasion that would have rid Cuba of Castro, had it not been for the amateurish interference of President Kennedy. Sitting to my right is John Adamson, retired CIA. He was a young agent on his first assignment in that CIA training camp. He's helping us because he knows that camp intimately. John went on, as some of you know, to head clandestine operations before his retirement twenty years ago. We've briefed him on Isfahani's activities, especially since the time Isfahani first went to Guatemala a few years ago.

"You all have read about a University of Florida law professor, Maxwell Hunt, who, while acting as a lecturer and consultant for the State Department, helped us three years ago in Guatemala. You know Professor Hunt first met Isfahani when he and Guatemala's notorious Juan Pablo Herzog were graduate students at Professor Hunt's university in Gainesville. Maxwell Hunt is now in a protection program, with a new identity and location. There is no need for you to know the details of that. Any comments thus far?"

No one stirred. A few of the agents in the room started their careers when John Adamson was still active and Malcolm Whitney was in mid-career. Adamson and Whitney were folk-loric figures in the CIA. The agents asked to attend knew that this was not so much a question and answer session as one to convey what Whitney and Adamson had already planned.

Nevertheless, a nondescript, pudgy, middle-aged agent finally spoke. "It appears you're contemplating using Maxwell's new persona to deal with Isfahani. It seems we should know his new name if he's to work again for us."

"He won't work under his new name. We'll use a third name, once he agrees to carry out what we've planned," said Whitney.

A fourth agent, the most senior woman in the group, inquired, "If the plan, as I understand it, is to have Isfahani terminated as a threat to the U.S., why don't we use one of our in-house agents? We have people trained and anxious to undertake a sanction."

"Anxiousness can be a negative. It happens that Maxwell, as he now exists, knows parts of Guatemala better that we do. He has decades of experience in and out of that country. He first saw the activity around El Molino Alemania a dozen years ago. He knows Isfahani by sight and voice. We think Maxwell's perfect. He will be known as Ben Roth for this mission. Let's begin using that name now."

The mention of Ben Roth brought murmurs; heads turned with surprised looks, mouthing the name: "Ben Roth?"

The pudgy agent spoke again, "Malcolm, you know, as we all here know, that Ben Roth is the most ruthless assassin for Israel's Mossad. Roth is known to have killed Arab targets in several countries. *What* are you planning?"

Whitney smiled and responded, "I wondered how long mentioning Roth's name would take to cause a response. Roth is indeed the real name of a Mossad agent whom we know has killed at least five suspected terrorists. Two in Syria, one in Israel, one in Frankfurt, and the last in the Sudan. The Mossad does not currently operate in Central America, at least according to *our* information. We believe the Mossad doesn't know about Isfahani, and, if they have heard about him, they don't know he's in Guatemala. Nothing we've been able to discover from our contact in the Israeli embassy in Guatemala City suggests otherwise. That makes sense because Guatemala is very unlikely to draw any attention from Israeli intelligence."

The youngest agent present commented, "We have a lot of trouble with the administration regarding what to do about 'known' terrorists. The President's dead set against assassinations of *any* kind, at least without his approval."

"We'll be here long after the President's gone," Whitney responded. "Some administrations leave us alone; others interfere with our work. John Adamson and I could tell you about more assassinations during our careers than there have been presidents. Our current President wouldn't approve a sanction in Guatemala, even of an al-Qaeda terrorist. Which is why we're going to make the assassination look as though it were done by the Mossad's Roth. When we were changing the identity of Maxwell Hunt, Dan Wilson, head of our protection program, noted the resemblance between Maxwell and Ben Roth. A little plastic surgery, tucks and nose reshaping, and hair coloring, changed Maxwell enough that he could pass for Roth. Maxwell's new identity may have Roth's features, but retains Maxwell's far lighter skin tone. When we want Maxwell to be Roth, we'll instruct him to let his hair grow longer, remove his moustache and glasses, and we'll add some temporary skin toning.

"First, we'll convince *our* new Ben Roth to agree to help. We have certain leverage we can use, as you'll see. If you recall Hunt's background, he was a superb marksman growing up. He still practices. He *likes* shooting. And, behind a little sarcasm, he's patriotic. He'll agree. When he's picked up at a private air strip near his current home, he'll be 'touched-up' on the flight to Guatemala — to look like Roth. We also have clothes similar to what Roth wears, including his signature black turtle-neck T-shirt and jeans. Our Roth will be flown to an airfield, owned by a Guatemalan nickel company we operate as cover for Central American operations. It's well-guarded, ostensibly because of a worry about theft by local Guatemalans. Our Roth can move between that airfield and El Molino Alemania without going through Guatemala City. He won't go anywhere near our embassy, and no one there will know about his being in the country, except for the two agents at our mission in the embassy who are working with us. We know Isfahani jogs every morning along a road near the camp. The operation will be a simple sanctioning of a known terrorist who is a direct threat to the United States."

"The Supreme Court might not agree with that," said another agent.

"The Supreme Court is not always supreme," Whitney mused, with a smile that showed his long success in averting interference from "other" government entities.

Another man at the table, a stoic, trim agent, recently returned from an operation in the Sudan and showing a not-yet-healed red scar starting just below his left ear and tracing his jaw bone to a small cleft, had listened carefully. He said, "I think that convincing our Roth to risk his current identity in the protection program will be difficult. How do you plan to get his cooperation? Secondly, how will Guatemalan officials and perhaps the terrorist group that Isfahani works for in Afghanistan be convinced that *Israel's* Roth did the killing?"

Whitney's face showed a slight, wry, appreciative smile. "Our Roth *will* agree. As I said, we can exert pressure in the way of 'adjustments' to the support he receives under the protection program. We also. . . ."

The questioning agent interrupted, something not taken lightly by Whitney. "Adjustments! That's extortion! If it's known an agent in the protection program is subject to threats to remove his protection, the program is useless."

"I think I should have been clearer," Whitney interjected, surprisingly not showing any irritation with the interruption. "Maxwell's successor lives in the United States. We would *never*, or let me say never except in *extreme* circumstances, do what you're implying — intentionally reduce the protection the program provides."

Whitney went on: "Maxwell Hunt had Thanksgiving dinner last year and has been communicating regularly with a woman who has a large ranch near his cabin in the West. She's an investment broker who works in Manhattan. Her south-facing window office is high in the Chrysler Building. She owns an expensive apartment on East 67th, and she works long hours. From what she's told some friends in New York, according to one of our female agents who has mutual friends, this lady is quite enamored with Maxwell's successor. She has plane reservations to leave Manhattan Christmas Eve to join him in Montana."

After a pause that may have been due more to age than giving his listeners time to consider questions, Whitney continued, "Now let me shift to Abdul Khaliq Isfahani. The reason we must kill him is that he is the principal in an al-Qaeda plan to attack targets in the United States. He's an accomplished pilot.

As we speak there are two Gulf Stream jets at the Teterboro Airport in New Jersey, quite near New York City, that are registered in the name of a Liechtenstein corporation, a subsidiary of a Cayman Islands corporation we know has terrorist links. Most important, we have *specific* plans for such a proposed attack, obtained from a double-agent who is a close colleague of Isfahani in Afghanistan. Our counterplan is code-named the 'Ides of March.' It will take place next March 15th. Isfahani is known to avidly read Shakespeare, and you may recall the warning to Caesar in the play, *Julius Caesar*."

Whitney took two photographs from a folder and laid them face down on the table. "We know that two Manhattan buildings will be the targets. We plan to make certain that the planes will never leave the ground at Teterboro. But we also want to arrest or dispatch everyone showing up to fly them or assist on the 15th. Isfahani is scheduled to fly one plane, the double agent the other. The reason the latter came to us is he has second thoughts about killing thousands of people. We want to throw a wrench into this plan as soon as possible. We want Isfahani killed. He's willing to sacrifice himself by piloting one of the planes. We'd like to sanction him before he has that opportunity. We know someone will take Isfahani's place, but it will be less organized without him. It's a risk to wait until that day to stop the flights, but we know we can stop them, and we may catch some important al-Qaeda figures."

John Adamson relieved Whitney. "You might be curious about the two buildings." Adamson turned the photos over. "Look at the photographs. One is the Empire State Building, the other is . . . the Chrysler Building. Maxwell's lady friend's office is circled — it faces south on an upper floor, on the path a plane would take into the building. If Maxwell's successor knows what Malcolm has told you, we think he'll play the role of Ben Roth."

After a pause reflecting his age, Adamson continued: "Malcolm mentioned that we think we can make Israel appear responsible. Israel doesn't want Ben Roth's name in the papers. We will arrange with a Guatemalan CIA agent to pay someone from the area of El Molino Alemania to swear that he saw a person with a rifle whom he will describe exactly as Roth."

Another agent asked, "Where will the real Ben Roth be at the time? He can be in only one place, and that could be where there are witnesses who will provide him an alibi."

Whitney re-entered the conversation. "That's a little sticky, we know. We've set the date because we know Ben Roth will be vacationing with his family in an exclusive hotel in Cayo Costa, Cuba, flying in from Europe on a commercial jet. Cayo Costa is on the northeast coast of Cuba. Who will believe the Cubans or Israelis if they say Roth *never* left the island during his vacation? Our story is that the Mossad planned the whole operation, using Cuba from where to send Roth to Guatemala. A small jet will leave Cayo Costa and fly along Cuba's north coast to Guatemala the day before the event, and return the night after, about the same time as our Roth is flown back to the U.S. The jet over Cuba will be seen. That jet will have been sent to Cuba the week before, carrying a half-dozen Department of Commerce officials on a quiet trip approved by the Cuban government to talk about expanding trade. The pilots work for us, not Commerce. The trade mission will be meeting in Havana while the plane, with temporary Israeli markings, is flown round trip to Guatemala."

"What have we missed?" Whitney asked, with a hint of expectation that there should be no further questions.

"Will we meet again?" asked the pudgy one.

"No, and we've *never* met. No one's given me reason to believe this hasn't been well thought-out or that it's unlikely to work," Whitney said.

He lifted his body from the chair with difficulty and left the room. Back in his office he called the cell phone number of Macduff Brooks in Montana.

38

MALCOLM WHITNEY MADE ME AN OFFER he was certain I couldn't refuse.

"I'll think about it," I said, "and call you back."

"I can't wait," responded Whitney. "You'll receive a sizeable payment."

"No."

"No?"

"I'm not for hire."

"So you won't do it?"

"I didn't say that."

"Don't mess with me, Brooks."

"I'll do it."

"You changed your mind."

"No."

"You mean you'll do it, but not for pay."

"Yes."

"Why?"

"Isfahani wants to kill me."

"That's the only reason?"

"No."

"May I know the other?"

"A woman."

"The one who has an office in the Chrysler building?"

"Yes."

Sleep wasn't easy that night. It rarely is after talking to anyone at Langley. I tossed and turned, thinking, "What if I said no? What would happen to Lucinda? To thousands of people? I know Whitney didn't tell me any more than he thought was necessary to get my agreement. Abdul Khaliq Isfahani has become part of the network of terrorists that's determined to strike the U.S. again. But if the CIA knows they've targeted the Empire State and Chrysler buildings, *and* knows the date, why can't they be ready? Close down all air traffic over the East that morning? Shut Kennedy? Newark? La Guardia? Every airport five hundred miles in every direction? Evacuate the two buildings? I think I can convince Lucinda to stay away from her office that day. It may require telling her some things about me I'd prefer to keep secret. But what would she think if she learned I wouldn't try to save the people in her building?"

Even if I kill Isfahani, another radical could take over piloting one of the aircraft. Or the other pilot might fly one plane and strike the Chrysler rather than the Empire State building? Whitney said they were convinced they could stop the other pilot. He didn't tell me that pilot was a double-agent.

I could back out. I called Lucinda that evening and tried to concentrate on her voice. The tone and the rhythm. The phrasing. The laughter. All that held me under a spell at her ranch. I didn't talk about the ides of March plans. Hearing her was enough.

Malcolm Whitney called me the next morning.

"I thought I agreed yesterday," I said.

"You did. Start letting your hair grow."

Wondering whether he'd been drinking at breakfast, I hung up.

39

LUCINDA ARRIVED AS SCHEDULED on Christmas Eve. Not *exactly* as scheduled, but on the same day, three minutes before midnight. Something new for the airlines. Same day service like my dry cleaners.

Her flight was delayed in New York for six hours. She was on the plane, belted in, book open, ready to taxi. The door was shut. She was thinking departure *on time* at a little before five would get her to Bozeman *on time* at 6:45 p.m. — Montana time. The weather was predicted to be clear and more than cold.

Unfortunately, some confused airport passenger at Kennedy, trying to find her lost little girl, had walked around a security checkpoint. The child was looking for Santa. Flights were delayed for three hours while every plane at the airport was emptied, the passengers rescreened and repatted. Incoming planes were diverted throughout the Northeast to other airports. They never found Santa, but they found the kid. Then Lucinda's plane couldn't take-off because of the sheer number of planes waiting. Her flight was told that passengers would have to wait a half-hour before reboarding. In a half-hour they were told another half-hour and that repetition continued for five hours. The airlines call that updating the passengers.

I reached the Bozeman airport on Christmas Eve twenty minutes before Lucinda's flight was *originally* due. She had phoned me as her plane's door shut. Content that she was on her way and couldn't call me until she landed, I turned off my cell phone. I learned about the delay when I reached the airport. My cabin's an hour and a half away. Three hours round trip. It didn't make sense to drive home, so I drove into Bozeman and walked a couple of miles through the old residential section. There were Christmas lights throughout the town. Carolers were going house-to-house singing. One group asked me to join them. I didn't feel like singing. Joy to *my* world would be when Lucinda arrived. I managed to kill a couple of hours and drove back to the airport. I was chilled, bought the maxi-size coffee, tucked myself into a chair in the lounge, and opened a book. With some laps through the airport, a few more coffees, and an equal number of trips to the restroom, I managed to pass the final three hours without too much frustration and anxiety. Frustration and anxiety weren't an appropriate prelude to meeting someone I wanted to embrace in good spirits.

Thirty minutes before Lucinda's flight was to land, I walked to a huge glass window and watched for that first, tiny speck of landing lights. When the plane came within sight, I followed it down to its 11:57 p.m. touchdown at the end of the runway, with as much focus as if I were in the pilot's seat. When Lucinda walked into the airport, our embrace *was* in good spirits: warm *and* long. It was strange to realize we'd only spent that one Thanksgiving evening together. Our friendship had developed mostly by phone. When you're not with someone you like, but haven't gotten to spend much time with, you tend to conjure an image that evolves toward perfection. Lucinda looked better than that.

I'd planned to take her to dinner at Livingston's Montana Rib & Chop House, in an old building along the Burlington and

187

Northern Railroad tracks. But it was after mid-night. The Chop House was closed. Albertson's was open — we dined in my SUV on cut-up fresh fruit, chicken tenders, and a $95 bottle of French *Château Lafitte* red. Even the *label* looked expensive. We used paper napkins and plastic forks. They felt like fine linen and antique silverware.

With the window down a bit, the motor running and the heater struggling, we parked in the side lot next to a Livingston church where they were singing Christmas carols at the end of a midnight service. "Silent Night" never sounded as good. It was Christmas Day. Joy to the world!

40

CHRISTMAS DAY LUCINDA DROVE her Jeep to my cabin around noon. Wuff met her on the porch, gave her a thorough sniffing, welcomed her soccer ball present, and began to knock it about the cabin.

Lucinda received the grand tour of my cabin, but not the music room. I'd moved photos of Maxwell and El from my bedside table to a drawer and did my best to vacuum dog hairs.

"Your cabin's like you, Macduff, private. It's out of sight among the trees, yet so close to the creek. . . . Where have you hidden the *guy* things . . . the mounted heads, elk antler chandeliers, and bear skin rugs?"

"An hour ago I moved them all to the basement. I'll put them back when you leave. . . . Not really, I'm not a hunter."

"Not a hunter? There's a rifle over the front door, one over the living room mantel, and another by the back door!"

"My dad gave me the .22 by the back door when I turned sixteen. I use it a couple of times a year to shoot at cans. The rifle over the mantel hasn't been fired for more than a century — it's an antique Winchester 73. The one over the front door is protection, a .44 magnum lever-action Henry. There's another gun by my bed, a side-by-side shotgun with short barrels. If you look a little further, there's a .44 magnum pistol in the drawer beside my bed. There are also some knives in the kitchen and an axe in the garage. And a knife on a Leatherman on my . . ."

"*Easy.* You're *sensitive* about this. I didn't mean anything. My dad always had guns. I have his Luger he brought home from the war. Dad dragged me into duck blinds when I was seven. I keep a small, loaded, S&W by my bed in Manhattan. I promised him I would before he died; he worried about my living in the city alone." Abruptly, she changed the subject. "I like your Latin American and Spanish art. From travel?"

"Mostly. I enjoy surrealism." It's like my life.

While logs crackled in the fireplace, before I could sit down next to Lucinda on the intimate, two-place sofa, Wuff jumped up with her new ball, curled up against Lucinda, placed her head on Lucinda's lap, and fell asleep. I sat on a hard, single chair, and sulked.

"I know we promised no Christmas presents, but I have a late, housewarming something for your cabin wall."

It was a framed, platinum-print photograph entitled: *The Chrysler Building*, taken in 1931 by Margaret Bourke-White. I shuddered to think that the building might soon be gone.

"Here's something for *your* wall." I broke *my* promise, handing her a seven-foot bamboo fly rod I finished a week ago, inscribed: "to Lucinda from Macduff — Christmas in Montana."

"*Must* I put it on my wall? Won't you take me fishing."

"Next summer. If you promise not to catch bigger fish."

"Do all your clients have to agree to that?"

"No."

"Why me?"

"You're not a client."

"What am I?"

"I'm not sure."

"I'm a girl."

"I can tell that. But I have girl clients."

"Do they catch bigger fish than you do?"

"Sometimes."

"Why am I different?"

"I'm not sure, but you are."

"In a good way?"

"Very."

"For example?"

"You're here; they're not."

"I'm the first gal in your cabin?"

"No."

"Others?"

"Yes."

"For example?"

"Mavis, our shared housekeeper."

"And?"

"Wuff."

"Your lady companion."

"Yes."

"Do you want *me* to stay with you?"

"Yes. I have a guest room."

"You want me to stay in the guest room?"

"No."

"Macduff, you told me about your wife El. How you proposed on the second date. This is *our* second date. Are you proposing?"

"I hadn't thought of it that way. But . . . probably."

"*Probably*?. . . May I think about it?"

"Carefully."

We spent the evening talking at Lucinda's lodge. Wuff was invited and resumed her place next to Lucinda. I know Wuff will go home with me and scramble for the best spot in my bed. I was hoping the same about Lucinda. But not a word was spoken about our conversation in the afternoon.

Malcolm Whitney called early the next morning. He wants me ready to fly to Guatemala the end of February. I have over 200 yards along my road to set up a practice shooting location. Noise shouldn't be a problem. My CheyTac has a suppressor, and gunshots are common to this area.

During the hours Lucinda worked at her place, I shot a dozen rounds of .408 caliber, steel-jacketed bullets. They're more than bullets. My lever-action .22 shoots bullets. The CheyTac shoots shells. With the tactical, ballistic computer and linked rangefinder, each of the .408 cartridges is like a tiny guided missile. For practice shooting prone in our Montana winter, I put down an air mattress and insulated pad. The ground is frozen several inches deep by Christmas. If I use a pad in Guatemala, it will be protection against crawling things, not the cold.

On my third day of practice, I did a dress rehearsal. Over insulated underwear I put on a coverall Whitney sent me, made in the foliage colors of Guatemala's highlands in March. The outfit includes the same foot-long fringes on the hat, jacket, and pants that make sniper movies scary. Everything was going fine until I began a series of mistakes. I was lying on the ground along my entrance drive, sighting, when a voice behind me spoke.

"*Macduff!* What on earth are you doing? If you're wearing that outfit to Yellowstone, you chose the wrong season's colors. Maybe I should also ask why your letting your hair grow."

Lucinda was embarrassingly early for our overnight trip to Snow Lodge at Old Faithful. Ear-plugs had kept me from hearing her walk along the drive behind me. There was snow on the ground, but no more expected for a couple of days. The roads were clear. A snow coach would take us from Mammoth to Old Faithful. I was anxious about what might happen when we got to Snow Lodge. Lucinda had reserved the only available room — with one king-size bed. And Wuff was staying home!

I looked up at Lucinda to answer, but I was tongue-tied. Anything that came out would be wrong. "Hi . . . Lucinda," I responded insipidly, showing surprise, and struggling to gain another moment to think of something convincing. "I'm sighting in a new scope."

"Wearing green, *summer* camouflage? With fringe? And I haven't seen *that* rifle in your cabin. That's no lever-action! What do you use it for, shooting Dall sheep on top of a mountain?"

"I like target shooting."

I picked up the gear and put the gun in its case. We walked side-by-side toward my cabin, our shoulders occasionally touching. Not a word was shared between us. I wanted my pulse rate to go down, but looking at her didn't help.

As we passed the target I'd hung between two trees, she stopped abruptly . . . and stared. No traditional bulls-eye with radiating circles. With a black magic marker, I had drawn the torso of a man wearing a kaftan. The dress was clearly Muslim. There were six holes in the middle of the forehead and four in the heart. Lucinda looked at me, wrinkled her brow, and quietly said, "*That's* no Dall sheep!"

It worsened at the cabin. Lucinda's seeing my CheyTac and the target had unnerved me. I wasn't thinking. She stepped into the cabin a few paces ahead of me. On the far left side of the main room, the bookcase that hides the stairs to my music room was swung open. Light emerged from the stairwell. She looked at the bookcase, walked over, and peered down the steps. It hadn't been on the cabin tour I'd given her Christmas Day. Visible from the top of the stairs was a chair, a music stand holding the score for Marcello's *Concerto in D*, and my oboe and English horn.

"Mac! You *do* play the oboe," she said, as she scampered down the stairs. But when she reached the bottom and glanced around, she saw a full-sized image of Isfahani on one wall. A red circle surrounded his face, above which was scribbled: "Isfahani — dead by the ides of March."

Lucinda turned and looked at me with a face that expressed a little of the terror I last saw in El as the Snake River current carried her away. Lucinda rushed up the stairs and started for the door. I followed and grabbed her arm, far too tightly.

"*Sit down!*" I said forcefully, not conducive to calming her. She dropped into my deep, leather armchair, looking tiny and frightened. Wuff went over to her, leaned up against her leg and put her head on Lucinda's thigh. I didn't present as comforting a picture. I was standing in my sniper's fringed camouflage, the rifle case in my hands. Lucinda had seen the image of Isfahani, my arsenal, and the tables in the music room that suddenly looked, even to me, more like a command center than a simple computer on an office desk. On that desk was a bottle of Chilean *Camanere*, with the name of the winery — *Casillero del Diablo* — prominently displayed on the label.

Lucinda was scared. "Mac, that room *is* the Cellar of the Devil! Can I get up and leave? *Please!*"

Quietly and calmly, I said, "Of course. I'm sorry I grabbed your arm so hard." After a pause I added, "There are reasons for everything you've seen, . . . and reasons you don't know about that room. Some I can explain to you; some I can't."

"If we're headed anywhere you'd best explain it all."

I needed time to think through what I could say. But I had to say something, before she ran.

I struggled with, "If I tell you everything, I'll have drawn you into my life so deeply I will have risked *your* life. It's become even more complex over the past month. But I can't have you walk out that door without knowing more. . . . I'm going to tell you a few things, and then I want you to get up and go home to Manhattan . . . and think carefully. We'll talk on the phone . . . soon."

She sat quietly, listening. She didn't say a word, but her eyes expressed her feelings. I had to provide more than a few "yes'es" to any questions.

"The day I met El I knew I wanted to spend the rest of my life with her. We married and were on a magical ride that came to a horrible end. An end I won't ever fully get over. But you've helped me — by our conversations — to live with it as part of my past, and to understand my future doesn't have to be one of grief and self-pity. El died in an accident on a drift boat. I should have saved her. I wasn't a guide. I was a law professor at a fine university, loving every day I walked into my office. I lectured abroad, and met officials who formed national policy. My opinions increasingly were sought by our embassy. Our State Department began to sponsor my trips, arranging speaking tours in various countries. The *quid pro quo* was an initial briefing on what the U.S. would like to learn more about — mostly public opinion — and a de-briefing at the end. I went to a dozen countries, rarely doing much more than listening and conveying my perceptions to the local embassy staff. Unfortunately, a decade after El died, some corrupt parties in one country interpreted what I was doing as being contrary to their personal ambitions. The result was an aborted attempt on my life. I was severely beaten before our embassy people intervened and saved me. They flew me back to the U.S. in a private plane and . . . well . . . maybe I need to stop."

"Please go on, " she said, in the softest voice I'd yet heard her speak.

"I had to leave both my law teaching position and my Florida home. And assume a new name. Since that day, I've never spoken with *anyone* I ever knew before, including several close friends who helped me get through the dark times after El's death. . . . You've stumbled into a situation you don't deserve, into the complex life of someone who has come to feel strongly about you, but can't tell you that directly."

She was flushed. No words. No tears.

"One final thing. If you speak about this to anyone, the life I've been trying to establish for nearly four years, and especially since we met, will become so at risk I could never forgive myself for drawing you into a dilemma you don't deserve. Whatever you decide, I *must* have one promise from you. Will you trust me?"

I hadn't given her enough reason to make a very clear decision. I was surprised when, without looking up, she nodded.

"*Please*, don't be in New York City on the 15th of March. That's a warning as prophetic as the soothsayer who warned Caesar. Accept this advice *whatever* you think of me. And, if anything happens to me between now and March 14th, take my advice knowing it will probably save *your* life."

I got up, walked slowly to her, *gently* took her arm, helped her from the chair, and walked her to the door. "May I drive you home?"

"No, Mac, I *need* to be alone." She went down the two steps, paused, turned, came back up and threw her arms around me, tucking her head against my neck. She was trembling.

She turned and ran. I thought it might be the last view of her I would ever have.

41

I N LATE JANUARY A MONTH LATER, while the snow fell and drifted to create an undulating, white landscape, and I plodded along in a winter funk, I had an unexpected call from Manhattan. It was Lucinda. She was having lunch. Her voice disclosed little, but the tone was welcome and warm.

"Are you at Sardi's?" I asked.

"No."

"The Plaza?"

"No."

"McDonald's?"

"Getting closer. I'm having soup and a sandwich from *Au Bon Pain*. I'm in my office looking out at the Manhattan skyline. . . . Macduff, I'm not as strong as I thought. All the glamour and glitz from working in Manhattan . . . having enough income to enjoy this city . . . season tickets to the Met and special openings at museums . . . long weekends flying to London or Paris. I'm too much a conservative, home-spun, Midwestern girl to hold up very well when you talk about attempts on your life, and untold secrets. . . ."

There was a pause; I didn't know whether it was my turn to speak. I waited a little more and said, "I understand. I've realized the past few weeks how selfish I've been, letting my judgment be influenced by how I feel about you. What I've told you has been true, but I've left a lot out. I did that to protect you, and, to be honest, to protect myself. . . . I've been trying to see myself through your eyes; it doesn't look very good. I understand your need to break off what I hoped was. . . ."

"You *klutz!* When I said I'm not holding up very well, I meant *alone* here in Manhattan. Without you around to prop me up. I shouldn't have left Montana so abruptly. Remember, *you* kicked me out. *I* wanted to go to Yellowstone. And *I* reserved the room at Snow Lodge with only one bed. I'm not going to cut the bond we've developed. I want to stick around a while longer. At least to learn what you meant by 'probably'! You're a mysterious guy, and I'm a curious gal. *When do I see you?*"

"Wow!" was the best I could respond. "Wait until the middle of March. You'll know why then. Keep being that good, conservative, home-spun, Midwestern girl, and *please* do what I asked. Be *out* of Manhattan on the 15th. After that, you'll be entitled to have me tell you *my* life story, beginning with being born a lot earlier than you, in an old house on Main Street in Farmington, Connecticut. Sound petty ordinary? It was — for four decades. And *I* want to hear *your* life story."

We talked along the edges of our relationship for another hour before we hung up. I hope I'm not telling her too much. I'm not worried about *her* saying anything, but about wiretaps — even by the CIA! . . . I poured a glass of wine. It was a little early, but it *was* lunch time in Manhattan. The wine was from the bottle of Chilean *Camanare* I'd left on my desk in the music room. I'd intended to take it with us to Old Faithful. But that day didn't end as planned. I think I missed something special. I sipped the wine. It had aged a little since Lucinda left. I've aged a *lot* more.

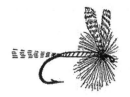

42

ON A LATE-FEBRUARY DAWN, as the sun began to ignite the tops of the Gallatin Range to the west, I drove south on 89. Snow was piled high on each side of Yankee Jim Canyon. It was like driving *up* a bobsled run. A Gulf Stream jet was waiting for me at Gardiner, registered in the name of a Guatemalan nickel company which, in turn, is owned by a Panamanian corporation whose owners are not public record.

Paula Pajioli's black SUV was the only vehicle at the airport. Paula's the Montana contact for people in the protection program. That means me — no one else has chosen Montana. I wouldn't have if I thought I'd have to stay through many winters. Right now I should be in Florida. When I walked to the jet with my bags, it was five degrees. But *getting* warmer. Maybe it would hit twenty by two in the afternoon, when the sun reached its low, winter zenith for the day. It's continental America's best imitation of Fairbanks.

Settled at cruising altitude, a make-up specialist who works for the agency sat down facing me, removed my glasses, and shaved off my moustache. Then she began her magic with creams, powders, instant tanning oils, and other unlabeled bottles. I'm certain I saw a can of Kiwi shoe polish in her bag. Styling my longer hair was her final attention.

We landed in Guatemala about two, at the nickel company's airfield in Las Verapaces. The temperature was eighty-five — I was still dressed for below freezing. I was driven to a vast cattle ranch owned by a wealthy Guatemalan cattleman, Lázaro Beltran, a longtime friend of the U.S. I changed into more appropriate clothes — tropical weight slacks and a white guayabera. Malcolm Whitney arrived an hour later, wearing an impeccable suit. With him were staff from both D.C. and the mission in Guatemala City. The scheme was simple because it had been planned carefully. Or maybe we were fooling ourselves. Maybe we were the ones who were simple, and I was more simple than any of the others.

We spent the evening relaxing on the hacienda's veranda. I admired Beltran's collection of his country's pre-Columbian and Colonial art. Many pieces had been in the family for generations. On the lawn in front of the veranda stood a twelve-foot-tall Maya stela. His grandfather had "acquired" it decades ago from the forests near Quirigua, a ruins site off the main road from Guatemala City to Puerto Barrios. The national archeological museum in Guatemala City has been trying to confiscate all of his collection.

Lázaro Beltran was an impressive figure. He wore a handsomely embroidered, pale-blue guayabera and razor-creased, white linen trousers. Whitney said he thought Beltran was nearly eighty, but in person he looked and acted a youthful sixty-five. Beltran turned to me and spoke, in English with an educated Bostonian accent, "Please forgive me, Señor Smith. I have been a poor host telling you about my art without first serving you a drink. What may I offer you?"

The agency had not told him my name was Brooks, and certainly not Hunt. *Smith* was fine.

"Do you have bourbon, Señor Beltran?"

"Please call me *Lázaro*. Will Gentleman Jack be satisfactory?"

Gentleman Jack was just what I needed. But Beltran's knowing my drink preference was information the CIA has recorded about me that keeps me from sleeping at night.

Politeness suggested I had to ask Beltran to use my first name. What was it? Mac? Max? Malcolm Whitney had seen my questioning look when I was called *Smith*. He offered me a small empanada. He had written *Alex* on the edge of his hand.

"Gentleman Jack is perfect, Lázaro. . . . Please call me *Alex*."

The next day we worked for several hours going over the plan. When we finished, we took a break and soon began again. Whitney was finally satisfied. He sat me in front of a large mirror and held a full-size, front-face photograph next to the mirror. It was hard to tell the difference between my face in the mirror and the face in the photo. I knew the face in the photograph was Ben Roth, Mossad's most notorious assassin.

"Malcolm," I asked, "is the resemblance coincidental?"

"Of course. Maybe *almost* of course. Dan Wilson noticed how you resembled Ben Roth when you were in D.C. about to undergo your change. He suggested we make the minor changes, which *had* to be made, to appear like Roth. He's considered very handsome among his people."

"You mean among *assassins*? And I'm *not* one of his people."

"You may remember there was talk of making you look like Frankenstein. Isn't Roth better?"

Whitney is full of surprises. Now I know that Dan Wilson's team had something sinister on their minds when they did the surgery on my face. They planned more than a new identity. They were crafting a new agent. I hope that meant only for *one* mission. Before the temporary darkening of my skin, with my glasses and moustache, no one would have mistaken me for

Roth. But now the resemblance was obvious. So it was Ben Roth who was going to kill Isfahani. At least someone who would be identified as Ben Roth. Was that supposed to make me feel better?

I went into the bathroom and threw up

43

Lázaro Beltran's cattle ranch was not far from El Molino Alemania — as the crow flies. But we faced a four-hour drive on winding roads into the mountains. Whitney remained at the ranch. Four of us left the ranch before sunrise the following morning, using an aged truck with a met-al-framed open back covered with canvas. It was a truck commonly seen in the area — nothing about it would attract attention. A dozen diminutive, plastic, religious figures dangled from the cab's overhead or stood imperiously across the top of the dashboard, a feature frequently seen in the cabs of vehicles in this impoverished Catholic country. Small banners of the local and national futbol teams were strung above the figures. It looked like a World Cup parade led by the Vatican. A marimba group from Huehuetenango was playing *La Paloma* on the truck radio. I thought the dove was a symbol of *peace*. Our mission was anything but. We should have been listening to Rachmaninoff's *Isle of the Dead*. Or *anything* by Schoenberg.

Whitney remained at the ranch. I rode in the back of the truck with one of the agents from Washington. It wasn't comfortable sitting on boxes with no view forewarning us about dozens of gut-wrenching curves.

The two Guatemalans in the cab were nationals employed by the CIA mission. The same lady who made me look like Ben

Roth had added some character to their appearances. The driver now appeared unshaven with scraggly hair and a drooping moustache; the other looked neat and clean in his "borrowed" uniform of the Guatemalan Presidential Special Guard. The uniform that gives the local *indios* the kind of fear the SS uniform once did in Nazi Germany. It was unlikely we'd meet any national police on the road; the few patrols the government could afford kept to major roads close to Guatemala City. And, if we did meet a rural patrol, the Presidential Guard uniform outranked them.

The location selected for the shooting could have been better. The shot had to be taken from a little further than I'd been told, closer to 200 than 150 yards. But I had a fairly unobscured view of the road that passed near the training camp. CIA agents had been in the area for weeks, keeping well-hidden and tracking Isfahani's patterns of movement. Isfahani prided his personal fitness. Each morning after prayers, he changed into navy blue workout clothes and ran a little over four miles. He *always* returned the same way, passing the spot the agents had chosen for the shooting.

The truck dropped me off and I quickly merged with the foliage. I was wearing the same outer garments that had scared Lucinda, they blended with the Guatemalan surroundings better than against Montana snow. The truck went on a quarter-mile, pulled off, turned around, and waited for my pick-up call. The two Guatemalans in the cab pretended they were napping.

The shooting spot offered a decent view of where Isfahani would pass behind some trees and emerge into an open space. I checked my CheyTac and adjusted the scope. A slight mist common to these highlands should further absorb what little sound the suppressor allowed.

I hadn't considered that some runners move up and down as they run. But Isfahani would be running toward me at a slight angle as he rounded a bend, so his motion wouldn't be a serious problem. By habit he would be on the far side of the road, facing infrequent oncoming traffic. The few Guatemalans who might happen by were not apt to be very careful drivers and wouldn't expect to see a darkly clad runner.

Beads of perspiration formed on my forehead as I stretched out in a prone position amongst the foliage. The sweat wasn't from the prospect of shooting, but the Guatemalan humidity. I *wanted* to pull the trigger. And I wanted a clean kill. Anything other than a quick death was unsatisfactory. I didn't want Isfahani to suffer a lingering death, even with his fanatical hatred for America and Americans. Hatred for me. And Lucinda by association. He's willing to trade his life for the lives of two to three thousand innocent people. It almost certainly means killing Lucinda *if* she's at work in Manhattan. If I saw Isfahani point a gun at Lucinda and cock the trigger, would I fire at him? *I'd empty the magazine.* I kept that in mind as I loaded five .408 cartridges in a single-stack clip, and lay on a far warmer ground than when I'd practiced at Mill Creek.

Soon, a tiny, lone figure appeared a half-mile away, running smoothly toward me, visible only for an instant in gaps in the dense highland forest. He was moving gracefully, most of his effort moving him forward without noticeable bouncing. That would make the shot easier.

Isfahani increasingly filled my scope as he approached the target point. He was handsome in the tropical sun that glistened on his sweating cheeks. Wearing a blue baseball cap with orange trim. I focused the scope on the hat. On the front was the Gator logo of the University of Florida. It was a perfect target, I've never been gator hunting before.

His face flashed a slight smile as he finished the steepest part of the road, knowing that within ten minutes he would be standing in a shower with visions of piloting the small jet into the Chrysler Building. Giving up his life killing a thousand infidels and entering everlasting sanctification. I hoped to change that and send him, only days earlier, to wherever failed Muslims go. I moved the cross-hairs of my scope to a little below the gator, a touch below Isfahani's eyebrows, and about where glasses would rest on the bridge of his nose. Take out that bridge and kill the gator.

I sensed only a shudder of the gun as the bullet started its journey. There was a modest crack from the suppressor, a sacrifice to have better velocity than using a quieter silencer. Isfahani's head jerked to the rear as a red spume erupted from his face while his body toppled to the side, falling off the paved road into an area where spring wildflowers were blooming. He lay motionless in a bed of yellow blossoms. His Gator cap lay on the edge of the road in a circle of red. I kept the scope on him until the truck stopped to pick me up. No movement came from the body.

There were no smiles on my face on the return drive to the ranch. But before I put away my CheyTac, I cut a small notch in the stock. It was the second notch and the first in more than half a decade.

I'm determined it will be the last.

44

I WAS SAFELY HOME in my Montana cabin within eight hours after the shooting. When I turned onto my road at dusk, I stopped, got out, and breathed deeply the clear, cold Montana winter air. Another *blood-red* sunset was unfolding in the western mountain sky.

Twenty minutes later, I stood on my porch in the plummeting temperature and sipped Gentleman Jack. The last daylight slipped behind the mountain peaks. John Denver was singing *Wild Montana Skies* on my stereo. Abdul Khaliq Isfahani may still be lying dead in his bed of flowers.

Lucinda is safe.

45

ON MARCH 16TH, *The New York Times* was headlined: SECOND BIG APPLE TRAGEDY THWARTED BY COMBINED OP. The article read:

Combined efforts of the FBI, CIA, NSA, and various New York and New Jersey police authorities, with the participation of Israel, thwarted a planned al-Qaeda attack in New York City that was to occur yesterday, March 15th.

Information available indicates that al-Qaeda terrorists were to have flown two private jets from the Teterboro Airport in New Jersey to Manhattan, remaining close to surface level down the Hudson River and turning east over Manhattan, flying at roof-top level along 38th Street. One plane was to turn north at Lexington Avenue and crash into the Chrysler Building, the other to turn south at 5th Avenue and strike the Empire State Building.

The privately owned planes were the largest version of the popular Gulf Stream jet manufactured by General Dynamics. While they lack the size and weight of the commercial jets that flew into the Twin Trade Towers on September 11th of 2001, they had been loaded and armed with newly developed, high-explosives that could easily have toppled each building.

The attacks were to be carried out by a group of al-Qaeda extremists. One of the intended pilots was identified as Abdul Khaliq Isfahani, an Iranian born radical educated first in Khartoum, Sudan, and later at the

University of Florida in Gainesville. He was to fly the lead plane into the Chrysler Building.

The pilot of the second plane was to be Mohammed Haqqani, a third-generation American of Syrian ancestry, who studied at Harvard and the School of African and Oriental Studies of the University of London, where he joined a jihadist group and converted to Islam. The second plane was to crash into the Empire State Building.

Abdul Khaliq Isfahani had been under surveillance for the past three years by unrelated investigations of the CIA and the Israeli equivalent known as the Mossad. Mohammed Haqqani had been under investigation by a joint operation of the CIA and the UK's MI6.

It is believed that an al-Qaeda training camp for this operation has been functioning for the past two years in Guatemala near El Molino Alemania, a former coffee plantation some ninety miles northwest of Guatemala City. The site was previously used for training by the CIA, leading to the miscarried Bay of Pigs invasion of Cuba.

The two terrorists were to have been allowed into the United States, but confronted and arrested at Teterboro. U.S. authorities said that they were to arrest additional persons assisting the attack. Of the two expected pilots only Mohammed Haqqani arrived at Teterboro on the evening of March 14th. He was immediately taken into custody by federal marshals.

The United States learned only yesterday that an attempt to assassinate the other pilot, Abdul Khaliq Isfahani, was made in Guatemala only days before the planned attack, while he was jogging near the al-Qaeda training camp. Photos obtained by the CIA of a person seen leaving the El Molino Alemania area, carrying what was likely a gun case, indicate that the killer was the Mossad's most notorious assassin, Ben Roth.

Some doubt exists whether Isfahani was killed or critically injured because others interviewed in the El Molino Alemania area had heard ambulance sirens in the vicinity shortly after the estimated time of the shooting.

Guatemalan authorities have confiscated all information about the training center, which the Guatemalan President's office insists was never functional and also had never been used for training for the Bay of Pigs invasion.

The participating U.S. government agencies are not clear who was to replace Isfahani as one of the pilots, but it is believed that the substitute pilot was one of those taken into custody at Teterboro. There were very tense days immediately preceding the 15th. Authorities added, however, that the two planes had been disabled by the CIA and could not have been flown. Furthermore, the bombs loaded onto the planes had been defused. In an interesting turn of events — continued on page A4.

When my cell phone rang on the morning of the 16th, I wasn't in Montana. I was in Manhattan having an early breakfast with Malcolm Whitney at a small, private hotel. Ironically, my room had a view of the Chrysler Building from a few blocks south. Several times during the night, standing in the window, I counted up the fifty-five floors and guessed which windows were Lucinda's office.

Whitney had insisted I come from Montana when rumors arose that Isfahani might not have been killed. But I knew I had shot him in the head and that he couldn't possibly have taken part in the planned attack. Whitney would not waver and when dawn broke yesterday on the 15th, there were over eighty agents secreted throughout and around the Teterboro Airport. Whitney, three serious looking heavily armed agents and I were sitting inside the Gulf Stream jet Isfahani was scheduled to fly.

The call for me was from a house in Farmington, Connecticut. I turned off the cell phone speaker, put the phone to my ear, and said, "Yes?"

"Have you seen the paper? . . . I'm sorry if I woke you; I know it's only 4:15 a.m. in Montana."

"It's 6:15 where I am, Lucinda. In Manhattan! Are you OK?"

"I'm fine. It's front page of *The New York Times!* I'm walking over to turn on the TV." She sounded stressed. Without my insistence she would have been in her office yesterday, and while unharmed by the plot, she would have been horrified to learn about her building being a target.

"Calm down. Try CNN. . . . Are you safe? Where are you?"

"I'm in Farmington, staying with an old friend who teaches here at Miss Porter's School. Somewhere, I think, on the street where your family lived when you were born. I did what you asked. I left Manhattan two days ago and took the train to Hartford where my friend met me. I even walked Farmington's Main Street last evening looking for a plaque on a house that said 'Maxwell so-and-so was born here.' I didn't find one, and I don't know Max's last name, but it's a beautiful, peaceful village."

Her voice gave away her nervousness. She was trying to make small-talk and avoid contemplating what might have happened."

"You *knew* something was going to happen . . . you had to . . . or there was no reason for you to be so insistent I leave the City. . . . Why are *you* in Manhattan?"

I excused myself from the table and went into the hall to talk. "Lucinda, I more than knew about the plot. I was given little choice but to become involved. I knew people in Guatemala from my trips there years ago. I had information essential to dealing with Abdul Khaliq Isfahani. He was my student in my earlier life. Only a small group within the State Department knew he was in Guatemala and that an al-Qaeda cell was operating there. I can tell you more, if you still want to see me. . . . And, I'm fine. A little shaken from yesterday, but fine. And much better hearing your voice. Can you get a train back to Manhattan this morning?"

"Yes. I'll call the concierge at my apartment. He'll let you in. I can't wait to see you, Mac or Maxwell or whoever you are. You know, from the drawing in the *Times* this morning, you look a bit like the Mossad's Ben Roth. I bet you wish *you* had been the shooter! If Roth *was* the shooter, he saved a lot of lives. He deserves a medal." She hung up. My work was over. As for public knowledge, I never existed. Ben Roth did the shooting.

And I don't want a medal.

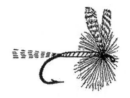

46

LUCINDA'S APARTMENT is on East 67th Street between 2nd and 3rd avenues. Once the home of a single, wealthy family, a decade ago the four-story brownstone was converted to small, elegant apartments. Lucinda's is on the third floor, high enough above the sidewalk to deter at least New York's "second story" thieves.

The concierge must have been a bouncer in an earlier life. An imposing six-and-a-half footer with something like 250 pounds spread where it should be, he buzzed me in and smiled when I entered.

"Are you Mr. Brooks, sir?"

"I am. Miss Lang apparently informed you I was coming."

"Yes, she called a few minutes ago. But I believe 'warn' is the better word, sir. I'll have to search you . . . please."

"For?"

"Shotguns, rifles, pistols, knives, and explosives."

"Are you going to search me when I leave?"

"Of course . . . for silverware, securities, jewelry, and art."

Lucinda had left her apartment without the slightest thought I would see it before she returned. That meant she'd left things around she might have put away. Maybe the four silver-framed black and white photos on an antique Chinese table in the foyer, showing the two of us in her lodge in Montana. I didn't recall she had taken any pictures. Two showed us sitting in the room with the fireplace, the other two at the dinner table.

In the living room, more photos were clustered along a low table in front of a window that overlooked 67th Street. The most dominant were of an attractive couple I assumed to be her parents. In several the man is in an Army uniform, first as a young lieutenant during WWII. Lucinda mentioned at Christmas that her father parachuted into Belgium a few minutes after midnight on D-Day, was injured a month later by a land mine in France, but returned to combat until the end of the war. Serving in London after the war, he fell in love with a High Court judge's daughter who had spent the war helping the British break the German codes. When he proposed, she gave him her answer in encrypted wartime German. It took him two miserable months to break her code, during which time she refused to see him. Her answer was, "I hope it doesn't take you as long to break this code as it did to propose. I would love to marry you." They eloped the following weekend.

I felt uncomfortably invasive sitting alone in Lucinda's living room, though I was peculiarly content and at ease. A Japanese 18th-century triptych screen in mostly black and gold, depicting five wading herons, separated the living room from a small dining area that sat at most six. Her mix of Stickley furniture and Oriental art was striking.

The living room had none of the Western art that decorates Arrogate Ranch. Indian, Japanese, Tibetan, and Chinese pieces dominated, starting in her entry foyer with a pair of powerful Chinese ancestor portraits that stretched from close to the floor to a foot below the high ceiling.

Her small library included a large selection of non-fiction and historical novels set in Europe during the war. Her father's service had influenced their lives for decades thereafter.

One item in the library reflected Lucinda's Montana life. Over a small fireplace was the bamboo fishing rod inscribed "to Lucinda from Macduff — Christmas in Montana." That was a little presumptuous. It was only our *second* time together, and a few days later she fled to New York confused about with whom she was becoming entangled.

I was overwhelmed by a dozen, large black and white photographs in her dining room that were taken at her ranch. They expressed the velvety tone of platinum prints. My favorite was a moonlit view of a small spring creek joining Mill Creek. The moon appears twice, once directly rising above the outline of the hills behind her lodge, a second time as a reflection in a still pool of the spring creek. She must have hired a professional photographer from Bozeman, or maybe from New York.

I didn't go into either her kitchen or bedroom. Kitchens scare me. Her bedroom scared me even more.

When Lucinda arrived I was like Wuff waiting for me to come home to the cabin. I wished I had a tail to wag. I opened her door, picked her up, and hugged her in the doorway so hard I thought the maid for the next-door apartment, who was cleaning in the hall, would call 911. When we closed the door, Lucinda threw her arms around my neck, and both of our bodies trembled, until the throbbing, if it wasn't subsiding, was at least in unison. She moved a hand from the back of my neck and her fingers searched and found the nick in my ear, as if that were more tangible assurance that it was me. Not Maxwell something. Not Ben Roth. Not Alex Smith. Just Macduff.

She looked at me and said, "Macduff, you've shaved your moustache and let your hair grow. All for me?"

"In a way *just* for you."

We were both physically and emotionally exhausted. By nine, I tucked her in bed and went to sleep on the big sofa in front of the fireplace, covered by a massive duvet she brought back from one of her long-weekend trips to England. Just in case someone slept over. She'd never used it.

In the middle of the night I woke because my hand was being pulled. It was Lucinda, outlined in the light of a nearly full moon coming through her front windows. I didn't say a word, but I didn't let go. I let myself be abducted, still wrapped in the duvet. And I slept much better. At least when we finally fell asleep.

It took three days for us to approach normal in our conversations, when we could look at each other and talk about something that didn't soon shift to the terrorist attempt and often end in tears.

Lucinda was a little beside herself about going back to her office in the Chrysler Building. We waited until Saturday when we walked down Lexington Avenue and went up to her office together.

No one else was there. We stood, an arm around the other's waist, and looked south out her office window. Without comment. I was sure she was thinking what I was — what if she had been standing in this very spot, taking a sip of a surcharged morning latte, casually looking out as a plane turned sharply a few blocks south, at her level, heading straight for her building, the pilot's angered expression growing increasingly vivid. In only a few seconds it would be over. Another stain would be left on the city — the Big Apple, the "I Love N.Y." place. Giving those who enjoy the macabre media a few weeks of non-stop replays on the TV.

On Sunday I left for Montana.

47

AMONG THE USUAL PILE of catalogues, solicitations and other junk mail waiting at the Pray Post Office, half-way between Emigrant and my cabin, was a letter forwarded from Bruce Samson at the fly shop in Jackson. I knew the handwriting.

Dear Macduff

It's been over a year since I wrote to you after what you must now recall only as the "float from hell." I've wanted you to know how much you helped me. After a few months home I started practicing law again.

I had passed the Maine Bar exam right after law school, and a class-mate and I began what we planned as a month-long tour of the west coast. We flew to Seattle, rented a car, and drove south. My friend had an old college boyfriend we visited in L.A., staying to see if there was any bloom left on the their rose. There wasn't, but I met his friend Park and another rose quickly bloomed, proving as you know to have been a particularly thorny variety. After two months we married!

I still don't know how it happened so fast. Call it a small town girl goes to Hollywood and sees stars. I found a job at a law firm and passed the Cal Bar, but once the daily life began, I started to understand my role. I was more a trophy than a treasure. Park controlled me. He made me quit my job, and I was pretty much a housekeeper for the next two years. I think he took me to Jackson only because he didn't want me out of his sight.

You know what happened next. But what you don't know are events that occurred after I arrived home here. Park sent some nasty letters to my parents, insisting they tell him where I was. He finally flew to Maine to look for me. After a lot of threats, leading up to a day when he knocked me down in front of my mom, I got a restraining order. He hasn't been back. But he writes and sends e-mails. And calls. He is certain I'll eventually go back to him. Not a chance!

I took the Orvis fly casting course you told me about. And, if you can believe it, I fished last summer . . . in Scotland! I was on legal business in Edinburgh and drove up to an area famous for its trout and salmon fly fishing, the River Spey north of Aberdeen. I stayed at a charming hotel, the Craigellachie. They had arrangements with a local ghillie, who put me onto some beautiful Scottish trout. He said the hotel would cook them for me, but I wanted them thrown back. And I squeezed off the barbs of the hooks, as you taught me. I loved Scotland, and thought of you. Macduff is as Scottish as they come.

My last note to you ended with a thought we might float again together. I would like that.

P.S. Thanks for the flowers after my last note.

Affectionately

Kath Macintosh

Bar Harbor, Maine

I read the letter three times. I wondered what "affectionately" meant. Kath sounds in need of some companionship other than her aging parents. Maybe she's romanticized her brief time here. If she knew more about me, she wouldn't have written. She isn't the first client to ask for private lessons. Most have come from married trophy wives in Jackson Hole and Paradise Valley. I find them about as attractive as a combination of Barbie on the outside and Disney's Cruella de Vil on the inside. I think Kath's different, but we spent only one afternoon together, and she was justifiably distraught. I won't answer her letter.

I wouldn't know how to deal with telling her about Lucinda. But I'd like to hear from her that she's exorcized Park and latched on to some great guy who knows he's getting someone special.

I called to order some flowers for Kath. When they asked for her name and address, I changed my mind and sent them to Lucinda.

48

MALCOLM WHITNEY CALLED the first week of August. "Mac, I'm sorry to have to tell you, but we think Isfahani survived. Your shot destroyed his jaw, but a doctor from a nearby village heading to see a patient came across him within what must have been minutes of the shooting. The doctor gave him some first aid. Isfahani was stabilized and transported to Guatemala City. He was flown to a Zurich hospital for a half-dozen operations to reconstruct his jaw. He's no longer the swarthy, handsome, Omar Sharif type. We lost track of him when, without permission, he left the Zurich hospital in late June, still wrapped in bandages. He's thought to be in one of the terrorist sanctuaries in the Mid-East. Or maybe Afghanistan. Or even Somalia.

"Any possibility he's in Guatemala?"

"We don't think so."

"Or in the U.S."

"*Probably* not. But Isfahani won't take the shooting lightly."

"Probably" and "we don't think" aren't reassuring words. "Do you think the *Israelis* might try to kill Isfahani?" I asked. "After all, the Mossad doesn't want their best assassin killed?"

"Good thought . . . and exactly what we're trying to encourage."

"I'm headed to Missoula today to do a couple of floats for a charity. I come home in three days and stop at the Bozeman airport to pick up Lucinda."

"Do what you need to do, Mac. But be careful."

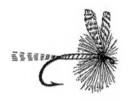

49

RETURNING FROM THREE ENRICHING but exhausting days teaching fly casting and guiding for Project Healing Waters in Missoula, I met Lucinda's plane in Bozeman. Lucinda insisted we go directly to her ranch for a meal our shared housekeeper Mavis left for Lucinda's arrival. I approved; I wouldn't have to feign cooking. We picked up Wuff at the vet's on the way.

After an early meal, the summer evening still filled with light, I towed *Osprey* down to my cabin. Lucinda drove behind me to borrow some books. When we reached my locked gate, she leaned out of her window and called, "Did you see that small, parked car facing us, about thirty yards before your gate? For some reason, it looked out-of-place. As soon as you turned in, it left in a hurry, tires spinning on the gravel, fishtailing a little as it U-turned and headed south. I may be jumpy, but it bothered me."

"I saw it. Probably nothing," I replied. "This *is* Montana, most likely some hunter scouting places to poach in the fall. This is all private land, but a lot of locals think it's theirs for hunting. They read 'No Trespassing' signs as including an implied exemption for native Montanans. We might feel the same way if we'd been born here."

When we reached my cabin and parked our vehicles between the garage and the house, I let Wuff out. She headed directly for the front door. It was past her meal time. Bounding up two steps to the porch, she stopped abruptly, and then walked deliberately up the remaining step, sniffing all the way to the front door. She turned and barked. Wuff's not a barker. Something attracted her. I knew she was hungry. I called to her, "Wuff, as soon as I get that door open, I'll get your supper," aware that only the first and last words — "Wuff" and "supper" — made any sense to her.

When I reached the porch, Wuff grabbed my pants cuff and began pulling me away from the door. I had my key inches from the lock when Lucinda took my arm and said, "I don't like this, Mac," resorting to my nickname as she does when something is troubling her. She pulled my arm from the door. "Could anyone have been here while we were gone?" she asked.

"Our cleaning gal, Mavis, has been in Great Falls with her family. She came back yesterday morning. I told her I'd be away. There shouldn't have been any trouble, unless someone's broken in. Wuff probably smelled a raccoon searching for food. But let's look around before we go in, and see if there are any traces of a break-in. If someone wants in badly enough, they can do it. But they won't get in without leaving some sign."

My doors are extra heavy, and the window glass is supposed to keep out everything from UV rays to .30-30 bullets. Sometimes frustrated hunters like to shoot at things. Not just road signs.

We looked carefully along the edges of the front door, but saw nothing unusual. The windows and the back door were untouched.

"Lucinda, I don't see how *anyone* could have gotten in. Let's go in and make some morning coffee. I'll grind some of your favorite Antigua coffee beans."

I started up the porch. Wuff began barking again. This time not at the front door, but beyond our vehicles around the rear of the garage. Lucinda and I walked over.

"My extension ladder is where I left it, against the garage rear wall." As we started back to the house, I looked back at the ladder. "Wait a minute. The ladder looks *reversed*. The part that should lean against the building is facing outward." I walked back. Sure enough, it had been turned around.

I looked at Lucinda, who was between the cabin and me. "Look on the roof of the cabin. That flat aluminum vent helps disperse hot summer attic air. It *could* provide access to the attic, where there's a pull-down ladder into my bedroom. Could anyone have tried to go *down* that vent?"

"Can it open enough for a person to get through?" Lucinda asked.

"Possibly," I said, as we walked back to the cabin. "You take a look through the windows of my bedroom and see if there's anything unusual inside. I'm going up on the cabin roof and check the vent."

I carried the ladder to the back of the cabin and leaned it against the eaves. When I placed the ladder, the bottoms of the two sides fit perfectly into two depressions in the ground. My ladder had been placed there recently. As I climbed the ladder, I yelled to Lucinda, "Stay away from the house!"

She came running around the side, calling, "There's a ladder hanging down from the ceiling of your bedroom!"

"I've never pulled it down. It's hard to pull up or down. The angle is so steep I doubt anyone *inside* the attic could pull it up. Someone's been here! They got into the cabin using the ladder.

224

I think they removed the vent and dropped into the attic. Then pushed the ladder down into my bedroom. I'm going in that way."

"Careful," she said, looking both curious about the possible intruder and concerned for my safety.

I climbed onto the roof. Someone *had* removed the vent and later put it back, roughly fitting the flashing and shingles back into place. I pulled the vent aside. There was a makeshift rope ladder nailed to the inside frame for the vent, dangling to a couple of feet above the attic floor. It was not *my* rope ladder.

I climbed down into the attic. As Lucinda had seen, the attic access ladder in the bedroom ceiling was hanging down into my bedroom. There were footprints in attic floor dust that had accumulated over the past three years. Someone had been here and taken careful steps to get in and back out. I climbed down the attic ladder into my bedroom, looked around, but saw nothing unusual. I walked carefully to the living room, looking for any wires that might have been strung across the threshold. There were none. But when I saw the inside of my front door, I froze.

Stacked from the door sill to the top were plastic explosives, wires running in ways I couldn't comprehend, connected to a small box that had to be a device to trigger an explosion when the door opened. It wouldn't have just blown out the door; it would have blown the whole cabin and anyone within twenty yards of it into small, unidentifiable parts.

I didn't have any idea how to disarm explosives. Trial and error didn't seem wise. Nothing was ticking; there was no clock visible attached to the explosives . . . it wasn't on a timer. More likely the explosives would have been set-off when the door opened. The bomber wanted more than to blow up my cabin. The bomber wanted to *incinerate me*.

I called Dan Wilson but couldn't reach him. I tried Paula Pajioli in Bozeman and caught her heading for lunch with her husband. When I described what happened, she said, "Get away from the cabin — immediately. There could be more explosives rigged in your garage or elsewhere. I'll be there in an hour. *Just get away!*"

Lucinda and I used the wait to drive to my gate, where we'd seen the car when we entered my drive. The car had left tracks a foot off the road; the driver had been in a hurry to turn around and leave.

Searching along the car's tracks, she called out, "Here's some paper that might have been tossed out of that car." Opening the crumpled paper, she added, "they're receipts from the machines that take credit cards. One's for gas in Emigrant, dated this morning. The other's for lodging two nights ago at a Las Vegas hotel."

"Maybe the guy was a hunter who liked to gamble," I said. "We'll give them to Paula."

Paula arrived in fifty minutes; a few minutes behind was another person who never gave his name. He climbed onto the roof, dropped down into the cabin, and disarmed the explosives, all in about twenty minutes. We watched from a hundred yards away.

"Who could have done this?" asked Lucinda, out of Paula's hearing. "That Arab who was killed by Ben Roth in Guatemala is gone. His colleagues?"

"Isfahani might not have been killed," I confessed. "But I don't think he could have recovered enough to do this alone. It would mean he knows who I am and where I live. I assumed he'd be in Israel searching for Ben Roth."

My cabin was a busy place for the next two days, while a half-dozen unidentified people swarmed in to investigate. They were close-lipped and told me nothing. Paula gave them the gas and hotel receipts and mentioned what Lucinda and I had discussed about the car that had been parked near my entrance road.

Malcolm Whitney phoned the day the agents left. "We have a problem with the bombing attempt. There were enough explosives to destroy everything in the neighborhood. But it was *not* the most up-to-date explosive device that's being used by al-Qaeda terrorists. We have a lot more to analyze. Dan Wilson and I want you to get out of there — soon. Not many here know about your place in Florida. I suggest you go there and lay low. Do it today. We'll take care of cleaning up, have the vent replaced, and the cabin set-up for winter. Send me a list of what needs to be done. But *get out!*"

I didn't need any more bad news, but I feared the worst when the phone rang again an hour later and it was Dan Wilson.

"I know you talked to Whitney. I have some more uncertain news, Mac."

"Might as well drop the other shoe, Dan."

"And then some! I've just had a call from one of our agents in Denver. Juan Pablo hasn't been on our radar screen for some time. He is now. A few days before your cabin was rigged, a man was stopped at customs in Denver after a private flight, allegedly from Oaxaca, Mexico. His passport stated he was a Mexican national named Alejandro Hernandez. He drew the bad card — one of our purely random searches. His documents checked out — he had an entry visa. Customs didn't find any reason to hold him. He said he was on his way to a private preserve west of Denver to hunt birds. But the day after they let him go, one of the customs agents mentioned that he had reservations about the guy. He didn't have any clothing in his suitcase that suggested he was going hunting. He wasn't carrying a shotgun case. That didn't trouble the agent as much as a book he had in his suitcase. It was a novel entitled *Deadly Blasts*. The agent thought it looked interesting, the back cover described the story as being about a serial killer who used explosives to kill his targets by rigging their homes while they were at work, to explode when they returned home and opened their front door. The agent went on line at noon to order a copy. The only Amazon review said the book's description of building the bombs was so detailed that a teenager could make them. That all bothered the agent. He searched Hernandez in some government databases. The U.S. had never issued a visa to a Mexican named Alejandro Hernandez. The entry visa was forged. One of our agents in Denver was called in. He took over and has learned that there is no such person, and that the plane quickly returned to where it actually had flown from, not Oaxaca — from Guatemala City! The plane belongs to a Cayman Islands corporation owned by *Juan Pablo Herzog*. The customs agent was shown a photo of Herzog this morning and identified him as the person who entered the U.S. posing as Alejandro Hernandez. The Denver agents don't know about the attempt at your cabin.

"You're telling me that Juan Pablo's here in the West! You don't know where? Plus he's reading about planting bombs? Dan, he's doing a lot more than reading!"

"Take it easy, Mac. We're trying to trace him. There's no reason to believe Juan Pablo knows who Maxwell Hunt is, *if* he believes Hunt didn't die. It's a big jump from his thinking Hunt didn't die to knowing who you are and where you live. You need to head to Florida. I'll keep you informed."

"Juan Pablo doesn't know where I am! Who rigged the bombs? The book's author? I don't need to be kept informed. I need to be kept alive!"

"Mac. Get out soon. The bomber may not know that the bombs didn't go off. He may be far away waiting to read about the blast. But we don't know that. Just get out!"

I told Lucinda only that we had to leave. That night I slept on her couch, my packed SUV out-of-sight in one of her barns. She didn't come to get me in the middle of the night. I didn't sleep, wondering what I should tell her, and what to do about Juan Pablo. I have to live my life. If I live scared all the time what's left? In the morning we headed north to Livingston and then east a couple of hours to the Billings airport. It was further than taking her to the Bozeman airport, but was on the way east, where Wuff and I were headed.

It gave me a few more hours before I let Lucinda go — but we had little in the way of conversation on the drive.

50

WHEN I FINISHED the leg of each day's drive to Florida, I couldn't have named a single town I'd passed through. My thoughts were on the bombing, the whereabouts of Juan Pablo, and how to keep Lucinda from being further drawn into my problems. I didn't develop one sensible idea.

Crossing the Florida border, on a final tiring day from Mississippi, I saw a sign on a bank that said it was August 31st, 6:47 p.m., and ninety-three degrees. It was humid in the oppressive way I'd been determined to escape by choosing to live summers in Montana. I diverted a little south to pass through Gainesville. I miss the town. Driving through felt good. I drove by the law school and stopped to pick up the Gainesville paper at Wilbert's. There was one item I hoped might be there. The women's soccer team was to open the season Friday night, three days away. I'll be there. High in the stands, where few sit. Wearing sunglasses and an old, wide-brimmed Gator hat I never threw out. Trying not to think of the past two weeks.

51

LUCINDA IS IN MANHATTAN. Working hard. We talk every week, sometimes twice, sometimes increasing to daily, when some mutual fear in our personalities says: "slow down," and we don't talk for two weeks. It becomes a game of chicken to see who'll call first. It's usually me.

Thanksgiving passed and Christmas arrived with no news about Juan Pablo or the bombing. My cottage was quiet and lonely. A lot of silent nights had passed. I hadn't asked Lucinda south to Florida. She hadn't asked me north to Manhattan. She settled the last details of her dad's estate, made difficult by claims pressed by one of his former business partners. I knew she needed time to sort out the attempted bombing. But I wanted her here. I finally called her late on Christmas day.

"Hi . . . Merry Christmas . . . I'd sing 'White Christmas,' but you'd mistake me for Bing Crosby."

"More likely for the chipmunks," she said. "Macduff, it's so *boring* here. I miss you. The business parties at holiday season are silly. I've seen more dreadful apartments than you can imagine."

"Would you be interested in visiting a snake-, gator-, and mosquito-infested marsh a little south of St. Augustine?"

"Any shelties to protect me?"

"Just one."

"I'll be there."

I'm tired of eating alone in restaurants, shopping alone in grocery stores, and even being alone in my flats boat. It's not companionship I miss; it's a *certain* companion. But, like El, Lucinda could do much better if she'd look around. I don't want to get closer and then learn she has looked and found someone better than a fishing guide who flinches when he sees his shadow. Who's living a phony life, lost a client on a float, and was nearly blown up in his own cabin. That's a pretty disconcerting existence for someone like Lucinda. For the moment, I'm content with keeping the relationship going the way it is and avoiding talking about hard decisions, like explaining what I meant by "probably." I'm not sure I even know.

My Florida cottage is large enough for a guest. If Lucinda needs some space between us, she can have my bedroom. I have a small office off the living room with a pull-out bed. I'd like to believe we could share the bedroom, like we did in New York. I have to think hard to remember we've done that. But then she came to me because she was scared. I want her to come when she isn't.

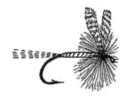

52

WE'RE A STRANGE PAIR — the Park Avenue lady and the Montana fishing guide. But when Lucinda arrived for a week in early February, she loved the cottage and kayaking in the narrow creeks of the salt-marsh. Especially on seventy-five degree days with clear skies, and then reading in *The New York Times* about thirty-seven degrees with soot and slush in Manhattan.

We left the cabin once, to visit St. Augustine. First to walk the old streets and in the evening to dine on the balcony of the A1A restaurant, where we ordered coconut-battered shrimp over Cuban black beans and rice. Plus a fruity, mild Tuscan *pinot grigio*. The town's holiday lights had been extended another two weeks because the King and Queen of Spain were arriving to talk about the city's coming 450th anniversary. Tens of thousands of tiny, white lights enveloped the downtown. Every building was outlined. From our table we could see strings of lights hung like umbrella-ribs down from the old market plaza's tree-tops. It was an unseasonably balmy early-February night in my Florida. Our Montana was deep in snow. Her Manhattan was deep in uncollected garbage.

I looked at Lucinda across the table. She was wearing creased, pleated, tan Bermuda shorts and a broadly scooped, short-sleeved, lime green top.

"Your *trapezius* are beautiful," I remarked.

Her face reddened. "You've never noticed before?"

"Your shoulders aren't bare much in Montana. There's a slope from your neck to your shoulders that tapers gracefully. It exudes athleticism."

"Exudes? Wow! Does any other part of me exude?"

"I hope to find out."

She was even redder, but leaned toward me and whispered, "Wait till you see my *iliopsoas*."

"I can't wait. I don't know where they are, but I'm willing to search extensively."

The waitress interrupted, and asked, "Is everything OK?"

"It's getting better by the minute," I said.

Lucinda choked and hid her face in her napkin.

The hostess sat two women at the table beyond us. I recognized one as a former neighbor in Gainesville, Nancy Sawyer. She'd often saved my mail and papers when I was away. I last saw her the day before I left for Washington, almost four years ago, never to return as Maxwell Hunt. Nancy sat facing me, but I don't think she noticed me. I put my sunglasses back on.

Lucinda asked, "You all right?"

I said, "I'm fine. I'm supposed to wear sunglasses whenever I'm out. My older brother developed macular degeneration before he was killed. I have some early symptoms. Nothing serious." It probably sounded pretty silly.

"That sounded pretty silly. It won't work. There's no sun on this porch. You've seen someone you know. Should we leave?"

"No," I said, quietly. "It's a neighbor . . . a *former* neighbor. In another life you know very little about. But I looked different then. That's another thing you deserve to know about."

Lucinda leaned toward me and spoke quietly, "There's enough breeze to blow their conversation this way. One just

234

said you remind her of a former neighbor in Gainesville — a Maxwell Hunt!"

"I know her. Or rather Maxwell knew her. What else has she said?"

"That there's still a lot of talk about Hunt's death. Even after four years some Gainesville people don't believe he died of a stroke in D.C. There was never a burial . . . no body or even ashes were ever returned to Gainesville. The most current rumor is that Maxwell was working for the CIA and was killed in Guatemala. . . . Now they're talking about something else . . . getting a child into Flagler College."

Fortunately, Nancy and her friend moved inside. The evening temperature was dropping under a fresh northwest wind. It didn't bother Lucinda or me. We're tough Montanans.

When they left, Lucinda looked at me with a disconcerting concentration, and then whispered, "I don't think Maxwell Hunt died. Do you?"

I whispered back, "What do you expect me to say?"

"That you have a lot to tell me when we get back to the cottage. And this time — no gaps."

53

IN THE CAR I turned and said, "When we get to the cottage, I know you're expecting a detailed autobiography. While we're driving, tell me more about yourself."

"You're the mystery person. Not me," she said. "I was raised in a strict, middle-class family, in the Midwest. German immigrant stock. Lutheran parents who tried to pass on to me all their positive values. They mostly stuck — except the Lutheranism. I went to Oberlin, played tennis, and had good grades. I started reading *The Wall Street Journal* to balance a required economics course that was pompously and dogmatically taught by a onetime Keynesian socialist who struggled in class to explain his newly adopted but misunderstood Marxism. The *Journal* was to him like a cross to a vampire. I used *Journal* articles to write down questions to ask in class. Questions he didn't like. It was my only D, and my only grade below *A*."

"So you didn't take to Keynesian economics, much less Karl Marx?"

"Not a word. Von Hayek and Schumpeter made more sense to me. I went on to complete a doctorate degree in finance in London, worked for a Paris branch of a English bank for six years, and decided it was time to move back to the U.S. A New York investment firm offered me a job, and in a dozen years I've confused myself and my parents with my earning capacity.

I've saved far more than I'll ever need. I've used some to travel, first mostly Europe, but more recently, aware that the furthest west I'd ever been was my Midwest hometown, to the American West."

"And that took you to Montana, *Dr. Lang?*"

"Finally, due respect! But I won't call you 'Professor' on condition you don't call me 'Doctor.' Eventually, I traveled to Montana. A few of my friends had bought second homes in Jackson Hole and encouraged me to do the same. I visited, but there was something about Jackson that wasn't *me*.

"You didn't want to stay and be a Jackson girl."

"I couldn't really define that, until one day I watched a pretty gal about my age walk toward me across Jackson Square. She was borderline anorexic, which wasn't the characteristic I attributed to the Jackson trophy-wife norm, which usually meant noticeably well-fed. But she did have big gift-boobs. It wasn't the amount of visible flesh that amused me about the young woman, but the cover wrapping. From the ground up, she wore a pair of stiletto-heeled cowboy boots that had seen neither horse nor dirt corral. They had pointed toes and a beige hide that changed to bright red panels around the instep, where a large gold star announced her as Texas weaned. Her butt-tight, bell-bottomed pants went just to the top of her boots, with enough rhinestones stuck on from the knees down to start a costume-jewelry store. The pants were cut low and magically supported six inches below her navel by a four-inch-wide belt that probably had some leather behind the glass studs. At least six sizes too long, with the silver tip flapping. The buckle was enormous, silver with large dollops of turquoise."

"She sounds posh, classy, chichi, maybe even . . ."

"Macduff! She *wasn't* your type. . . . The view got sillier as she passed by. Above the belt was an expanse of bare skin, and then a lot of long fringe, best appreciated when she walked down the street in a good headwind. The top half of her torso was mostly quivering silicon. A ragged-edged top was scalloped low enough to show a gold rattlesnake tail hanging from a chain attached to a wide, jewel-studded collar around her neck. She wore a wide-open buckskin jacket that was two sizes too big. When her arms were down, her hands disappeared into the sleeves, but when she raised them, out popped a display of bracelets that just jingled and jangled in perfect tempo with her boobs. She had rings on her fingers everywhere but the ring finger of her left hand, so I guessed she was available and looking. Her bleached hair looked like a Dallas import and had to have been sprayed with some silicon left over from the boob job. Not a hair moved as she worked her way through the crowd. What a picture! For me she will forever be 'the Jackson girl.'"

"Cultivated, polished, restrained, even soigné. Are you trying to tell me you want an outfit like that for next Christmas?"

"You do and I get to dress *you*! There's so much money in Jackson. I always thought that money improved taste, not misconstructed it to a ponderous *mauvais goût*. I thought the town of Jackson was an offense to gentle eyes."

"Wow, *doctor! Mauvais goût!* . . . I think my grandfather died of that."

"*Mauvais goût* is bad *taste* — *professor* — not bad *joints*."

"I never took the SAT French exam, Lucinda. I studied Latin."

"I don't believe you. Say something in Latin."

"*Ad nauseam*."

"Now we're back to Jackson."

"I think you were about to *leave* Jackson."

"I was looking for something I hadn't yet defined. I chose north as the most scenic way out of Jackson. As I drove through Yellowstone Park, my spirits soared and pressures plummeted. It was late September and most of the tourists were gone. I stayed a week at the Lake Hotel, walking the trails and trying to decide what to do with the rest of my life. Driving further north, leaving the park at Mammoth, I discovered Paradise Valley. It became my *Valley of Decision*. I booked into the Chico Hot Springs Lodge and the following day discovered *my* Shangri La further north, up along Mill Creek. A large but poorly maintained piece of land was available. It had more than a mile of the creek meandering through on its drop to the valley. I bought the property and immediately set about merging architecture and landscape with my determination to preserve forever every square foot of the land. I donated much of the land to the Nature Conservancy, and built the lodge and ranch buildings above the creek where they're hidden. Not feeling that *anyone*, much less myself, deserved to own such a place of peace, I called it the Arrogate Ranch."

"And then you went searching downstream for me?"

"I *accidentally* learned about a creepy neighbor who had built a cabin further downstream. A very quiet, fifty-plus-year-old hermit, who occasionally used the same person, Mavis, who I use at my place, to help him at his cabin."

"So I'm a *creepy hermit?*"

"*Very* creepy, as I think I'll learn tonight. Mavis described you as shy, easy to work for, often gone, about middlin' in keeping things where they belong. Except for the garage, where everything was in place around the current jewel of his kingdom — *Osprey*."

I was pleased Mavis left out the music room when describing the cabin to Lucinda, suggesting Mavis hasn't found it by accident or otherwise.

"Mavis told me you had a lot of art in the house and loads of fishing gear. And a few guns. But nothing about the Glocks, Sigs, and the CheyTac sniper rifle in the music room. She also told me about a beautiful, small, rescued sheltie that you sometimes left with her. She adores the pup and told me it would be a very lucky woman who was treated with the love that Wuff received."

"*Very* lucky. I feed Wuff on time and clean up her poop. What more could a lady companion want?"

"I won't even begin to answer that."

We reached my cottage and went up the dozen stairs. Inside Lucinda pushed me into a single, comfortable, leather chair, handed me a glass of Gentleman Jack, pulled a kitchen chair in front of me, turned it backwards, and straddled it so her knees were touching mine. Then said, "OK *creep*, talk."

"Lucinda . . . I'm dragging skeletons; they're rattling in my subconscious. Actually they're not *mine*, at least not *Macduff's*. What I tell you, *I* don't fully understand. Most of all, I dread putting you at risk."

"Talk, Macduff."

I began talking — emotion leading thought — having no idea where my words would lead. Maybe I wasn't doing it for Lucinda. Maybe it was personal therapy. A secular confessional. But at least I began.

"I'm wanted by some people. They will kill *you* without hesitation or regret if they find us together. And they'll kill me — much more slowly and with insatiable pleasure. You know a little about Isfahani, but not very much about my time in Guatemala, nor about a man named Juan Pablo Herzog. He makes

Isfahani look ready for sainthood. Isfahani apparently isn't dead. Juan Pablo is very much alive. What these two would do to us is unimaginable." I sat back and breathed deeply.

"Don't stop."

I told her the whole story about Juan Pablo, including the carnage at the cemetery, the beating he gave me in the hotel room in Guatemala, and my return to Washington. But not about his recent entry into the U.S., and possible involvement in rigging my cabin with explosives.

"I've done some things I was asked to do by our government . . . *noblesse oblige*, perhaps. . . . Macduff Brooks was fashioned from the remains of Maxwell Hunt by some government people in D.C., around a conference table, in early May almost four years ago."

"*Are* you in the witness protection program?" she asked, confirming that her hunches were right.

"Something similar."

That was a tough question. Her next two were more so. "Are you Ben Roth?. . . Are you a professional assassin?"

I knew what she meant. . . . Had I shot Isfahani, and do I shoot people for a living, with guiding merely a cover?

"I never killed anyone as Macduff Brooks until I shot Isfahani. *If* he's dead. We made it look as though Israel's Mossad agent, Ben Roth, did the shooting. But I *wanted* to kill Isfahani. . . . I was willing to go to that extreme because one of his targets was your building. That made dealing with him easy, as though he were holding a gun to your head and I had a chance to kill him before he could pull the trigger."

"If you hadn't known me, would you have shot him?"

"I think about that. But I can best focus on *him* by imagining him trying to kill *you*."

"You told me in Florida about the float near Jackson when your client was shot. Was that killing related to you as Macduff Brooks? Or as Maxwell Hunt?"

"*That* killing occurred two years *after* I became Macduff. I'm pretty sure the shot was meant for me. The Teton County Sheriff's Office continues to believe the shot was intended for Ander Eckstrum. I've never tried to dissuade them. Nothing has been resolved . . . the investigation is *ongoing*. Meaning, they haven't a clue who did it. But the FBI and the CIA believe it may have been arranged by Juan Pablo."

"Don't tell me anymore about the Guatemalans tonight. I do want to hear it. But, *please*, let me ask some questions about things troubling me. You've often spoken about the law. I *know* you're law trained. . . . You may not like what I've done. It's because of how I feel about you. Before I came here, I did some investigating. I knew you had some connection with Gainesville. I looked up an online list of *Gainesville Florida lawyers*. I found no one who seemed to be at all like you."

With unsteady hands rattling the ice, I poured us *each* a little Gentleman Jack.

She went on, "Next, I searched the University of Florida website. Specifically the law faculty. Again, nothing that helped. Shifting to *Gainesville Florida newspapers,* I tried *all law faculty at UF over last ten years.* That brought up a few obituaries. One had an accompanying article. It was about a law professor who suffered a fatal stroke in D.C. A law professor . . . who had a lot of experience abroad. . . . He was, as you've now told me — Maxwell Hunt. Shall I call you Max?"

I reached for my glass — to hide in the last half-inch of liquid bronze. I couldn't speak. If Lucinda could do this, could Juan Pablo? But he had to work the opposite way. He would try to find Macduff Brooks knowing only about Maxwell Hunt, rather than finding Hunt knowing Brooks, which is what Lucinda had been doing. I held onto the slimmest thread of hope that Juan Pablo thought the fatal stroke actually happened.

"OK," I conceded. "I'm law trained. After college, the Navy, and law school, I practiced briefly and began teaching. Soon after I met El." I walked over to my desk and pulled out a nameplate. Holding it up facing her, I said, "This was on my door at the law school for twenty years." The name plate read: "Professor Maxwell W. Hunt."

"I knew you were married and lost your wife. And about an expected child. I'm sorry. The photo of Maxwell with his obituary was handsome. I can see why El fell for you."

"Thanks a lot. Are you going to ask me to undergo more plastic surgery to again look like Maxwell?"

"If you did, you wouldn't have that nice moustache. Or look like Ben Roth. Can I have a rain check?"

She grabbed my hand and pulled me to the couch, where we sat closely and talked far into the night. Nothing remained hidden. She fell asleep close to dawn, her head against my chest.

Back in Manhattan, Lucinda immersed herself in work. As the days and weeks became large "X's" on her office wall calendar and summer approached, she was increasingly less fulfilled with New York City, and especially the investment business. Less and less she imagined retiring from her job at the firm's compulsory sixty-five; she wasn't sure she could endure the work even until fifty. But when she thought she wanted to spend more time with Macduff, regardless of his skeletons, ghosts, and nightmares, she wondered if she were a foolish romantic. And then she thought of days floating rivers and hiking along creeks. She wanted to fish more with Macduff. She often sat in her office, hoping he would call, but afraid to call him.

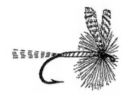

54

I WAS SITTING ON MY COTTAGE PORCH with a Heineken on a seventy-degrees early March evening, distressed over the latest about Juan Pablo, when I read of the untimely death of law professor and friend, Roy Palladio. He was struck by an errant baggage cart while walking to the plane at the Gainesville airport on the beginning leg of his trip to visit the mud huts of Mali, a long-time dream. He must have turned fifty-three or four this year, far too young for someone so active. Roy's funeral would draw many of the law faculty and dozens of town friends. I *had* to be there, whatever Dan or Malcolm might say. I'd wanted to call and say goodbye to Roy when I left D.C. for Montana — a foolish thought — and far too soon to breach my promises to Dan not to compromise my new identity. Roy died believing both El and I had predeceased him.

On the mid-March day of his funeral, I woke to a mysterious mist ghosting through the air and hanging in droplets from every leaf and branch on the salt marsh, obscuring the depth of vision and taking the horizon hostage. The mist slowed my drive to Gainesville. Arriving late I pulled in to the far end of a vacant lot next to the church where the service had started. I was downwind and an occasional organ note drifted through the narrow, open slit in my car window. I wasn't prepared to enter a group where Roy was known to so many persons — a lot of them also my acquaintances. I remained in my SUV and trailed the burial procession to the cemetery, a hundred feet behind the last car that burned its headlights to define its role. We drove through corridors of unfinished fog that draped the monuments in the cemetery, mingling with the tears many shed for their friend.

Avoiding the crowd surrounding Roy's gravesite, I knelt by a faded, marble marker, thirty yards distant, from where I watched a white pine box slowly lowered below the surface of his productive life. Ten years earlier, visiting a Shaker settlement in New Hampshire, he ordered the simple casket with all the care given to purchasing a custom-tailored suit.

Mourners at gravesites often stare off in disbelief and sorrow into personal memories of the deceased. A few such stares directed toward me by old friends made me wonder how much I resembled Max. But I was wearing mourning black, sunglasses, and a wide-brimmed black hat with a downward curl I'd worked into the brim. I strained to hear the final words of praise for this rare person. Turning to walk back to my car, another figure was kneeling, as had I, away from the burial site, but also facing the ceremony. When his head rose and turned briefly in my direction, I was startled and distracted. *It was Juan Pablo Herzog!* Reaching my car I looked back. He was standing by the grave marker where I had knelt, looking at the marker and then looking at me.

I remembered little of the drive home to my cottage, preoccupied with my sighting Juan Pablo. I poured a glass of Gentleman Jack and had an abysmally frightful, sleepless night.

55

W UFF AND I RETURNED to Montana in early May, pushing the weather because of some early scheduled floats. It was hard to leave my Florida marsh in the best of the spring. But Floridians soon will wake one morning to discover the humidistat had jumped abruptly to mid-ninety percent and would hug that range until fall.

I picked up accumulated mail in Pray on the final leg to my cabin. There was a letter from Maine, which I held until the evening, after removing some of the grime from *Osprey* that seeps into the garage each winter. At dusk, I cooked some bratwurst on my grill and half-filled a wine glass from a bottle out of a case that Mavis had placed in the cabin. It had a card that said, "Save at least one bottle for the night I arrive. Love, Lucinda." She's trying to plan a four-months leave from work — July through October. She especially wants to see the fall colors. I hope that they're second on her priority list. I plan to limit my guiding after the first of July.

"I guess I'm free to drink the other eleven bottles," I said to Wuff. She gave an approving nod. The case had a dozen different wines. I chose an Argentine *Malbec*. With Interpreti Veneziani playing one of their specialties, Vivaldi's violin concerto *l'inquietudine*, I sat before a fire and opened the letter:

Dear Macduff

Please don't think poorly of me for writing again, but there are some developments you might want to know about Park and me. I've sensed you believed I was having second thoughts about divorcing Park, but I assure you that's not been the case. The divorce went through last week. I'm once again Kathleen Macintosh.

Unfortunately, any property settlement with Park is going to be dragged out. My L.A. lawyers have discovered Park has more assets than we thought, spread over a dozen places with names like the Cayman Islands, Turks and Caicos, Bermuda and Liechtenstein. All places that seem to have laundry franchises owned by the very same international banks Park used. Those banks have names I've never heard of — have you? Like the Southeast Caribbean Bank & Trust, Ltd., and the Offshore Banking Company of Liechtenstein? Thus far IRS investigators have located about $18 million. Park is furious; his tax returns showed no evidence of any such accounts. I suspect that much of what he has will be forfeited. Anyway, I hope so. I got what I wanted — the divorce. I can do well enough on my own; I don't need a dime of his dirty money. But I'd like him to be parted from it.

Park has shown up here a couple of times and stalked me. He's ignored the restraining order. There's a local warrant out for his arrest, but he hasn't been found. He hasn't even been at our old house in L.A. for weeks. I worry about what he might do.

I met a guy here, Geoff Moor, who's been helping me and my parents with some estate planning. He's a former rugby player from York in England, recovering from two knee transplants that I told him he wouldn't have needed if he'd acted like most sensible Brits and played cricket. He's a law-trained LSE grad turned chartered accountant. Everybody likes him here; I'm not sure whether it's his natural charm or his accent. He's been a terrific help to us.

I worry about my parents. I was their little girl who came late to them, and they're now in their eighties. I'm living with them in the house where I was raised. My dad's parents built the house; it overlooks the harbor on a slight crest that rises from the rocky coast. The yard is filled with the most wonderful smelling juniper. My folks plan to pass the house on to me. I think they'd like to see me married, with children who'd someday inherit the property.

It's been a few years since our float. I still dream of doing it again. I'm trying to interest Geoff in fly fishing, but he has this idea that fly fishing is for wimps; rugby is for real guys. He showed me a DVD of a rugby game when the UK national team beat Argentina. He said he played "hooker" for the UK, which makes me a little suspicious. The video shows a group of big boys who never grew up, still wanting to wear team uniforms and play in the mud. I've got a lot of work to do before I buy him a fly rod.

Best

Kath

I'm sorry Kath's having trouble with Park. Some men don't understand a wife is supposed to be a partner, not a low-level, unpaid employee. Maybe that tendency increases with the wealth husbands accumulate. I wonder how Lucinda would view me if we were married. Guiding isn't exactly high paying. I could probably practice law in a small, low-profile firm. But I like being here in the summer and Florida in the winter — not a good arrangement for an investment broker *or* a lawyer. I don't know what would happen if I walked into the UF law dean's office and said, "Dean, I'm back and ready to work." That's apart from what would happen when Juan Pablo and Isfahani learned I was alive and available for pleasant reminisces, preluding an unpleasant finish. If I did try to go back, the first things I would buy are a cemetery plot and a pine box like Roy's.

Geoff sounds good for Kath, an admission tinged with a little jealousy. Losing nice gals has happened to me before — it could happen again. When it didn't with El, I captured a rainbow and never looked for the pot of gold. The rainbow was enough. But that rainbow no longer colors my sky. Anyway, I've got one great gal — Wuff. Long ago, in a speech someone, whose name I forget, said, "The one absolutely unselfish friend that man can have in the selfish world, the one that never deserts him, the one that never proves ungrateful or treacherous, is his dog. When all other friends desert, he remains."

When I finally put Kath's letter down, I'd finished the full bottle of *Malbec*. It's the first time I've done that in a long time. Around four, I woke with a horrible headache and a mouth like the Gobi desert.

I sat up and made a note to send Kath flowers.

56

SPRING AND EARLY SUMMER GUIDING proved alternately thrilling, freezing, hot, wet, windy, exhausting, and, I readily admit, a much better way to spend the summer than being in a law professor's office teaching a summer session.

Once the Yellowstone River cleared, more than a month after the stonefly frenzy ended, the local guides settled down to dry fly fishing, routinely using nymphs as droppers. I didn't drive through Yellowstone Park to fish the Snake in Wyoming as often as I wished. That drive takes several hours. Especially since our leaders in Washington decided adopting *free days* would make the national parks look *better used*. On those days, Yellowstone is overrun with visitors who don't believe the parks are worth the price of admission, unless that price is zero. I hadn't thought of free admission to our parks as another entitlement.

Although I didn't speed driving through the park, it could be frustrating to be behind an aging RV, driven by two fossilized retirees who stopped in their tracks every time they saw a buffalo, ground squirrel, or chipmunk within their declining range of sight, peering out of the RV's front window like two meerkats.

On one trip through Yellowstone, I watched a Mexican standoff between a Winnebago and three large Turkey Vultures which, before they were willing to lift off, were determined to finish some apparently tasty parts of unidentifiable road kill. The vultures held their ground until an irate skinhead in a black, sleeveless T-shirt, with WOLVES SUCK stenciled across the front, got off his noisy, low-rider Harley, placed his rusting Nazi helmet on the seat, and walked up to the feeding birds. He pulled out a .22 caliber automatic that was a look-a-like for a German Luger and emptied eleven cartridges in the general direction of the vultures. He killed one by a shot that ricocheted off the road, wounded a second, which began screeching and running in circles flapping two broken wings, and completely missed the third, which when the shooter was out of bullets, returned to the middle of the road to consume the remains all by itself. An eleven-year-old-girl with pigtails got out of a waiting car, walked up to the last buzzard and yelled "shoo." The bird lifted off and disappeared, letting the now hundred-plus vehicle column proceed. The little girl looked at the skinhead and said, "cool bike!" and walked back to her folks' car.

57

ON A DRIZZLY AUGUST AFTERNOON after picking Lucinda up after the airport, I asked, "Stop at my cabin for a late lunch?"

"What are you serving?"

"Nothing beyond my skill level."

"I'll take a chance."

At the cabin, Lucinda wandered down to the creek. She seemed reluctant to go inside. I realized the last time she was here, the cabin had been wired with explosives. I'd worked hard to eliminate every sign of that episode. I suggested she sit on the porch. The drizzle had stopped. It was seventy-two, some twenty degrees cooler than Manhattan had been yesterday.

As soon as I opened the porch door, Wuff bounded out to greet Lucinda as though she were a long-lost friend. Wuff gave a confidence with her *joie de vivre* that I failed to do with words. I went inside to work on lunch, while Lucinda played ball with Wuff in the yard. When Wuff had enough, she began to run circles around Lucinda, working her closer to the cabin. Wuff had doubled her herd to two.

"Macduff, you've trained Wuff to herd me to the cabin! Does she do it to all your guests?"

"Nope, only ones she approves of."

"She's herded me to the porch and now wants me to go into the cabin. Am I supposed to get her meal? It's only two in the afternoon."

"She isn't taking you to the kitchen. It's her nap time. She's taking you inside to the bedroom."

"The guest room?"

"Nope, *my* bedroom."

"Do you nap also?"

"Of course."

"So all three of us nap together?"

"Yes, it's called a Montana *ménage à trois.*"

I diverted Wuff's attention and seated Lucinda on the porch. The cabin could wait. The nap might have to wait even longer.

My lunch was fresh fruit, an assortment of roasted vegetables and a Montalcino Tuscan wine. Roasting vegetables sent my kitchen reputation soaring. While I set our table on the rear porch overlooking the creek, Lucinda placed a small digital camera on a railing, set the timer, and sat next to me, one arm tightly around me and her head tilted against my shoulder. She smelled much better than the roasted broccoli. The camera clicked; she retrieved it from the railing and, showing me the photo, said, "This is better than any I have in my apartment or office in Manhattan or here at the ranch. I think I'll blow it up, maybe make a wall mural at my lodge."

"You have a dozen, large, black and white photos of your ranch hanging on your dining room walls in Manhattan. Who took them for you? Someone in Bozeman?"

"No, someone from New York."

"I thought you might have had a professional come out. They're spectacular. The guy who took them could become the Ansel Adams of Montana."

"What do you mean *guy*? *Women* take photographs — like Margaret Bourke White — one of *your* favorites."

"Was it a gal?"

"Yes."

"Do you think I could hire her to take photos of my places?"

"Not a chance."

"Why? Is she dead?"

"Not when I last checked."

"When was that?"

"About four seconds ago."

"*You* took them with that little camera?"

"Not this one, but one not much bigger."

"You should be showing your work."

"Should? Or could?" she replied.

"Sorry. *Could.* When — *and if* — you're ready . . . I'd like to help."

"Thanks. *If* I showed, it would be under another name. You're not the only private person in this *duo*."

After lunch and the nap, on our drive up to her lodge she turned and said, "I want us to talk more tomorrow at your place, when I finish some work I promised a client. We've been together a *very* few times, even considering it's been nearly four years since we met. I'm not sure either of us was ready for anything serious for all that time, even with the romantic, balmy evenings at your Florida cottage. I want to continue our conversation we started in Florida. Could I come by your cabin?" Before I could answer, she dug her elbow in my ribs, and added, "Do I *really* need an invitation?"

"If Wuff concurs, you're invited. Breakfast at the Howlin' Hounds and back to my cabin after that?"

"Perfect."

That evening the temperature dropped enough to have a fire. Lucinda was busy working at her lodge. Wuff and I sat together on the sofa, watching and listening to our fire. I wondered what Lucinda wanted to talk about. And why at my cabin . . . she said it would be a "continuation" of our talk in Florida. I thought we'd finished the conversation there. She said we were a "duo." And implied we're past the time of not being "ready for anything serious." I haven't yet explained "probably." It should be an interesting conversation. I wandered from room-to-room looking at every wall, every item on every table and bookshelf, for signs that might disturb her. I didn't see any. But she views the world differently.

When Lucinda walked in the next morning after our breakfast, I cut some fresh fruit and we sat at the table in front of the window overlooking the creek. The temperature was twenty degrees lower than during lunch on the porch yesterday. I tried to second-guess Lucinda's impressions of the cabin. There were some grins that made me think I hadn't cleaned very well or left something on a table I hadn't intended. I wanted to show her the music room on better terms than she saw it when I was rehearsing, not for a music performance, but to kill Isfahani. I wouldn't subject her to any oboe solos. Mendelssohn's Violin Concerto was enough music — it played quietly in the background.

I knew I had to help Lucinda deal with what was troubling her. I didn't know how she felt about the attempted bombing last summer. We hadn't talked about it during our week together in Florida. It was never in the papers because the CIA handled the details. The local police were never informed. I wanted to tell Ken Rangley, but was overruled by Dan Wilson. The CIA continues to believe it was the work of Juan Pablo. I don't like what that suggests. Maybe they'll want me to move again.

Lucinda began. "I'm still trying to fit pieces into the Macduff Brooks puzzle. Usually, one begins a puzzle by sorting out all the straight edges and establishing the perimeter, then filling in where there are patterns to several connecting pieces. You're different. I started, at our first dinner at Thanksgiving, hearing about the more obscure pieces inside the edges of your life. And they were mostly *blank* pieces. I wanted to fill in the most important pieces. We talked in Florida about how little I knew about you. You told me a lot. For the first time I thought I knew you. I like it. Even more so just sitting with you yesterday. I want to enjoy being around you. Maybe for the next fifty years. I know you're full of stories."

Then the entrancing grin returned.

"And after fifty years, then what?" I asked.

"Ask me then . . . I may want a younger man."

I had to warn her about the gamble she faced in any future with me. Forgiving the past was not the same as confronting the future?

"Lucinda, some of my chapters don't have clear endings. I don't know for certain who was the target when Ander Eckstrum was killed. I've thought about it more since Florida. Kris wasn't the target. If Ander was, it leads to the obvious assumption that it was Islamic terrorists angered over his remarks. But I don't feel good about that. I think the terrorists have better targets to focus on. . . . That leaves *me* as the target. But there's a problem with that line of thinking. The shooter should've known *I* was the guide and sat in the middle . . . but he shot the person in the *front* seat. I don't think our wearing headgear was the reason. Guides sit in the middle, period."

"Is there anyone else *unrelated* to Guatemala and the Islamic groups who might have tried to kill you?" she asked. "Have you considered others in some of the countries you visited? You told me about your time in troubled parts of Yugoslavia: Serbia and Macedonia and Montenegro. Did you alienate anyone there?"

"With all the lectures I gave and the people I met, I must have said things that threatened someone's turf. But nothing significant enough to send assassins to the U.S. to hunt me down. And, they would be searching for Maxwell Hunt, not Macduff Brooks. As would Juan Pablo Herzog and Abdul Khaliq Isfahani."

"Let's consider only people you've met *since* your identity conversion. Anyone in Florida?"

She thinks logically, I think presumptively. I've never worked through who I might have irritated as *Mac*. I've *presumed* the shot was for Maxwell.

"I've kept a *very* low profile. I know only a few people in Florida as Macduff. My housekeeper Jen, of course, and her husband Jimmy and son Tom. There's the fellow who sold and maintains my flats boat. Plus the realtor, Janet, and a few guides. Other than those people, no one else."

"What about people here in Montana or Idaho or Wyoming? You know a *lot* of people."

"I do," pleased with being reminded of the number of friends I've made in the last five years. "I've paid all my bills. I know a lot of guides. I've become a kind of father figure to some of the young guides. I've tried hard to get along. There are the gals who do the shuttle services for my different floats. There's Sue Gomez at the Reel Food Café in Jackson. The owner of the Howlin' Hounds Café. Maybe one of those scruffy chic 'Jackson girls' you've described has the hots for me and I rebuffed her."

"We won't go into that," she said. "The only other group would be *clients*. Remember Park what's-his-name, your client from hell? Or any other of your 'three-percenters'?"

"I've only had the one certified obnoxious client, Park Salisbury." I hadn't told her about Kath's letters. I did now, but starting with the fact that she had met a nice guy, and it looked like they were a steady pair. "Salisbury's problems focus on money laundering, not murdering someone he knew only one day."

"Only *part* of one day," Lucinda observed. "And he spent most of the day walking through bushes and along gravel slopes. Plus you made him look *awful* in front of his trophy wife."

"*Lucinda*, Salisbury's in California. He's under a court order to stay away from Kath and Bar Harbor. He can't have held a grudge for all these years. He's *never* approached me."

"It's not 'all these years.' It's only been two since Ander was shot. And I think you said he was shot the year after you left Park on the river bank. So three years of festering hate?"

"If you're trying to scare me, you're succeeding. But I still suspect Salisbury has better sense. He apparently has a lot of money stashed away, and I doubt he'd trade that money for getting even with me and spending the rest of his life in jail."

Three hours passed. We were both tired. Lucinda hadn't mentioned our relationship; she was focused on my safety. She stayed the night. I didn't sleep much. I sat up in a chair next to my bed watching her bathed in as much accrued light as a half-moon acquiesced. She slept in trusting innocence.

58

BRUCE SAMSON CALLED from his fly fishing shop in Jackson two weeks later. "Can you take a float sometime in the next couple of days? I know you're probably packin' for Florida."

"Bruce, you know I don't think even a couple of hundred dollars tip is worth spending eight to ten hours with two obnoxious, wealthy, good-ole-boys from Texas, who want to boast about their money, drain a couple of dozen Buds, and carry on endless debate over which one is out-fishing the other, whether the Longhorns are going to beat the Aggies in two weeks, and who's sleeping with whose wife at their country club."

"It's a *single*, Mac. The guy's Thaddeus Calloway — from *Oregon*, not Texas. He's 'bout to begin buildin' a wooden drift boat — like yours. Wants to fish from a wooden drift boat and talk 'boat buildin'' on the float. I thought that'd interest you. But if you don't. . . ."

"Sorry to rant . . . the float does interest me. Is it a Montana Boat Builders drift boat he's interested in?"

"Yep. Calloway said he spoke to Jason Cajune up in your neck of the woods. Cajune suggested he try to book *you* for a float. Sounded to me like a float you'd enjoy."

"I'll check my schedule and get right back."

I wanted to ask Lucinda if she'd like to do the float, and perhaps some wade fishing on the streams in Yellowstone Park — weather permitting. She said fine. I called Bruce back.

"I'm clear the day after tomorrow. . . . I'll use *Osprey.*" Normally, new clients get my plastic boat. But Calloway's interest in wooden boats is why he booked.

I added, "Bruce, *one* condition. You've met Lucinda. I want to bring her with me. She wants to photograph a float. She'll sit in the back and won't fish. Along with my sheltie, Wuff. Agreed?"

"In case the guy's scared a dogs or dames, I'll ask him."

He soon called back. "Calloway's beside himself at floatin' with someone who's built one a Jason's boats. He asked me to tell you he'd enjoy seein' any photos taken durin' construction, if that's OK. He's never built a boat before. But he said he's pretty handy with tools. No problem 'bout bringin' Lucinda and Wuff. See you."

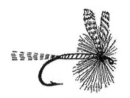

59

THE FOLLOWING MORNING I hooked up *Osprey* and called both my shuttle service and Sue Gomez in Jackson. Sue will make lunches for the drift. For three people and one dog. That's all Sue wants me to tell her — *how many* to make. Not *what* to make. She's pretty sensitive when her idea of a nice lunch gets tinkered with. She knows a few of my eating quirks, what Wuff likes, and always asks if the client has any food restrictions. I do like good wine. But *I* don't drink it when I'm guiding. I take one decent bottle of wine for my clients to split for lunch; I don't want drowsy clients throwing droopy lines with big hooks back and forth over my head. Hopefully *over* my head.

Lucinda and I had a relaxed day driving through Yellowstone and Grand Teton parks. In Yellowstone near Canyon Village, we stopped at an old favorite brook trout stream, an enchanting, corkscrew stream in a meadow hidden by woods, only fifty yards off the road. We caught a few small brookies on matching #18 BWOs.

As we walked back to the car, Lucinda leaned against me and said, "How many did I catch?"

"One or two."

"I caught *four*," she corrected.

"That's the sign of a great casting instructor."

"You were thirty yards away from me!"

"Do you know how embarrassing it is for a guide to have a gorgeous lady friend along for the ride . . . who out-fishes him?" I never tell her I get more pleasure from watching her catch one than my catching a dozen.

"You won't be fishing in *Osprey*. You have to row. And find us a lot of fish."

"How do you think Calloway will feel if you out-fish *him*? He's paying for the full-day float."

"Maybe not so good. Wuff and I will sit in the back and be very well behaved. Like that lady on your flight to Denver years ago who you told me about. I'll sit demurely, with my hands in my lap. Do you have some white gloves I can wear?"

"Don't remind me." But it did remind me that Lucinda has found room in her memory for some of the trivia of my past I've told her about.

Not long after we left Yellowstone Park and entered Grand Teton, we were settled in at Dornan's at Moose and walked up to a leisurely dinner at the Pizza & Pasta Company, on the outside deck. We ate Thai linguini and drank Spanish *Crianza Rioja* wine.

"Desert?" I asked Lucinda.

"No, but you have some. I *never* order desert."

The waitress appeared. "Desert?"

"One *crème brûlée*," I said.

"And you, Miss?"

"A spoon please."

"What's the spoon for?" I asked.

"I might want to *taste* your desert."

"You said you didn't *want* any."

"But I might want some of *yours*."

The waitress brought the *crème brûlée*. She placed it between us, a little closer to Lucinda. I was losing already. She gave us each a spoon, looked at me, and said, "good luck."

I had two spoonsful before Lucinda finished it. "Did you enjoy *my* desert?" I asked.

"Yes, thank you."

"Are there any deserts you *don't* like?"

"Wait and see."

We finished with Italian cappuccino. I ordered two without asking Lucinda. I got to drink all of mine. We ended the evening sharing a small snifter of port from the Douro Valley in northern Portugal, watching the sun set over Grand Teton and its supporting cast neighbors, confirming the range as one of the most spectacular in America. For a final moment the sun was a sizzling, fuzzy-edged mandarin orb, edges sitting on top of the mountain crest. Then the dusk slowly withdrew the sun behind the granite ridge, the sun's bottom flattening imperceptibly each few seconds, until it became a perfect half of its former self, then slowly diminishing to a quarter, an eighth, and finally a tiny dot of orange, which burst in a last struggle to survive. And suddenly it was gone. I shivered, either from the cold or sharing the fright of the earlier inhabitants, wondering if the sun was lost forever. Reappearing in the morning had to be a blessing and a mystery.

I asked Lucinda, "Do you think the sun will come back in the morning?"

She grinned and said, "I'm sleeping in. You tell me."

Dornan's is comfortable. No TV. There's a great view of the mountains from our porch. Nothing on TV could trump that. I'd been lucky to get us a cabin at Dornan's on short notice, but I stay there if possible. I'm still trying to convince them to take Wuff. No luck — yet. She'll sleep in the car. Maybe I should park it next to the manager's bedroom and tell her to howl like a wolf every hour.

In the morning, just before sunrise, I fed Wuff in the SUV and walked her. Lucinda was up when I returned. She made coffee and we huddled on the porch, wrapped together in a blanket, and watched the mountains begin to reflect the dawn's *earliest* light. There was a reddish glow to the sky.

"Macduff, this view is stunning. Breathtaking. Astonishing. Beguiling."

"Wow! I would have said, 'Oh, my! Good heavens! How 'bout that! Or maybe even zounds!' I bet you scored higher than me on the vocabulary part of the SATs. After all, you have a doctorate."

"Probably. But you score high with me." She grabbed my jacket sleeve and pulled me inside.

We didn't see it happen, but the sun reappeared in the east.

The cabin was hard to leave, but we had to meet Calloway in Jackson. The sunrise and clear sky were a silent recommendation of what the day should bring. But the red sky made me think of the old saying: "Red sky at night, sailor's delight; red sky at morning, sailor take warning." I wondered if "sailor" includes a drift boat rower.

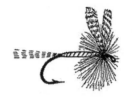

60

WE WERE EARLY ENTERING JACKSON to meet with Calloway, enough time to drive beyond the town square to Albertson's. I went to get two coffees; Lucinda went searching for sunscreen. As I opened a sugar packet for the coffee, my cell phone rang. It was Huntly Byng at the Teton County Sheriff's Office. We hadn't talked in months. Hopefully he was closing in on who shot Ander, who ironically was killed less than a quarter mile upstream from where we would start the float in a couple of hours. Nothing could make me feel any better than doing the float knowing *that* mystery was solved.

"Well, we've got trouble," Byng began. His tone wasn't encouraging. I took the coffee to a small table in the corner, where I wouldn't be overheard. "A lady called us yesterday afternoon, just before dusk. She wouldn't leave her name. But she doesn't understand modern communications. Her call was from a cell phone registered in the name of a wealthy Jackson real estate broker. But he wasn't the one who called. We used new voice identification. It was the voice of a prominent Jackson woman, also in real estate, twenty years younger than the guy. She's not his wife. We did some more checking. The two were in Yellowstone Park for two days. The lady didn't want it known who she was with. I know there's no property for sale inside the park. She was showing off something other than real estate. If we need to I can bring them both in. Coming home the lady said they decided to drive through Grand Teton Park and visit the old Bar B-C Ranch. They bounced over the old, rough RKO road that runs out to the bluff above the river. The lady wanted to do some photography, looking down on the old Bar B-C cabins. She's a very competent landscape photographer. When she looked through her telephoto lens, she saw a man backing a motor bike out of one of the old Bar B-C buildings. Before he closed the door, she thought she saw a vehicle in the barn. The man took a pistol out of his belt and put it into a backpack. He took off on the motor bike, across the ranch and up the slope of the moraine, and disappeared. It concerned her and she called us."

"It sounds suspicious," I said. "Is it related to Ander's shooting?"

"*Possibly.* I went to the Bar B-C location last night. The lady was right. There were motor bike tracks. Inside a Bar B-C shed, we found a Jeep Wrangler with oversize tires. The Jeep had been stolen yesterday from a Jackson parking lot. There were several .30-30 cartridges in an empty rifle case that had once been white. We disabled the Jeep. . . . Could you come down from Montana?"

"I'm at Albertson's in Jackson right now. I have Wuff and my Mill Creek neighbor Lucinda with me. We're heading to pick up a client at Bruce Samson's fly fishing shop and then to Deadman's Bar to float."

"*You mean your floating Deadman's Bar to Moose today?*"

"That's right. I'm doing a guy a favor. Lucinda and I thought of coming down here soon anyway before we both head east. Having a client makes it a paying trip."

"Well, I don't like the idea of you two floating the Snake today. We *will* have the area covered with SWAT team snipers.

We'll see if the guy with the motor bike returns for the Jeep. I don't like thinking of you or Lucinda, or your client, as bait. Who's your client?"

"His name's Thaddeus Calloway. He's from Oregon. Wants to build a drift boat and asked to float with a guide who uses a wooden boat."

"Do me one favor, Mac — drop by my office to pick something up before you stop at Bruce's shop. Better yet, park in the public lot north of the square, where a lot of you guides park. I'll look for you there."

Lucinda joined me at the table. "I leave you for ten minutes and you look bewildered. You OK?"

"Fine. Trying to think through the day. Thanks for remembering the sunscreen." While we sipped our coffee, I picked up a crumpled *USA Today* newspaper someone had left on the table. I happened to open to the page that has one trivial news item from each state. It's interesting to see what different brief state items the editors chose to print. Since it's not *The New York Times*, I guess it doesn't have to be "all the news that's *fit* to print," just that *fills* the space.

The Wyoming piece was about new gas drilling leases for the Pinedale area. Montana's contribution mentioned a rancher who shot three wolves who were "threatening" his livestock. And in Florida, four Miami Dade County officials had been indicted. That's probably fewer than the number last month. I glanced through the rest of the states and stopped at Maine. I couldn't believe what I read; I was shaking and spilled the coffee refill Lucinda had set in front of me:

MAINE. Police continue a statewide search for the killer of Bar Harbor attorney Kathleen Macintosh. Ms. Macintosh and a friend, Geoff Moor, were murdered while biking on the Acadia National Park summit road. They were shot as they approached the top. The police believe the killer used a high-powered rifle.

"*What* are you reading?" Lucinda asked.

"Two people were killed in Acadia National Park in Maine a couple of days ago. The parks aren't the serene and safe places we think they are. It reminded me of Ander's shooting, also in a national park."

I didn't want her to worry. I'd told her a few days before about Kath and Geoff. If I'd developed a relationship with Kath, I could have been there with her, instead of Geoff. Kath was building a new life that might have included me if she hadn't met Geoff. And, if I hadn't met Lucinda. Now, it's over for Kath. I hope their killer is found quickly.

61

BYNG WAS WAITING FOR US in the Jackson town parking lot, looking unusually tired. I introduced him to Lucinda. He already knew Wuff.

"Lucinda, I need a couple of minutes with Macduff." Lucinda nodded with a squint that reflected her curiosity. Byng and I walked a couple of cars away. He removed a Glock pistol from his jacket pocket and slipped it into mine.

"Loaded. One in the chamber, ten in the clip. Ever handle one?" Byng said, quietly. He wasn't looking at me as he talked, but glancing quickly and nervously across the parking lot.

"You're a little melodramatic," I said, "A pistol isn't going to help if there's a sniper a hundred yards away. Or do you think someone in another drift boat might shoot at me?"

"Don't put the gun in one of your boat guide-storage compartments. Have it in your jacket pocket where you can reach it. *Do* it!"

I agreed only because he was determined. No gun, no float.

"By the way," Byng added, "I checked out Thaddeus Calloway. He's authentic. Lives in Oregon, in a town along the Deschutes River. He's originally from one of the Carolinas. Calloway's a master carpenter. He should have little difficulty building a drift boat. He's an avid and skilled fly fisherman. Solid reputation in his town. Churchwarden. Little League coach."

Byng left, and Lucinda and I walked to the fly shop to meet Calloway. He was finishing paying Bruce for the day's trip. That means a couple of hundred dollars as my share and, hopefully, an additional tip directly from Calloway. It'll cover our expenses for the two days. I looked at it as a paid holiday for us before we split and returned to New York and Florida.

Thaddeus Calloway was magnificent! Except for his girth, exactly my image when I envision Jim Bridger, the legendary 1800s mountain man who most historians agree discovered the upper Snake River, and maybe Jackson Hole. He got there long before the first "Jackson girl" arrived to strip him of his beaver pelts. Calloway sported collar-length, jet-black hair, a dense moustache and sideburns that merged with a four-inch ragged beard. He wore a weather-stained, wide-brimmed leather hat, with a dozen enameled pins in the brim from places he'd fished, mostly Oregon and Washington rivers. His eyes were hidden behind sunglasses. Jim Bridger didn't wear sunglasses or have little fishing logo pins. Scalps were more the fashion of his day.

Calloway had arrived ready to fish — waders, boots, and vest already on. His vest size has to be a triple XL. He must weigh 280 or more; I wonder if I'm up to handling that amount of weight. *Osprey* weighs a little over 350. The three of us add almost another 600. And then there's Wuff. I hope she's not the straw that breaks *Osprey's* back. I'm going to be rowing a thousand pounds. I should add an obesity surcharge to Calloway's bill.

In stark contrast to his size was his voice — a quiet, soft, southern accent. He was gracious being introduced to Lucinda, scratched Wuff in all the right places, and loved *Osprey* as soon as he saw her.

"Macduff," he said, "Ah'm lookin' farrd to buildin' one of these here boats. Ah'm verah sorry if ah'm a pest durin' the float. Ah've got lots of questions to ask 'bout buildin'."

Calloway showed me some photos he took on his cell phone at Jason's shop in Paradise Valley. "When do you plan to start building?" I asked.

"Ah've ordered the plans. They should be in Or'gon in 'bout a week."

"Thaddeus, I'll send you a disc I've made — hundreds of photos. I took several after each day of work on *Osprey*."

"That'd be most gracious of y'all."

Talking about *Osprey* comes easy. I've been stopped at dozens of gas stations when towing the boat. People walk over and ask questions, which I answer, until others waiting for gas lose patience and honk.

Calloway had left his car at the back part of the public parking lot. We all got in my SUV and headed for Deadman's Bar. I've floated Deadman's Bar to Moose only twice since El's death fourteen years ago — with John Kirby and then a week later with Kath and Park Salisbury. I was a little anxious driving down the steep incline to the Deadman's Bar launch. I tried not to think about El or guess where the sniper hid and shot Ander.

Calloway rigged his nine-foot five-weight Loomis rod, which held a 5/6 Ross reel — both good choices — while Lucinda and I loaded gear into *Osprey* and slipped her into the river. I set the anchor, asked Calloway to make sure the boat didn't drift off without us, and went off to park the trailer. My shuttle service will have the SUV and trailer waiting for us at Moose.

When I lifted the SUV's tail gate to see if I'd forgotten anything, which is often the case, there was a wrapped package. Plain, brown paper with a piece of Scotch tape holding a single wildflower and a note: "Macduff — the other half of the pair, Love, Lucinda." I opened the package. It was a Simms Guide jacket. The version with Simms' signature burnt orange panels. It fit perfectly. Only because I'd promised Byng, I slipped the Glock into the right side pocket.

On the other side of the note, Lucinda had written, "I have one too, Macduff. Even if we don't catch any fish, we'll look great together!" I turned around. There she was. Cheshire cat grin, in her matching jacket.

"You *can't* wear that jacket, Lucinda." I said.

"Why not? It fits perfectly. It's *beautiful!*"

"That's the *Guide* model. *I'm* the guide!"

"But I catch more fish," She responded.

The truth hurts. And she needs the jacket. I hadn't outfitted her very well for the changes in weather on fall floats. She's always borrowing my dry-bag clothes half-way down a river. The new jacket's perfect over her sweaters. We were beginning to feel the front edges of a cold spell, and on the drive home through the park we might even confront one of the occasional early October nights when a couple of inches of snow fall.

"Lucinda, do y'all fish? And please call me Thad," said Calloway, as we stepped into the boat. He sat in front, leaving Lucinda and Wuff the rear. Calloway was paying for the float, and it was thoughtful of him to think of her fishing. "Ah surely hope y'all will. It's such a fine day, and ah'm sure Macduff will put us both onto some splendid trout."

"Thanks, Thad," Lucinda answered. "I'd like to fish a little, maybe on this first run, and later when we stop at one of the gravel bars for lunch."

There's a productive, quarter-mile run immediately after launching at Deadman's Bar. Half-way down the run, we had on a double. Floating a #12 Chernobyl Ant, Calloway quickly landed a sixteen-inch cuttbow, the increasingly prevalent and controversial cross of cutthroat and rainbow. Lucinda, casting her favorite Adams Trude, hooked a true Fine-Spotted Snake River Cutthroat about a foot long. Not the size of Calloway's, but Lucinda produced the prettier smile.

We set up for lunch along the same bank we'd stopped at on my client from hell trip. Despite that day it's my favorite stopping point because the sand and gravel bar provide good holding ground for trout. Clients can fish while I'm performing wonders in the "kitchen," meaning unwrapping whatever Sue Gomez had made for us.

Lucinda cast her Adams Trude off the bar — her graceful movements reminded me of Park Salisbury's wife Kath. Thaddeus Calloway didn't remind me a bit of Park Salisbury. Calloway waddled along the bank and had trouble when he caught something because he couldn't lean over with his enormous stomach.

While I was cleaning up from lunch, my cell phone rang. I usually wait until after a float to answer calls, but Calloway had gone off into the brush to relieve himself, so I opened the cell phone's lid. It was Jason Cajune at Montana Boat Builders.

"I have the lightweight, carbon-fiber spare oar you ordered, Mac. Do you want to pick it up, or shall I drop it off at your cabin?"

"I'll stop by and pick it up next week. I want to talk to you about how to rig a better tie down for *Osprey*. I'm using a juryrigged strap that's too narrow. It works, but it's slow. Lucinda and I are on the Snake, above Moose. My client is the guy from Oregon who was at your shop yesterday and ordered plans."

"Mac, *I'm* the only one who writes up orders for plans and finished boats. I haven't sold either in the last month for the Guide model. What's his name?"

"Thaddeus Calloway," I answered.

"Oh, yeah. Nice guy," said Jason. "He drove in here early yesterday. We talked about him building a sixteen-foot Guide. I showed him one I finished last week and another about half completed. He snapped a bunch of pictures and went on his way. He asked about the cost of plans and a building-time estimate, but he never placed an order."

"He might not have had his check book with him," I commented. "You'll be hearing from him; he loves the boat. He was even willing to wait a few days to float with me because he wanted to float with someone who had built a wooden drift boat, and specifically one of your designs. But, we get some strange clients, Jason. Calloway's a character, a real live mountain man — beard, moustache, scraggly hair — he must weigh nearly 300 pounds. Kind of a contrast with his soft southern accent."

"Macduff, he *was* big. But I didn't recognize any southern accent. Got another call — talk to you later. And see you next week. Drop by anytime."

62

Wondering whether Jason was confused about Calloway, I started to clean up the lunch table. My cell phone rang. It was Dan Wilson in D.C.

"I know you're in Jackson Hole, Mac. What are you doing?"

"Floating the Snake with a client. We're about to start the afternoon's float down to Moose. What's up?"

"Not good. We almost caught up with Juan Pablo this morning. *In Jackson!* But he's gone . . . again. He spent most of yesterday at the Jackson Hole Historical Society museum, going through the newspaper records from the week El died! Our agents have just checked what he read; there's nothing that would help him find you. But he *may* be in town. I'm going to have an agent join you at the end of your float. He'll see you get on the road back to Montana safely. I'll call you if I hear anything new."

If Juan Pablo is here checking papers when El died he likely hasn't learned about my new identity — yet. But I don't want him to see me. I'll make sure I keep sunglasses on, and try to look like just another local guide. I'll feel better when we finish the float, hook up with one of Dan's colleagues, and are on the road home to Mill Creek. I'm not sure how much I'll tell Lucinda. I haven't told her about Juan Pablo being in Denver recently.

63

WHEN YOU PACK UP AFTER LUNCH and begin the afternoon portion of a float, you know pretty much how the day's going to turn out. I know Thaddeus Calloway was pleased with his day. He'd caught a half-dozen trout and asked question after question about building *Osprey*. Lucinda was taking photos. Wuff was content with her treats Sue Gomez packed with the lunch, and will spend the afternoon sacked out on the floor between Lucinda and me.

Thirty minutes after we resumed the float, my cell phone rang again. I looked at the screen not intending to answer the call. But it was Huntly Byng. Alone, I use the speaker, but not in front of a client. I hoped Byng and his deputies had learned more about the person sighted yesterday at the Bar B-C.

"Hi, this is Macduff."

"Where are you?" asked Byng.

"An hour shy of the Bar B-C. Beautiful day! What's up?"

"Listen to me, and don't say anything other than an occasional 'sure' or 'OK,' but *nothing* else. And don't call me by anything official. Is Thaddeus Calloway with you?"

"Sure is."

"Brace yourself! Stay calm and don't act surprised. Your client is *not* Thaddeus Calloway. He's *Park Salisbury!* Kathleen Macintosh's former husband. Those names are familiar to *you*, but you never mentioned Park Salisbury when we were investigating Ander's death. We learned yesterday that Kath Macintosh was killed in Maine. Along with a male friend. The Maine state police found Salisbury's name and a Newport Beach, California, address on a letter he apparently forgot to mail that dropped down between the car seats of a rental car he returned in Portland. The rental agency found the letter, a map highlighting a route from Portland to Bar Harbor, and an Acadia National Park brochure about the hiking trails. They'd heard about the murders in Bar Harbor and called the police. The police learned that Salisbury flew from Maine to Jackson Hole after the shooting. That put him here four days ago. There's an APB out on him. We ran his name and discovered he was arrested here a few years ago for killing fish in the Snake River.

"When I saw you this morning I was concerned about Salisbury being in the area and up to no good, but not being after *you*. I'm sorry I didn't mention it. After you left to do the float I ran some more checks. I learned from the park police who arrested Salisbury three years ago that *you* were the guide Salisbury floated with that day. Well, that made me think about a link to Ander's death. I speculated Salisbury might be here to do another shooting on the river. Especially since the lady's telephone call yesterday about the man at the Bar B-C. I'm *now* assuming Salisbury killed Ander Eckstrum two years ago while trying to kill you. I really screwed up on this one, Mac. I never considered Salisbury as the killer. He was nothing more than an obnoxious fisherman arrested for killing a fish, not shooting a man. Salisbury had no motive to kill Ander. But apparently he did with you."

I was concerned Byng was talking too long for me to give only a few "yes" or "no" answers. I interrupted, pretending I was talking to Bruce at the fly shop, but increasingly nervous about Salisbury, who had turned around from watching the river ahead to watching me.

"Sure Bruce, I can do another float tomorrow. Tell me about the clients . . . what they expect. Especially where they want to float." That might buy some time so Byng could tell me more.

Byng understood, and continued, "A few pieces of the puzzle have only fit together in the last few hours. If you remember, people who saw a car leave Deadman's Bar soon after Ander was shot were not sure whether it was a Toyota or a VW. The Toyota that burned in Pinedale threw us off any further thinking about a VW. I looked at the Eckstrum investigation records after I left you this morning, and read the statement by the person who thought the car might have been a beige VW Beetle convertible. Another thing, last summer, when you told me — in strict confidence — about your cabin being rigged with explosives, you mentioned seeing a car parked when you entered your drive. I've just talked to the Montana State Police. They stopped a beige VW convertible beetle for speeding in Paradise Valley, about the time you returned to your cabin and discovered the explosives. The VW had California plates. The police issued a ticket to a Parkington Salisbury. After I left you in the parking lot this morning, I saw a *beige VW Beetle convertible* in the public parking lot, five lanes over from where I gave you the Glock. It has California plates — registered to Salisbury. Salisbury apparently drove it here and flew to Maine from Jackson. Now we think he may use the stolen Jeep. I never should have let you go on this float. But you're so damned stubborn. We don't know why Salisbury decided to *float* with you because we assumed the way he killed was with a rifle from a long distance. We thought he intended to shoot someone from the river bank near the Bar B-C Ranch, much the way he shot Ander thinking it was you because you switched hats. Something made him change his mind about shooting from the bank this time. Maybe he's afraid he'll shoot the wrong person again. But the land location provided an advantage; he might get away quickly from the land, like he did before. It's a different matter to be on a boat. He can't float down the river for a couple of hours and escape. He's *desperate* Mac."

Salisbury was sitting three feet in front of me staring at me with the concentration of a stalking mountain lion. Byng was talking a long time, but telling me what might save our lives.

"Mac, the river's banks are staked out. No one else has showed up. I'm pulling in as we speak behind a cabin not far from the barn at the Bar B-C where the Jeep was left yesterday. We took prints, but we didn't learn until this morning that they match Salisbury's. I'm sending deputies along the river, hopefully all well hidden."

If there's a shooting from the land this time, it won't be Salisbury doing the shooting. It'll be Byng's SWAT team snipers trying to stop the man sitting in front of me.

Guides don't stay on the phone talking when they're with clients on a river, unless it's an emergency. Salisbury didn't like the length of my call. He reeled in his line, set his rod down, took off his hat, and calmly drew a Glock from his pocket. When he removed his sunglasses, his eyes gave him away. I had seen those eyes stare at me with hatred three years ago when I shoved off the bank with Kath, leaving Salisbury to walk out. With his sunglasses on when I met him today, he was just another client preparing for a float.

He unzipped his jacket and began to remove padding, tossing piece by piece into the river. The sideburns, moustache, and beard all followed the padding. He wasn't a mountain man. He was Park Salisbury, ready to kill Lucinda and me a few days after killing Kath and Geoff. What troubled me most was the Glock Salisbury held. It was like mine. But his was in his hand pointed at me. Mine was in my pocket hidden behind a zipper.

Salisbury hadn't uttered a word. He stared transfixed with anger. I was still on the phone. Some people get a last meal. I was getting a last phone call.

I broke into Byng's warning, still pretending I was talking to Bruce Samson. "Bruce, I think I better talk to you later — my client needs a little help." I set the phone down on top of my gloves on the guide box, but I didn't turn the phone off.

Quick glances behind me told me Lucinda was no longer casting, she had turned forward and could see Salisbury's Glock. She laid down her rod, blew into her cupped hands as though to keep warm, and slowly put her hands into the pockets of her new jacket. I didn't see her right hand close over another Glock Byng had placed in *her* jacket pocket when it was in the SUV.

Everything was becoming clearer. I've spent four years looking over my shoulder for a shooter who was trying to kill Maxwell Hunt, living with the belief that my identity had been compromised. It hadn't. Juan Pablo and Abdul Khaliq weren't players on the Snake River — not today.

I hadn't given a thought to Salisbury being a murderer. Lucinda had pressed me on it, but I'd ignored her. I should have analyzed some clues better. Kath's letters repeatedly told me what Salisbury was like, but I always considered them with the proverbial grain of salt. They were written by an emotionally distraught woman who was being harassed and terrified by an estranged and vengeful husband.

Salisbury had stripped down to more manageable dress. The gun was in his hand, but he hadn't fired. He must want something. Maybe to scare me before he shoots. I've *been* scared for four years. Now I'm terrified. Salisbury had shot the man in the Stetson thinking it was me. Now he sits an arm's length away with a Glock that gives him eleven more tries. I have eleven tries too, but to paraphrase somebody: "A Glock in hand is worth two in the pockets."

Wuff's asleep behind me. Lucinda's holding her arms tight to her sides with her hands in her jacket pocket. She must be mired in grim thoughts about what I've done to her. She would have been killed if the cabin had blown. Or maybe if Isfahani had flown into her building. Now, Salisbury's about to empty his Glock into the two of us.

The only hope is that one of Byng's men will take out Salisbury before he decides to fulfill his paranoid determination for revenge. He's eliminated Kath — and her innocent guy. Now he wants me — and my innocent gal.

Salisbury's going to die. Unanswered is how many of us go down with him.

64

I HAD TO DELAY SALISBURY. I could see ahead how the river split. Carefully, I positioned *Osprey* so we entered the more dangerous side channel to the right — the one closest to the Bar B-C Ranch. It's where I vowed never to float again, where El was lost. Salisbury hadn't turned his head to look where we headed, he must assume I won't choose a channel we can't get out of.

Salisbury doesn't know what I know — that the pile of trees El and I hit fourteen years ago has been added to year-after-year, waiting for some fifty-year rarity when the whole river's scoured clean in a flood, and then the strainers begin to build again. If I can send *Osprey* straight into a strainer I'll lose *Osprey*, but I may save Lucinda. From her rear seat she might be thrown clear of the strainer. Salisbury wouldn't fare as well. He's in the bow seat, our figurehead. He'll be the first to hit the strainer's limbs. After that we'll take our chances. If that isn't rational thinking, maybe the circumstances excuse questionable judgment. But what are my choices? What might delay Salisbury? . . . Conversation?

"Killing us won't help you," I tried. "You have *no* place to go. Huntly Byng will be after you with a flock of deputies before you reach Moose. If you abandon the boat, they'll track you with a copter. This is a pretty irrational attempt. Did you think you could kill me here on the river and get away with it?"

When he finally spoke it was without any southern accent. It was the angry voice I'd heard years before, screaming at me from the river bank as I floated off with Kath. "I *will* get away with it. . . . She dies first," he said, nodding toward Lucinda. "Then the mutt, just because it's yours. *You* go slowly Macduff. You're the cause of all this. First a slug in your shoulder. So you're a little disabled but can still travel with me. We get out at the Bar B-C Ranch site. I stole a Jeep and left it in one of the old barns. I don't need the VW anymore. With you as a hostage we'll be over the Grassy Lake Road, through the Tetons into Idaho. I have a jet there. Another bullet to make you bleed and keep you weak and quiet in the plane. You'll go with me to a refueling strip in Central America. That's where you end the trip. I'll be in Brazil in a day from there, where I've hidden seventy-million for me and another five-million for bribing government officials. A Brazilian wife I married before I divorced Kath is waiting for me."

Salisbury's beyond angry. Paranoid. Irrational. Because I didn't close the cell phone when I put it down, hopefully Byng has been listening. If he has, he should be screaming at his men to shoot. I wish Salisbury would stand up and point the gun at me. It might be all Byng's men need to fire. But Salisbury had lowered the gun. It was resting in his lap. Out of sight from the riverbank.

My cell phone began to beep, the battery was low. The beeping told Salisbury the phone had been left on while he was talking to me. Telling me his plans. Now, Byng knows what Salisbury was planning. And Salisbury's aware that someone knows. Salisbury lifted the Glock, said, "Goodbye, *Bruce,* or whoever you are," and put a bullet through the middle of my phone. My first thought was that the warranty had expired a week ago. That's why I'm not much good in protecting people on my boat: my focus tends to be a bit abstract.

Salisbury pointed the Glock at my head. "Macduff, maybe I should put a bullet through that gold Maine lobster pin on your hat." The pin must remind him of our float with Kath. It was her pin; she'd sent it to me with one of her letters. I had planned to retire it from service before I had to explain it to Lucinda, and replace it with a little gold Florida alligator.

No more than thirty yards from the strainer, beyond Park's shoulder, I could see a shuddering, long limb prominent among the strainer's branches — pointed toward us. Its jagged tip was two feet above the water bouncing around like a prize fighter with one arm extended, feeling his opponent before he closes in for the knockout. At thirty feet Salisbury heard something behind him. It was the noise a strainer makes when its parts are bounced and slapped against tons of pressure from the water's flow. He jerked around, saw the strainer almost upon us, turned quickly back again, and pointed the Glock at my chest. Taking me hostage was no longer his intention.

I let the oars go and reached into my pocket for the Glock. Suddenly it sounded like Omaha Beach on D-Day. Shots came from in front of me. More shots came from the bank. And even more from behind me. Wuff and I were the only ones not in the firefight.

Salisbury had fired off four rapid shots. I counted them, but hardly heard the fourth. His first two shattered my left shoulder, tore through muscle and ligaments, and exited in adjacent holes, blood spurting like severed irrigation pipes. My head dropped, and I saw another flush of blood as the third bullet entered my leg at an angle a few inches above my right knee. I didn't know where the fourth went. It either missed me, or I was no longer feeling the impact. Three out of four is pretty poor shooting at this range, but I didn't want to tell Salisbury that. He had six bullets left, and it was the dealer's choice. This time the dealer chose a straight — Salisbury aimed at my mid-section and got off three more quick shots. Now I know what it's like to take three quick blows from a heavyweight champion. Strangely, although the shots knocked me back, I didn't see any more blood.

I wasn't sure how, but my right hand pulled the Glock from my pocket and aimed it at Salisbury. What little consciousness was left was trying to communicate with my right hand. Yelling at it to shoot. Finally, I got off three quick shots before Salisbury's next shot smashed into my gun hand. It was noisier than the New York Philharmonic ending Tchaikovsky's *Overture of 1812* with full cannon fire. But no church bells. If I'd heard bells, I'd know they were for me. I had a blurry view of Salisbury tipping to the left. Falling slowly or I was seeing in slow motion.

In a fraction of time, he'd been hit in his chest by bullets from behind me, by several more in his left arm and shoulder apparently from my gun and, finally, by several large caliber bullets from both shores — the only one I saw was a shot from one of Huntly Byng's snipers entering under Salisbury's right eye, expanding and blowing through the left side of his skull in a shower of emulsified bone and brain. But the *coup de gras*, more for show than effect, came as the jagged limb of the strainer I'd aimed for caught his back dead-on three inches below his neck, crushing vertebrae, pushing through flesh, organs, and bone, the limb exploding out of the front of his chest and coming to rest a foot in front of my face. Salisbury may have had more bullets remaining, but there wasn't enough of him left to pull the trigger.

The collision with the strainer twisted *Osprey*, broke the right gunnel and tossed her off to the side, luckily past the strainer, leaving Salisbury's body hanging from the killer limb. Blood was gushing from around the limb, from the side of what a few moments ago had been his face, and from two small holes in his chest near the protruding limb. His arms dangled and his boots were barely under the surface of the water, the current dragging his legs downstream a few feet before they flipped back. He was a human sweeper.

I struggled with consciousness. I had to know what was happening behind me. I twisted as I slumped back, turning just enough to see Wuff lying across Lucinda's lap. Wuff was bleeding. Not moving. Not even whimpering. Her eyes were shut. Behind her, Lucinda lay back spread-eagled across the top of the transom, holes in her new Simms jacket just where her heart was. But no blood on her chest. Her head hung back out of sight. She had to be bleeding badly from somewhere, the current alongside *Osprey* flowed deep-red. Her right arm dangled in the boat. Her hand held a pistol. She must have fired the first two shots that hit Park in the chest. Her left arm was holding Wuff's body.

I took those images down into an abyss. My last thoughts were that I didn't have any last thoughts. If unconscious bodies can cry, mine was bawling. Lucinda and Wuff were gone. Like El. And Ander. Maybe *if only* I had. . . .

65

THIS TIME IT TOOK FOUR DAYS before I awoke in that same vacuous, white, Salt Lake City hospital room that I landed in when El died. When my eyes first opened, I saw the same generic, square, soundproofing panels on the ceiling where I had tried to count all the tiny holes during my last visit. I wasn't interested in counting anything this time. I hurt. A lot. I was on my back. Tubes disappeared under the covers. I didn't know where they went. Or what they did. Something was dripping into my arm from a bag hung on a metal hanger. Pill bottles were lined up on the side table. Wuff's blood-stained collar lay beside a vase of flowers on a table by the window. With a struggle to rise a few inches, that sent lightning strikes of pain through my body but at least told me I had feeling in some parts I doubted were still attached, I could see the screen of a machine behind my head. A bright line slid across the bottom producing an even series of little peaks. That was my heart. I watched the line for a while, praying it wouldn't begin to look like Kansas — flat and dead.

A nurse came in and saw I was mimicking consciousness. She called the on-duty resident. He arrived wearing the identifying M.D. garb — blue scrubs, stethoscope, and a name tag that said Jacob Levy, M.D. Dr. Levy was reading papers on a clipboard. I guessed it was a list of repairs performed during my second recall. My SUV has been recalled only once. Levy told me the doctors first operated on my wrist and shoulder. Then twice on my leg. They think they've finished. I'll be feeding from tubes for another day. My mid-section was bruised and sore. For some unexplained reason, Salisbury's last three shots hadn't penetrated.

The medical staff is convinced guiding in drift boats is a dangerous profession. Floating with me is a death warrant. With Huntly Byng's help, friends had brought in the two nine-foot oars from *Osprey* and mounted them crossed diagonally on a wall in my room. With the help of the hospital staff, they filled in the middle with a stethoscope, a couple of blood transfusion bags, and a catheter. When Paula Pajioli came to visit, she added two toy, plastic Glocks and a sniper rifle. Hanging from the rifle barrel was my Stetson, with the little gold lobster pin. At the top was the side profile of a drift boat made from plywood and painted the same green as *Osprey*. Below it all was a label — *Brooks' Family Crest.*

I drifted off. When I woke again, I tried to talk to the resident. I thought I *said* all the words, but my sound system was on mute. Nothing came out. I made a little motion of scribbling. Hospital charades. It worked. The nurse brought pencil and paper, and held the paper. I scribbled — *Lucinda? Wuff?*

"Your dog's fine," the nurse said. "She's the first dog we've ever had brought in for emergency care. She lost some blood from a bullet that grazed her flank. Bloody, but no serious damage. We patched her up and made a little bed next to yours. A detective was with the three of you in the helicopter that came from Jackson. I think his name was Byng. He took your dog home with him. She has a new collar that isn't bloody. She's in Jackson waiting for you. We all wanted to keep her.

When Byng came to take her, she jumped onto your bed and crawled under the covers."

She'd answered only half my questions. I had to scribble again — *Lucinda?*

She didn't answer. Her expression wasn't encouraging. She left the room. In a few minutes a Dr. Walker came in. He was older and taller than Dr. Levy. He said, "Your wife was shot three times. The first two bullets went through your shoulder and then her neck . . . one severed an artery. She lost a lot of blood. The third bullet that missed you hit her in the heart."

I couldn't believe it . . . a bullet meant for me had killed Lucinda.

Dr. Walker continued, "That last bullet bruised her badly. But it didn't penetrate. She was knocked back against the transom and lost consciousness. She tumbled out of the boat, swallowed some water, and would have drowned if one of Byng's snipers hadn't waded into the water to help. When he pulled her out of the river and gave her first aid, she was still clutching a pistol in her right hand and holding your bleeding dog with her left arm. She'd fired several rounds."

He continued, "Her jacket saved her. Huntly Byng said the two guide jackets were specially lined with Kevlar. If either of you hadn't been wearing those jackets you'd be dead. Your wife's in a coma. We don't know whether she'll survive. She may have lost so much blood there's been brain damage. A specialist on her kind of wounds, Dr. Kent, will tell you more when she comes by."

My wife! I scribbled on the pad that Lucinda wasn't my wife. Dr. Walker said, "We didn't know her last name. She lost any identification she was carrying. Huntly Byng said to log her in as Lucinda Brooks. That if you had any sense she *would* be your wife."

Dr. Kent came by soon after. She'd been on duty when the copter brought us in. Dr. Kent said the bruises from the direct hits to the two vests weren't life threatening. The dangerous shots were the one that entered my leg at an angle and the two that struck Lucinda's neck.

"She's a very strong lady," said Dr. Kent. "She was in and out of consciousness until she was in the helicopter when she went into a coma. She'd been waving a pistol around until police pried it out of her hand. She wouldn't give up the dog. And she kept calling: 'Macduff.' I haven't seen anything so sad since I was a new resident in the emergency room here a dozen years ago. A young man was brought in from almost the same location. He'd been fishing with his wife. They hit some debris and capsized. Her body was never found. The man kept calling out for his wife. Her name was El."

I know.

EPILOGUE

Two weeks later Lucinda languished in a coma in her hospital bed in Salt Lake City — Sisters of Charity or Chastity or some name Macduff had forgotten. Lucinda's mother had come from Indiana. Her brother and sister came and remained for a week, expecting Lucinda to succumb, but returned to their jobs. After Macduff's discharge from the hospital, he rented a nearby one-room apartment. On a visit, Huntly Byng brought Wuff from Jackson. Wuff was recovering, the only sign of her trauma a slight limp that in time should disappear. Wuff stayed close to Macduff in the apartment. She didn't want him to leave, even for a few minutes to get the morning newspaper. The hospital let Macduff bring Wuff to the room where Lucinda lay immobilized by the mechanisms of life support. Wuff lay on the floor next to Lucinda's bed and whimpered. Macduff sat touching the bed and also did a little whimpering.

Macduff had never met Lucinda's mother or siblings. Nor her father, who had passed away a year earlier. Her mother was in her late seventies and in good health, a kindly, solid lady, with a lot of the steadfast character that Lucinda expressed. She retained a trace of English accent. She didn't know very much about the shootings. Macduff wasn't considered a favored suitor for her much loved daughter. Macduff understood. He didn't want to cause her any more grief than she was suffering. He kept away from Lucinda's room when her mother visited. But Macduff was there whenever she was not. He fell asleep in the chair in her room most every night, until exhaustion caused the nurses and doctors to make him stay away and get a full night's sleep. But he slept even less when he was away from her.

Macduff knew he didn't want the stark, hospital room to be where Lucinda died. If she had to die before him, he hoped it would be in his cabin, in the bed they sometimes shared, and in his arms. With no one else except Wuff in the room. When Macduff was with Lucinda, he passed the hours sitting by her bed, talking to her and holding her hand, despite her coma. He told her all the details he could think of about his life. And then repeated them. He had a lot to ask her about her life that he'd never learned.

During those sad days, Macduff had much time to think. Maybe guiding wasn't what he should be doing. In only three drifts on the same section of the Snake River, he'd seen four people die, and another was close to joining them. Plus Kath in Maine and her intended, Geoff. And the injuries to Wuff.

A letter reached Macduff one afternoon at the hospital, forwarded from the Jackson guide shop by way of Byng, who visited weekly. Macduff knew the handwriting. It was from Kath, postmarked the day before she was killed.

Dear Macduff

Geoff and I have announced our engagement. The wedding will be in six months. I'd love to have you here because you helped set me on a course that's far better for me than remaining with Park. Geoff is a nice guy and will be a good husband. I am sorry you never answered my letters. But I loved the flowers. I think you know that I dreamed you would someday show up in Maine and we'd become a couple. It was not to be. This will be my last letter. I wish you the best.

Kathleen Macintosh

Kath never knew about Lucinda. That was best. Kath carried her last hopes to her grave. Macduff used his cell phone to call a florist in Kath's hometown, Bar Harbor. He asked that flowers be placed on her grave. With no note.

Elsbeth had been reading her father's manuscript for hours. She read many parts twice. Some even more. She learned so much about her father — things she never knew. She had much more to ask about at Christmas. The sun had set over the Gulf, but Elsbeth hadn't noticed it was one of the most glorious sunsets of the year. Finally, she carefully replaced the manuscript in the package. She wondered whatever happened to Juan Pablo and Abdul Khaliq. That would be the first question she would ask at Christmas.

M.W. GORDON — the author or co-author of more than sixty law books that have won awards and been translated into a dozen languages, has also written for Yachting Magazine and Yachting World, and won the Bruce Morang Award for Writing from the Friendship Sloop Society in Maine. Gordon holds a B.S. and J.D. from the University of Connecticut, an M.A. from Trinity College, a Diplôme de Droit Comparé from Strasbourg, and a Maestría en Derecho from Iberoamericana in Mexico City. He lives near St. Augustine, Florida, with his wife Buff and sheltie Macduff.

AUTHOR'S NOTE

I enjoy hearing from readers. You may reach me at:
macbrooks.mwgordon@gmail.com
Please visit my website: www.mwgordonnovels.com
I am also on facebook at www.facebook.com

I will answer email within the week received, unless I am on a book signing tour or towing *Osprey* to fish somewhere. Because of viruses, I do not download attachments sent with your emails. And please do not add my email address to any lists suggesting for whom I should vote, to whom I should give money, what I should buy, what I should read, or especially what I should write next about Macduff Brooks.

My website lists past and future appearances for readings, talk programs, and signings.